# TIDE
### OF
# DARKNESS

Also by
Joseph L.S. Terrell

THE OTHER SIDE OF SILENCE

A TIME OF MUSIC, A TIME OF MAGIC

A NEUROTIC'S GUIDE TO SANE LIVING

# TIDE
## OF
# DARKNESS

*THE LOST COLONY* THEATER MURDERS

# JOSEPH L.S. TERRELL

TIDE OF DARKNESS
ISBN 978-1-933523-66-8

Copyright © 2010 by Joseph L.S. Terrell

First Printed: April 2010

Library of Congress Control Number: 2010903704

Printed in the United States of America on acid-free paper.

Cover photograph by Scott Geib

Book design by Bella Rosa Books

BellaRosaBooks and logo are trademarks of Bella Rosa Books

10      9      8      7      6      5      4      3      2      1

This story is dedicated to my children, now grown into fine adults, but who remain to me forever my children.

## Acknowledgments

I want to thank tough but kind professional editor Chris Roerden for her talent, insightfulness, and patient work with me; literary agent Leslie Breed for encouraging me to write this story; to Thomas Childrey, retired Special Agent with the North Carolina State Bureau of Investigation, for reading the manuscript with a critical eye, and for his many years of friendship; and to Suzanne Tate, Penelope Thomas, and Veronica Moschetti for editorial catches and suggestions. A very special thanks, too, to Rod Hunter of Bella Rosa Books for having faith in me.

## Author's Note:

Although this is a work of fiction, some readers may remember that years ago a popular cast member of North Carolina's *The Lost Colony* outdoor drama on Roanoke Island was murdered. After an extensive search, the young woman's body was found snagged on a cypress stump on the edge of Croatan Sound near the mainland. Her slaying remains unsolved. This writer covered the investigation for a true-crime magazine. That case serves as the germ for *Tide of Darkness*. However, none of the other events or people depicted should be interpreted as anything other than fictional. While many of the place names are real, I have chosen to compress time and set much of the action around downtown Manteo as it used to exist, including the picturesque old courthouse that housed the sheriff's office and jail in the days when the stunningly unique Christmas Shop was relatively new; when Dowdy Amusement Park squeaked and squealed on the Bypass, and when the Waterside Theater, home of *The Lost Colony*, was more rustic than it is today.

–JLSTerrell

# Chapter One

I was determined not to think about murder.

In that, I was wrong. Dead wrong.

I'm a crime writer for a publisher who has three magazines. But I was sick of writing about scumbags and the stench of death they cause. I needed to get away from it, maybe forever.

Late that Thursday night as I drove toward the Outer Banks of North Carolina, I ran into an August thunderstorm, but I didn't care. I figured it a crucible I had to pass through to get to paradise, where I planned to make my home.

I promised myself there were things I was going to do and things I wasn't when I reached the Outer Banks. I was going to loaf, and read and walk along the beach, and eat at my favorite restaurants from years ago.

Thinking about murder was not on the agenda.

It was after one A.M. when I reached Manteo on Roanoke Island and pulled in under the portico at King's Motel, where I'd stayed before. My car was loaded with stuff, including my bass fiddle and Janey, my parakeet.

In the sparse lobby, a large young man I assumed was Mr. King's son slouched in a chair in front of a television. He got out of his chair, still smiling at the TV, and lumbered behind the registration desk. He was taller than his father, with some resemblance, except for his pale skin. How could anyone living at the coast be as pasty as the underside of a snail?

I gave him my name.

"Weaver . . . Weaver . . ." He flipped through a spiral notebook filled with penciled notations. "Here we go . . . Harrison Weaver." He studied a note scribbled beside my name. "Oh, you're the murder writer," he said. "Pop said you were coming."

I was tired and didn't want to talk to him. I handed him my credit card and he made an imprint.

"Boy, I tell you that's something. I mean your timing and everything. You must really stay on top of things."

I was only half-listening—at first. "What do you mean, timing?"

"I mean getting here just when you did. Just when they found her body. Sally Jean Pearson. They been looking three days for her."

"Body?"

"Found her this afternoon before the storm, hung up on a cypress stump in the north end of Croatan Sound. Just about like the other one. *Lost Colony* girl, too. Worked backstage but danced or paraded around or something in the last big scene."

"Murdered?"

"You better believe it! Cord around her neck. And they don't know a bit more about who killed her than they did the first one, you ask me." He squinted, eager. "I figure that's why you are here. A murder. Just like you wrote about—four, five years ago."

"Four," I said. "But I didn't know anything about this one. I was in Virginia, working on a . . ."

He grinned. "Right." He handed me a room key.

I drove around to the back of the motel. Only a few other cars were parked there. My ground-floor room looked out across the parking area to a vacant lot edged with tall pine trees. The setting gave a feeling of cozy isolation I liked.

First thing I did was take Janey in, then came back and got my bass fiddle. Neither deserved to be left in the car unattended, especially in the heat of the next morning. I laid the bass on its side, out of the way. In its black canvas cover, like a shroud, the instrument appeared huge in the small motel room and vaguely ominous to anyone unaware of the rich, polished wood inside.

I got fresh water for the parakeet and gave her a short sprig of millet seeds. "Okay, Janey, you can rest now and get over all the bumping around in the car." She chirped and bobbed her head. After she settled in, I'd cover her cage for the night.

I took a shower, as hot as I could stand it, and tried to drive away thoughts of murder. But I couldn't get the thoughts, the images of dead and mutilated bodies out of my head. Death seemed to surround me. Four years earlier, writing about the unsolved slaying of another young woman with *The Lost Colony*, I had been fully introduced to the Outer Banks. The area fascinated me. After that, whenever I thought about the thin strip of islands that make up the Banks, I did my best not to think about the dead young woman and the killer who remained free.

But it bugged me.

Now there was another one.

And a killer still out there.

I went to bed in a foul mood, knowing what tomorrow meant. Instead of going to Whalebone Bait and Tackle Shop to find out about the fishing and maybe head to the beach to do a little surf-casting, I'd want to go straight to the sheriff's office. I knew I'd start sticking my nose into this case, despite my promise to myself.

Bright sunshine along the edge of the drapes woke me. I lay in bed, staring at the ceiling, until the telephone rang. Janey started chirping, as she did when she heard a telephone ring, wanting to get uncovered.

"Man, you know when to show up, don't you?" the voice said.

I struggled mentally for a moment to recognize the voice. "Balls?"

"You got it!" Pitching his voice deeper, being funny, he said, "Your gutsy investigator with four balls."

The caller was T. for Thomas Ballsford Twiddy, a special agent with the State Bureau of Investigation. We went back a dozen or so years when I was a newspaper reporter in Raleigh and later in Washington.

"Where are you?" My watch showed not quite seven-thirty.

"Here in Manteo, garden spot of the universe. Where'd you think I'd be when we got a real one going on?"

I had nicknamed him Balls after hearing about an arrest he'd made inside of what had to be the world's roughest juke joint near Raleigh. He had walked in, grabbed a suspect big as himself by the belt buckle and said, "You're under arrest." He hiked the guy practically off the floor by his britches and walked him out of the place backwards, nose to nose, with everyone hootin' and hollerin'. Any character in the place could have done Balls in and they'd never have pinned it on a soul.

When I heard about it, I told one of the other investigators that a guy'd have to have four balls to pull a stunt like that. The fellow investigator laughed and told another. The nickname stuck.

"When they found the body, I got called in to assist. Ran into old man King in Manteo. Told me you're coming to town." He was silent for a beat or two. "Case sounds familiar, don't it? *Lost Colony* member. Never makes it home from partying. Strangled. Body found snagged on a cypress stump. Sort of déjà vu all over again, huh?"

"A connection? I mean, four years."

"Four years, one month. First one was on a July fifth. Who knows? Maybe. Strange."

Balls would remember the date. So did I.

His voice got male-boisterous and jolly again. "Breakfast? Go somewhere we can talk." Then, "Catch up on how you're doing."

I felt the weight of that old sadness, something I tried to

push from my mind. He knew about my rough time after Keely's death. But I said, "Sure."

We agreed to meet at the Dunes Restaurant on the Bypass.

I opened the drapes all the way to what I knew, after the storm, would be a day that danced with sun and a light breeze. I dressed—one of two or three Outer Banks uniforms: khaki slacks, golf shirt, boat shoes, no socks. When I stepped outside the air was like a shot of adrenalin: fresh and clean, the pine trees just warm enough in the sun to give off a faint Christmassy smell. With all the rain, my car, a Saab 9000 I treated myself to before I left Washington, looked freshly washed. In fact, the morning was so bright and clean it was like the whole world had just been washed.

Yet, there was that dead young woman.

# Chapter Two

I drove east toward the beaches to meet Balls. The bridge across Roanoke Sound loomed ahead. As I crested the bridge, my spirits soared. The view did this to me. I could see Jockey's Ridge off to my left. Oregon Inlet lay at the horizon to the south, twelve miles away. With my windows open, air whipped across my face and the back of my neck. I was conscious of the ocean surging out there ahead of me, the sound of its surf, and the light salt smell that thrilled me, made me feel at home, at peace with the world.

I swung north onto the Bypass and a short distance ahead turned into the parking area for the Dunes Restaurant. A couple of dozen cars crowded the lot. As I got out of the Saab, I glanced around, thinking I might see Balls or recognize whatever he was driving these days. I knew his vehicle would not look like a standard-issue investigator's car. It never did. His would be a souped-up Pontiac or Ford with four antennas poking out of the thing, and a hood long enough to accommodate a powerful shit-and-get engine. I saw one that had to be his at the far end of the lot, nose out for a fast getaway.

I entered the restaurant and immediately spotted Balls. He grinned and beckoned to me from his seat near the rear where he had a view through the window to the parking lot.

"I saw you eye-balling those cars out there," he said, giving a crushing handshake, not rising from his seat.

"Trying to figure which one is mine, weren't you?" He'd grown a full Tom Selleck mustache since I last saw him. It made him look ruggedly handsome. He'd always been muscular and tough, just under six feet, with wide shoulders and a big neck. He had a habit of leaning forward when he smiled, eyes crinkling, as if sharing a joke.

I said, "Old yellow and white Thunderbird backed into the space at the end of the lot?"

"What do you mean, 'old Thunderbird'? Boy, that car is just getting broke in. They're not making them like that anymore. Got me a classic."

He already had coffee. He eyed me over the top of his cup. "I saw what you drove up in. Got yourself a Snob 9000, haven't you? Gone yuppie on us."

The college-age waitress in black Reeboks, baggy shorts and T-shirt, took our orders for two-egg specials with grits and ham on the side.

He cocked his head to one side. "You finally going to get moved down here?"

I'd talked about moving to the Outer Banks for years. King's Motel was a stop for only a couple of nights until the rented house at Kill Devil Hills was vacated so I could move into it. I had fuzzed over, even in my own mind, plans for moving, like I couldn't make a commitment. Maybe, on some level, I was having a harder time than I thought making life decisions after Keely's death.

"That's the plan," I said, "but, hey, I didn't know anything about the dead girl."

We stopped talking as the waitress put the plates down. Balls stirred a big pat of butter into his grits.

"Three days before they found her?" I said.

"Yeah. Not like the other one. Ten days. Remember that?"

I did. The picture clicked into my mind with the intensity of a strobe light—her body, swollen and discolored, the cord tight and cutting into the bloated flesh of her throat.

"If you haven't seen anything in the papers wherever the

hell you've been, you'll sure see something now." He produced copies of *The News and Observer* and *The Virginian-
Pilot* from the seat beside him, laid them facing me on the
table next to our plates. A photo of Sally Jean Pearson
smiled at me. It looked like a shot from a college yearbook.
Light-colored hair, neatly parted, almost shoulder-length.
Coed smile. All-American, girl next door. They always
seemed like that. Something about the picture bothered me.
Maybe because she was so young and healthy and I knew
she was dead. Something hauntingly familiar about her. I
turned it off. They all begin to look alike. The dead girls.

"Suspects?"

"One." Balls swallowed a wad of ham, egg and toast.
"The guy she went out with after the show. Said they drank
beer at the Green Dolphin Pub, left together, and started to
his place. She changed her mind, decided to walk home. Just
five or six blocks. Never made it."

"Christ."

He smiled. "Sounds familiar, huh?"

"What does the guy say? Her date?"

"Sheriff says he's either a real good actor—but, heck,
he's in the show, right?—or he's real broken up about it."

"Much of a suspect?"

"I don't know. We don't have anybody else. But he's not
as much of a suspect as that other one was."

"Bobby Ford."

"Not like him. He was a cool one, and ended up getting
right mean."

"He got pushed a lot," I said.

"Wouldn't break, though. Sheriff never more'n about
half-way convinced he did it."

"You?"

"Maybe. But he didn't do this one."

"Not a so-called serial killing, huh?"

"Didn't say that. Just said Bobby Ford didn't do this
one."

I let it slide for the moment. We ate in silence. Balls used a piece of toast to sop the yellow of his egg. I spread more strawberry preserves on my last piece of toast.

Balls said, "You think Bobby Ford did the first one?"

I shrugged. "God, I don't know. Tell the truth, I never was convinced either. Something just didn't fit."

Balls waved my hand away and picked up the check.

We stood in the parking lot. The sun had climbed higher and a nice breeze from the west brushed my face. Now I could see a few gray hairs mixed in with Balls' coarse reddish brown. He'd thickened a bit at the waist but still solid. I had the feeling that slugging him in the gut would be like punching a burlap bag full of wet sand. You'd just get bruised knuckles. I had to work at staying in shape. Balls was one of those guys born big and strong who never seemed to work at it.

He peered through the window of my car, packed with clothes, boxes, a small duffle bag filled with books. "Guess maybe you *are* moving down here." We walked toward his car. "You still playing that big thing, the bass fiddle? Where's it?"

"Back at the motel. Brought it with me. Along with my parakeet, Janey."

He shook his head. "In that car?"

"Fold down the passenger seat."

He poked vigorously at his teeth with a toothpick. Stabbing and sucking. Lot of metal in his mouth. It hurt to watch him.

I turned to look out toward the ocean. "A cord around her neck. Just like . . ." I didn't need to say just like the first one.

He sucked thoughtfully on a tooth, having apparently succeeded in dislodging the food he'd poked at. "You're not doing any daily stuff anymore, are you?" He referred to my newspaper days.

I shook my head.

He studied my face. "Good. We're not going public just

yet with what kind of cord. But it was a leather thong. You know, like a long leather shoestring or bootlace."

Again, I could have said just like the first one.

"It was wrapped good around her neck, single knot in the back. Then pulled tight. She was dead before she went in the water, we think. Not beat up, though. Just strangled. Still had her clothes on. Blouse and bra ripped a little but that was about all."

We had strolled to his car and stood near the hood of the Thunderbird. With the palm of his big hand, he dusted off a smear of dirt on the front fender. He glanced sideways at me. "And lipstick. Lipstick all over her mouth like a 1940s movie star."

I did a quick take. The clothes being ripped and the lipstick, especially the lipstick, got the reaction from me I knew Balls expected. I shook my head slowly. "Jesus, this is too similar."

A minivan with a couple and two pre-teen girls parked a few spaces away. As they started toward the restaurant, Balls nodded and the man and woman smiled and nodded.

"Where's the body now?"

"On its way to Chapel Hill, or already there. Doc Mordecai's doing the autopsy. She's chief medical now, you know. Tough ol' bird. She'll find anything there is to find— which isn't going to be much more than we already know, I don't think."

He watched me. We hadn't talked about Keely or any of that. He waited as I played a thought over in my mind. I said, "You're going back to the courthouse? Sheriff's office?"

Hell, I knew I was going to get involved in this, and Balls knew it, too. So much for settling in at the Outer Banks and forgetting about murder.

"Sure. Come on. Some of your old crowd'll be there. Sammy. Creech. The sheriff. The *new* sheriff, right?" We both still thought of Claxton as the sheriff, even though he had been dead three years. His replacement, Eugene

Albright, had been his chief deputy. "Albright won't mind if I bring you along. Won't do him any good if it does. You're my mascot. My lucky charm."

While Balls had been a great source of leads for me in the past, I had helped him solve a real sticky case once. He never forgot it. I'd also contributed a few thoughts that helped on two other crimes. That's when he started saying he had adopted me as his lucky charm. He said he liked the way I tried to make the pieces of the puzzles fit.

"What about Rick Schweikert? He still around?"

"Oh, yeah," he said, a smirk on his face. "Your good buddy, County Prosecutor Schweikert. Still strutting around, puffed like a peacock, and probably doesn't like you any more than he did last time."

I'd worked closely with Sheriff Claxton in writing the earlier story, becoming something of a local celebrity among the townspeople. This seemed to gall Schweikert. When a national magazine and later a TV series purchased my story, word came back to me that Schweikert was cussing me as an opportunist, a charlatan, and a person who'd used a county's tragedy for personal gain. To be honest, I'd taken a couple of snide swipes at Schweikert in my stories. Made him look like a neo-Nazi. Pretty damn accurate.

Balls said, "When we get to the courthouse, just stay out of his way."

I turned and started toward my car, but stopped and stepped closer again. "One thing that occurs to me. Does to you, too, I know. If she and this guy she was with got in an argument and got to fighting and he was going to choke her, wouldn't he more likely have done her in with his hands, choked her with his hands? Leather thong. Knot in the back. That's not what you use in the heat of a fight. Sounds like something to use if somebody slipped up on her. And the lipstick business just doesn't fit at all."

Balls got a sly, out-of-the-corners-of-his-eyes smile. He leaned toward me. "You're coming along, son. Getting right good at this detective stuff."

# Chapter Three

Balls followed me toward King's Motel, driving at a steady, even clip a careful distance behind me. As I crested the bridge at Roanoke Sound, the sprawling and pricey Pirate's Cove development lay ahead and below. Off in the distance, blurred and gray on the horizon, was Manteo. The first time Keely saw the town of Manteo—we had driven to Roanoke Island from the mainland in the central part of the state along highway 64—she thought it was quaint, as if it belonged to a past generation. I remembered how, even then, she would lapse into a private quietness, a terrible sadness that I couldn't penetrate.

I tore my thoughts away from Keely and concentrated on the good feeling I got seeing the sun glisten off the brilliant white boats moored at Pirate's Cove.

We dropped my car off to ride the few blocks together in the Thunderbird. Radio equipment consumed a good portion of the front console. When Balls maneuvered onto the main road, he gunned it and I exaggerated sinking into the seat. He flashed a proud grin.

As we got near the courthouse I saw a TV van, a car with a radio station's call letters on it, and four or five reporter-types bunched together near the vehicles.

"Uh-oh," Balls said. "Dare County version of a media feeding frenzy."

He parked in one of the "Court Officials Only" spaces.

From under his seat, he took out a mean and efficient-looking 9mm Glock and buckled it into a holster at his waist. "Don't always lug this into restaurants and places, but got us an official visit here. Move on in quickly."

Corny, I know, but I got a kick out of being Balls' friend and taking the courthouse steps hurriedly past two young deputies, who stood there like sentinels. Both nodded a solemn greeting to Balls.

We went inside and upstairs where an older woman whose face I recognized greeted us. A much younger woman, looking crisp and slender, stood beside the desk. They'd been talking. I remembered the older woman as having worked in the sheriff's office and as a part-time radio dispatcher. I saw the nameplate on her desk. "Good to see you again, Mabel. How've you been?"

"Legs and ankles. Arthritis. Same old problem but I shouldn't complain." She chuckled. "Who's going to listen anyway, huh?"

The younger woman's frank, open smile brightened the place. You get used to people at the beach looking salty and scruffy. She stood out by comparison.

We walked down the hall and Balls muttered, "Nice, huh?" I didn't respond.

Sheriff Albright glanced up from his desk, a tired smile on his big face. When he stood to motion us in, his large, beefy frame dwarfed his furniture. We shook hands, and he did his glad-to-see-you-again greeting. I felt it was genuine, and it probably was. He didn't seem surprised I had arrived at his office. Maybe he had heard from old man King, too.

"We've had outside reporters already, plus the locals and the TV guys and gals," Albright said, "but dern if you didn't get here quick."

"Just coincidence, Sheriff. Already had planned to be here."

Balls said, "Heck, he tells me he's goin' to move here—if all this killing off of citizens'll stop."

Albright didn't share Balls' smile. He said he was

pleased about my being back in the county, and settled into his big leather chair like a bear folding up. Although the room was cool, two creases of perspiration dampened the front of his shirt.

Balls sat in a chair he placed near the corner of the sheriff's desk. "We got us a serial killer here, Sheriff?"

"You know better'n that."

I think Albright meant that Balls should have known better than to say that in front of me.

From where I sat in one of the two chairs placed roughly in front of Albright's desk, I saw a stack of eight-by-ten color photos edging out of a folder on the corner of the desk. They had to be of the dead girl.

Albright said, "And those reporters out there and the TV folks, I've promised them a . . . you know, press conference. I've got to go tell them something." He took in a deep breath and then sighed before he continued. "We don't need any talk about a serial killer. I don't want folks talking about that. It might not be. Four years, you know. That's a long time."

Balls said, "Weaver's not going to say anything. He doesn't write daily stuff. Besides, he opens his yap I'll stomp on him."

Just then two deputies stopped at the door to the office and nodded greetings to Balls and me.

One of them, John Creech, had been on the Manteo police force when I first met him. Now he was one of Albright's deputies. With the uniform came an affected swaggering roll to his walk that I didn't like when I first met him. It reminded me of Hollywood's version of the redneck lawman. As I got to know him, I had to admit he was hard-working and appeared to do a good job.

"Sheriff, those reporters are getting antsy," Creech said. "I got them waiting downstairs outside the side door. Didn't want to let them in, cluttering the place. But they're ready for you. Six of them. Plus two TV guys now. Or gals." He grinned.

Albright took a deep breath. "Let's get this over with. You want to make this a joint press conference, Ballsford?"

"I'll pass, Sheriff. There's not much we can tell them now, anyway. Body's being examined. Investigation's ongoing. No suspects, no motive. We'll keep them informed on a regular basis . . . and so forth."

"I'm going to keep it short." He made a pass at smoothing down his hair. "Come on, Creech." As he and Creech started out the door, he nodded at the other deputy. "Sammy, you can entertain our guests."

If there wasn't a touch of irony in Albright's command, there should have been. Deputy Sammy Foster suffered from a terminal case of shyness. He looked embarrassed as he shook hands with us. I wondered if he acted shy and embarrassed when he arrested someone.

Balls slouched in his chair, maybe trying to appear relaxed to draw Sammy out. "What you think, Sammy? We got a serial killer? Copycat?"

Sammy eased his lanky frame onto the edge of a wooden chair next to the door. He shrugged. "Least we know it's not that other suspect, Bobby Ford."

Okay, that was the second time this was mentioned.

Sammy read my reaction. "Dead," he said.

Balls cut his eyes toward me, a slight smile hiking up one side of his Tom Selleck mustache. He enjoyed letting bits of information seep out.

"Drowned the first of this year," Sammy added. "February. At Lake Gaston. Creech thinks he was probably drunk or doing drugs. Fell off the pier. Maybe bumped his head as he fell."

Balls said, "You, Sammy? What you think?"

Sammy squirmed. "I know he got himself pretty well messed up. You know, emotionally, and with drugs." He cut his eyes quickly from one of us to the other, as if seeking help. "But . . ."

Balls, head hanging to one side and looking relaxed, said, "But . . . ?"

"Some things about the way he acted just didn't make sense. Sheriff Claxton always said things had to make sense, had to fit together."

Balls asked, "Did he still come to town every July fifth? Anniversary of that first girl's killing—Joyce Brendle—see that night's performance of *The Lost Colony*, then leave?"

I knew this story about Bobby Ford, how he showed up every July 5, saw the performance, and then disappeared.

Sammy nodded. "Bobby Ford came back one more time, too." Sammy cleared his throat, spoke softly. "He came back right after Christmas vacation. Not too long before he died. I saw him late one afternoon standing there by the Pioneer Theater just as I was coming in the courthouse. I thought maybe he was getting set to come in the courthouse. But when I got inside and looked out the window, he was gone."

I'd never heard Sammy talk this much. Maybe it was because we were quiet, not pressuring him. Or maybe it was something he'd been wanting to say.

Sammy had one hand in his pocket, absently rattling coins. "That same afternoon he was seen a couple more places around town. That night he drank a beer at RV's, then showed up at the high school basketball game for a while. One of our guys was moonlighting security at the high school. Bobby Ford sits there, doesn't cheer or nothing. Everybody else jumping and hollerin'. He just sits there and stares. Then he leaves. That was the last any of us ever saw him."

"So," Balls said, "the only thing we know is we can eliminate Bobby Ford as a suspect on this one."

I didn't like the way Balls kissed off what Sammy told us. It was too much of an effort for Sammy to hold forth with a discourse for him not to be telling us this for a reason. Something about that final visit of the late Bobby Ford bothered Sammy.

Balls reached for the folder with the photos. I leaned forward to get a closer look. He didn't try to keep them from my view. They were taken at the scene, apparently right after the body had been brought ashore. She was stretched out on a dark-colored tarp. An officer's feet could be seen in a few of the shots. The cord was visible around the young woman's neck.

At one of the pictures, I felt my body tense. It was a close-up of her face, focusing on her mouth. Lipstick smeared over her lips, onto her cheeks and chin, and under her nose. The lipstick was such a grotesque violation of the dead woman that I could taste the bitter revulsion that swelled in me.

My voice tight, I muttered, "That sonofabitch needs to be done away with. Eliminated. Wiped off the face of the earth."

Balls glanced at me and kept sifting through the pictures, shaking his head sadly from time to time. Except for the torn blouse and bra, exposing a small breast, her clothes appeared intact. Several pictures showed her full, knee-length shorts. One foot bore a strapped sandal, the other bare. Balls sighed and put the photos back in the folder and returned it to the desk.

I heard Sammy's pocket change.

I knew I needed to call one of the magazine editors I wrote for, stake out this story as mine. The case had all the elements these publishers loved. Writing about murder always filled me with mixed emotions—pulse quickened by the mystery, the chase, the efforts to solve, and at the same time my stomach repelled by the sordidness of it. And here I was again, steeped in death. It seemed I couldn't get away from it. Yet, overriding all else, deep-down anger at the scum who did this sort of thing. I burned to help get the bastard.

That morning, sitting in the sheriff's office, I swore that I'd stay with this case to the end. I was going to hang in there, dog this thing. This time I wanted to see it solved, ended. Put the needle to the son of a bitch.

# Chapter Four

We heard Creech talking to the sheriff as they topped the stairs and entered the office.

A lock of Albright's sandy-colored hair stood on end. I wondered if it would show on the evening news.

"That didn't take long," Balls said.

Albright sank heavily into his chair. "Long enough." He rubbed his face with the palm of his big hand. "Right away they asked was this connected to the other one. Was this a serial killing?"

I waited to see if Balls and the sheriff would elaborate on the serial killing business. I wanted to speak, but kept my mouth shut.

Balls stayed silent, too, giving Albright time to mull over his thoughts. But not for long. Balls sat straighter in his chair and said, "Let's don't get carried away with trying to speculate whether a serial killer, a copy-cat killer, or what kind of killer. We got us a dead woman, strangled and dumped in the sound. What else you going to do with a body in these parts except dump it in the water if you want to get rid of it? If you scuffle around killing somebody, clothes can get ripped. And not too many folks carry handguns around here, so if you're going to do somebody in, you do it with a stick or a rock or your hands or a knife—or strangle them with something."

I'm not at all sure he believed his own words. But I knew

he wanted to get back to the here and now, get his thought-action going, play out a scenario.

Balls continued. "What about the kid, her date, Bobby For . . ." He caught his mistake immediately.

The sheriff smiled slightly and Creech said, "Mind's the first thing to go, Balls. Or at least the second," and he giggled.

"What's this year's suspect's name again?" Balls asked.

"Charles Calvin Carlyle," Albright said. "He goes by Cal. Cal Carlyle."

"Where is he?"

"Back at his place. Mrs. Bailey's. He's not going anywhere. Just sitting there in his room."

"Scared shitless," Creech said.

I could hear Sammy's change rattling. The sheriff heard it, too, and frowned at his deputy. Abruptly, Sammy took his hand out of his pocket and tucked it under his arm.

Albright sighed. "I've talked with the dead girl's folks." In Manteo they spoke of the "dead girl," or they used her name. They didn't call her "the victim," a nameless reference more commonly used by cops in the bigger cities. A means of emotionally distancing themselves, I figured.

Albright's face registered genuine anguish at the part of the job that was so painful. "Her father, mother and brother been down here at the Elizabethan Motel since day before yesterday. The mother's just sitting on the bed crying and the father gets up and sits down, gets up and sits down. The son's threatening to kill half the town and especially Calvin Carlyle. They're going back to Winston-Salem today. Memorial services and all. They'll be back if we get a break in the case. *When* we get a break."

The sheriff turned to Sammy and Creech. "You two better go on back out and start knocking on folks' doors between the Green Dolphin and where she lived. Ask everybody if they heard anything at all. I don't care whether it was a dog barking or what."

"We've talked to about everybody who's old enough to

talk," Creech said, adding with a snicker, "and some was too old even to talk."

Sammy nodded dutifully at the sheriff's order, but his shoulders sagged with what had to be the painful realization he was to go out among the public again.

As the deputies left, I heard Creech's voice in the hall. "Yes, sir. He's in there, with the sheriff."

The erect military presence of County Prosecutor Rick Schweikert was framed by the door. He stared at me, thin lips compressed, eyes cold. He nodded toward Balls and the sheriff, then glared at me. "I might know you'd be here when tragedy strikes the county."

He always talked that way. To him, all slayings were "heinous crimes" and folks did one another in "with murderous intent."

Balls could apparently sense my body coiling, getting ready to blurt out, because he discreetly moved the fingers of one hand toward me to keep me quiet.

I forced myself to settle back. "Morning, Rick," I said. "Comforting to know that your views of the world haven't changed a bit." The sheriff shifted in his chair and actually groaned. "But just to set the record straight, Rick, I knew nothing of this 'latest tragedy to strike the county.' I came down here with purity of heart for a little R-and-R. And that's for rest and residence."

Sheriff Albright cleared his throat. "He's here with his friend, Agent Ballsford Twiddy, SBI."

"I know Agent Twiddy." Schweikert glared at me. "And I know Mr. Weaver here, too, and know how he capitalized on that other tragedy from *The Lost Colony*."

I said, "Look, if you think people aren't going to be writing about this case, you've got—"

"I don't care what other 'people' are going to do, Mr. Weaver. I just want you to know that I'm going to be watching to make sure you don't jeopardize this case just because you happen to be buddy-buddy with Agent Twiddy here, and—"

"Hold on there, Schweikert." Balls' voice, low and firm, cut through whatever it was that Schweikert was getting ready to say. "Nobody's going to jeopardize anything—and that includes you. If I'm correct, your job starts after we finish an investigation, wrap up the case, and hand it over to you—not before."

Albright raised his hands, palms outward. "Gentlemen, please."

Schweikert nodded curtly at the sheriff. "Sorry to barge in like this, Sheriff Albright, but . . ." and he turned toward me, "it seems strange that Mr. Weaver here just happens— just *happens*—to arrive about the time we find a body. It appears we can count on this exploitive writer being here when tragedy strikes us here in the county, when a victim's body is discovered. Just coincidence, I do suppose . . . although that becomes rather difficult to believe."

I said, "At least I'm not around town when the young women disappear."

Balls gave a chuckle.

Schweikert kept glaring at me, his jaw muscles working overtime. "Again, Sheriff, my apologies to you for storming in like this, but when I heard he was here, I. . . ." He nodded curtly to Albright, turned, and left.

Things were quiet for a moment. Balls said, "Coffee, Sheriff?"

"Sure, why not?" Albright stood and looked at me. "Maybe best if you do sort of keep out of Schweikert's way. Don't know why he carries on that way about you, like you're a real burr under his saddle."

I started to make a really snappy comment like, screw Schweikert.

But Balls spoke. "Weaver's with me. Period. That doesn't need to be any concern of Schweikert's."

Balls turned to me. "Notice that stiff white shirt Schweikert has on? He irons them himself. Doesn't trust the laundry, and says his wife can't iron them to suit him."

Just the same, what Schweikert said tugged at me. It did

look like death followed me around, as if I attracted it like a magnet. That was not a good feeling. And I came here to get away from death and violence.

# Chapter Five

We went downstairs and next door to Diane's Courthouse Cafe where town officials and courthouse people had coffee. Many would return for lunch. It was one of the few places where you could get vegetables cooked well and seasoned so they tasted like you were back home again. Even at the tail end of coffee-break time the place was busy, humming with chatter, the soft clatter of cups and saucers.

Maybe it was my imagination, but as we entered conversations became more muted.

Balls knew many of the people. A few looked familiar to me. As we made our way toward a table near the back, Albright carried on brief conversations with people at nearby booths and tables. His big frame towered above the tables, and he extended his paw-like hand in greetings. I realized that he probably faced re-election this November. I didn't see the likelihood of any serious challenges, yet he was still a politician, working the crowd.

"Any leads, Sheriff?"

"Checking things out."

"Was she raped?"

Politely, "We're checking things out."

I knew the guy asking the questions. Charlie Ferguson. He and his family own two or three businesses in town, including a variety store and an insurance agency.

Ferguson used the palm of one hand to caress the dramatic swoop of his silver-gray hair. "We're countin' on you, Sheriff." He smiled at us. Like a benediction. One of the town fathers, so to speak.

A younger man sat with Ferguson. I recognized him as the son-in-law, Dixon Nance. Ferguson was one of the towns-people who'd led the speculation about a local optometrist's connection to the earlier murder. The optometrist never recovered from being under suspicion, though it was brief. He was already drinking heavily, and the rumors apparently caused him to drift into deeper depression. That winter he used a .22 caliber target pistol to put a bullet in his head.

Even as Balls and I took seats at the back corner table, Albright exchanged words and a smile with an elderly couple two tables away. One of the waitresses, an older woman with heavy shoulders and hips, reddish gray hair, moved among the customers comfortably like a member of the household. She brought us three coffees without our asking.

In a booth on the other side of the room sat three people, one of whom I recognized, and didn't particularly care for— Jules Hinson. His name was plastered prominently on the front of his television sales and service place. He smoked and jabbed at the ashtray with his cigarette when he talked. He was always pissed off. Government, taxes, you name it. Rumors were that he had a goodly collection of porn videos in his back room. It made him popular among those who might have wanted to enliven a Saturday night for a few bucks. Hinson had been one of those who sided with Ferguson in tormenting the optometrist.

Hinson glanced at us through cigarette smoke curling around his thick horned-rimmed glasses.

Albright joined us at the table. He turned his big, open face to Balls, and said softly, "We got to get this thing solved. We can't have another one of these hanging over the county." He hunched his frame closer to Balls. "I'd like to hear any theories you have. Any at all. We've done all the obvious, ever since she was reported missing. Bartender, waiters, customers at the Green Dolphin. Nothing. People in the house where she lived. Up and down the street. Nothing. Like she vanished until she was found yesterday on that cypress stump."

Balls toyed with the sugar packets, stacking them, straightening them, and putting them back in the square white glass dish. "Motive. Puzzle's not going to fit together unless we got a motive." He looked up briefly at Albright, then continued an internal monologue addressed to the sugar packets: "Random killing? Naw. Not likely. You ride by and shoot somebody randomly. You don't grab them and strangle them with a . . . with a cord . . . randomly. If it wasn't this Carlyle kid, and you can't rule him out, not yet, was somebody lying in wait for her, bushwhack her? What for? Sex? He didn't get very far. I say he. Wasn't a woman. Rule that out. Strength and style. Whoever did it, did it quickly. Wasn't any screaming and hollering, apparently. Some neighborhoods nobody never hears nothin', the way they tell it. But in this neighborhood, this town, everybody sees and hears everything and not afraid to tell it. So it was quick. No noise, she was out. Probably dragged right into a vehicle."

Albright retrieved two of the sugar packets and emptied them in his coffee, stirring slowly.

Balls appeared to think about his last statement. "Almost had to be dragged into a car, or vehicle, quickly. Wouldn't want to run the risk of struggling out on the street. If she was on the street, and not killed in somebody's room and then put in the car, or maybe she was already in the car, parked. But she was supposed to have walked out of the Green Dolphin and then disappeared. You've talked to everyone in the Green Dolphin, and we need to do that again, see if there was anyone who came in, who else was in there. . . ." His voice trailed off.

Albright and I were both quiet, listening, letting Balls go on talking softly, staring at the table and the sugar packets as if he were trying to conjure the scene.

"There's not that many people around in Manteo after eleven o'clock at night. Did she start walking down the street, as that guy, her date, said, and then a guy is hiding, jumps out of his car as she approached? Wouldn't she run?" He was quiet again. He looked at the sheriff. "Or maybe it was someone she knew. Someone she trusted and didn't see any need to run. Someone she knew."

Albright nodded. "That bothers me, too. If it was someone she knew and trusted, it could be someone we all know—and trust." Perhaps unconsciously, he glanced around the room at the remaining group of regulars.

Balls and the sheriff continued talking, mostly rehashing what had already been reviewed, as if by returning to the few facts they might uncover something new.

We had been there a good thirty minutes and were about to finish our seconds on coffee and leave when Deputy John Creech hurried in the front door of the restaurant. He glanced around, saw us at the rear. Walking fast, he lost his swaggering, rolling gait.

Albright looked hopeful. "Got anything?" he asked quietly.

Creech took the remaining chair. He whispered, "Maybe. Just maybe." He put his handkerchief on the table and unfolded it to reveal a thin, circular compact, open: powder base, with pad, and mirror. "Very first place I went back to, the Johnston's little girl found this three or four days ago, her mother said, in the grass beside the street they live on, Fourth Street. That's in line between the Green Dolphin Pub and Mrs. Kennedy's rooming house where the victim lived. I went to Mrs. Kennedy's. Girl there said it looks just like Sally Jean's compact. She's pretty sure of it. Johnston girl's been playing with it, of course. Her prints all over it, but just the same . . ."

Other people in the restaurant cast discreet glances toward our table. I'm sure they could sense Creech's excitement even if they couldn't hear what he was saying.

Jules Hinson stared at us. When he saw me watching him, he put down a few coins and he and his two companions left.

Creech hunched forward. "Something else," he said, talking still lower and glancing around to make sure we still had privacy, "and I think this sort of ties it together. I had the Johnston kid go show me exactly where she found it, between the curb and the sidewalk, in the grass. And right there not two feet away mashed down in the grass was this lipstick thing." He had the lipstick in a business envelope, like the envelope for his cable television bill. "I carried it back to the girls at Mrs. Kennedy's. They said, 'Oh, my God, it's hers, I know it's hers.' They looked carefully at the end of it—I wouldn't let them touch it—to check the color. They were sure it was hers."

Without touching it, Balls inspected the color also. It was such a pale pink it was hardly more than lip balm. I thought about the grotesque picture of Sally Jean Pearson's lips and face smeared with bright red lipstick. Balls saw me looking at the lipstick. I started to speak but he caught my eye.

"If it's hers," Balls said, "where it was found could be the spot where she was hit, attacked." He thought a minute. "If she just decided to get in someone's car she knew, she wouldn't have dropped this stuff. Looks like a struggle. Maybe a brief one. But a struggle."

More to himself, Albright said, "That means she probably didn't know the person?"

Balls wrinkled his face, as if mentally flipping to the other side of the coin. "Not necessarily. It could just mean that she didn't want to get in a guy's car. Or she could have been a bit drunk and just dropped the stuff. And the girl at Mrs. Kennedy's could be wrong. It might not be Sally Jean Pearson's at all. Check it also with her parents, if they haven't already left."

Albright said, "About impossible to get any usable prints off the compact, just like you say, but we might have luck with the lipstick." To Creech, he said, "Nice bit of work."

Creech nodded, and appeared to swell with a bit of pride. He pushed back from the table, cleared his throat. "I guess I better get on back outside, keep checking." He walked from the restaurant, a hint of his old swagger evident.

"There's still an element missing," Balls said. "What was Sally Jean carrying this stuff in, if it was hers? A purse, wallet or something? What else did she have with her?"

"Let's go have us our little talk with Calvin Carlyle," Albright said. "He just might remember what else she was carrying."

As the lawmen started to rise, they both looked at me.

"I know," I said. "You'll do this by yourselves."

"Yeah," Balls said.

"While I'm here, Sheriff, mind if I take a look at the old Joyce Brendle file? I spent a lot of time going over that one four years ago."

"Yep, we can do that. I've got to speak to Mabel before we have a talk with Carlyle. She'll get the file for you." He smiled for the first time in a while. "She kind of likes you anyway."

"God knows why," Balls muttered. "Getting gray. Beat-up face. Look at those lines."

At the courthouse, Albright and I went upstairs. Mabel said, sure thing, she'd get the file, and pushed herself up from her desk. In her flat, cushion-soled black shoes, she rocked from side to side on her swollen legs and ankles as she led me to the file cabinets.

We walked past an open door and I saw the other woman, the pretty one, coming out of the office with a sheaf of papers in her hand. She glanced at us, smiled, and headed for the stairs back to the first floor.

Mabel opened a file drawer crammed with manila folders. "Here we go." She tugged at a thick file comprised of several folders, each at least two inches thick, secured with a large rubber band. "There's more stuff stored. But these are all the reports and main records." She took out another folder. "Here's one you might want to see, also. It's the newspaper articles, your magazine story."

I went into a room that I supposed was generally used by visiting investigators or maybe for an occasional interrogation. Government-type desk, telephone, three chairs, a wastebasket, and a couple of ashtrays that had been emptied but not wiped out. The wall calendar still showed July.

Picking up the last folder Mabel had given me, I sat down and flipped through scores of newspaper clippings, stopping when I came to a copy of the magazine with the article I had written four years earlier. I glanced at the lead paragraph and lightly scanned the text on the first page. It seemed written by a person I once knew. I turned the page.

Staring at me was a college yearbook picture of Joyce Brendle. What had bothered me at breakfast struck me immediately. Leaving the pages open, I put the magazine article down and went to the doorway of the office.

"Mabel, do you have *The News and Observer* from this morning?"

"Sure thing. It's around here. Two copies supposed to be." She came back a moment later with the newspaper. "All here but the crossword."

"I just need the front section." I folded it into quarters with the picture visible and laid it beside the magazine.

Mabel stood in the doorway watching. "I was wondering if you'd think what I think," she said.

"They do, don't they?" I studied the side-by-side photos. "They look alike. At least in these pictures. Certainly similar. Of course, both pictures are college yearbook poses, so . . . but just the same . . ."

"I think the girls look alike," Mabel said.

"Sheriff or anybody say anything about that?"

"I mentioned it to Sheriff Albright yesterday and he looked at the pictures real quick. He said, yes, there was similarity in hair color and height—both girls were kind of tall, for girls, although seems girls get taller every year—but that's about all he said. Of course things were hectic yesterday and maybe he didn't concentrate on looking."

I squinted to get a less sharply focused look. I wanted to compare the overall without the detail. The length and style of hair was the same—no wave, parted in the middle— reaching close to the shoulders. Both faces oval. The eyes similar, like large almonds that dipped at the bridge of the nose. Sally Jean Pearson may have worked on her eyebrows to give them more of an arched look, and they were thinner than Joyce Brendle's, but the eyebrows of both girls were nearly straight, hardly curved.

"Of course," Mabel said, "Sheriff Albright saw the Pearson girl in person, I mean, after she'd been dead for two or three days, so he's probably got a, you know, different view."

I closed the magazine and moved the newspaper. Mabel went back to her desk and I sat down with the old files. I skimmed through parts of it. After maybe twenty minutes, I felt I had a good grip on the story; it was all coming back.

I took the file with the autopsy report. The usual medical terms, as if this made the whole thing less personal, less human. Maybe depersonalizing is a way of dealing with tragedy. I skimmed through to the medical examiner's conclusion: death by asphyxia; method: strangulation. I flipped to photographs of Joyce Brendle's body. Not pretty. Her neck was so swollen the leather cord was practically buried in her flesh. In the text of the report, the forensic pathologist noted the ripped blouse and bra. Further on: "The left nipple suffered severe trauma resulting in contusion. Amount of discoloration suggest the injury was delivered shortly pre-mortem or virtually simultaneous with death, possibly pinched with great force."

I read further into the report. I wanted complete con-firmation of what I remembered, and I got it. "Despite the extreme discoloration of facial tissue and decomposition," the report said, "evidence exists of heavy application of lipstick on the deceased's face below the external nares to the top of the mentum. Heaviest concentration of the lipstick appears on the lips." Lipstick like a 1940s movie star. Just like this latest murder.

I looked at the pictures of the two girls again. Their lips were as pale as those of a six-year-old boy.

It's got to be the same killer, or a really clever copycat who knows all the details of the first one.

I glanced around the austere office, with its out-of-date calendar, two tin ashtrays that were stained with brownish cigarette tar from years of use. I thought this is one hell of a way to start off, as the poet says, loafing and inviting my soul at the Outer Banks. Reading a murder file.

I got up and stuck my head into the other office. "Mabel, the heck with reading this stuff now. Too pretty outside. I think I'll come back later to finish reading it, if I need to, if that's okay."

"Sure thing. I don't blame you. Seems like this is all we talk about around here. Murder and stuff." She gave a short chuckle. "Course, you could say that's what we're in business for. Just the same, used not to be that way at all. We talk about it so much that sometimes it doesn't even seem real—then all of a sudden you know it is."

One of those moments when you know it's real occurred right then. The side door of the courthouse opened and the sheriff and Balls came up the stairs. The young man between them looked frightened and vulnerable. Had to be the Carlyle youth.

# Chapter Six

As they herded Carlyle past me, the sheriff nodded slightly. Balls ignored me. I observed Mabel. She was expressionless, probably through practice.

I took the other stairs down to the front of the courthouse and stood on the porch. The year "1904" is affixed in big white numbers on the old brick building.

Even with the temperature rising, the light wind had shifted to the northwest, keeping the humidity down, and polishing the sky a bright blue, with only a few high clouds.

One of the Dare County deputies got out of his car and came on the front porch to enter the courthouse. He smiled and glanced at the sky also. "Yeah, nice day," he said.

I looked across the Manteo Waterfront to the spit of land two or three hundred yards away where the *Elizabeth II* was docked. A tourist attraction, the ship is a replica of the vessel that had brought the English settlers here in 1587. I could see a few people on the deck who seemed to be listening, as I had done on an earlier visit, to a "crew" member in sixteenth century garb going through his spiel about life aboard such a tiny vessel.

The history of the area and the efforts by a handful of people to colonize this place fascinated me. Directly across the street from the courthouse a historical marker noted that Virginia Dare, the first child born of English parents in what became the United States, was baptized on the island in

1587. After that, all the settlers disappeared. They became "the lost colony." Their disappearance and what happened to them remains a mystery to this day.

I checked my watch and thought about lunch, then decided to browse in the Manteo Bookseller around the corner. I liked the way the place smelled of paper and new ink, and how the aisles were arranged with great piles of books, many by North Carolina writers. Books that mentioned the Outer Banks were identified with a special plaque.

I bought a copy of David Stick's *The Outer Banks of North Carolina*, which I knew to be an excellent history of the area. A copy I once owned had been ruined in a rainstorm. I carried my book with me across the street to a restaurant on the upper level of the Manteo Waterfront complex, a mixture of shops and eateries, apartments above, a parking garage at street level.

My plan was to have a pleasant lunch and maybe read a few pages in Stick's book. I didn't figure on Schweikert ruining my appetite.

I sat in a booth by the window, looking out at the marina and Shallow Bag Bay. A power boat came in, throttled back, its sun-lit wake backing up on itself.

Then I heard Schweikert talking loudly to a couple of his cronies paying their tabs.

I kept my gaze on the boat. I heard Schweikert tell the others he would get with them later, had business he needed to attend to. I knew he strode toward me.

"There's a bit more of that conversation I want to have with you, Mr. Weaver, now that your watchdog isn't with you." He sat down in my booth.

I stared at him, keeping my face blank. "Didn't your mama ever teach you it wasn't polite to sit down unless you were invited?"

"This isn't exactly a courtesy call. There's that matter of the comment you made about—how did you put it?—'at least not being here when the girls disappear.' Just maybe that needs examining more thoroughly." He leaned forward, a smirk on his face that made me want to slug him.

I forced myself to wait a second before I spoke. "You got spinach stuck on your teeth, Schweikert."

Momentarily confused, he put one hand to his mouth, rubbed a finger on his front teeth.

"Just kidding, Schweikert. You probably didn't even have spinach." It was a juvenile trick, I knew. But I couldn't help myself.

He sat straight, a military bearing, eyes narrowed. "Be funny if you want to, Weaver. But I've got a theory. Let me run it by you, see what you think. Your career's stalled out. You know you had yourself a mini-burst of fame writing about that first *Lost Colony* tragedy. So, and here's the good part, Weaver, it occurs to me that you think you can jump-start your writing career again if you could, let's say, ensure that a very similar murder occurs—and then you just happen on the scene to write about it. What do you think about that theory, Mr. Writer?"

I stared in disbelief at the pompous bastard. But I learned a long time ago that frequently the most dangerous people are either very stupid or very self-righteous. Schweikert qualified on both counts.

Still looking at his smirking face, I forced myself to speak slowly and evenly. "Number one, Mr. Schweikert, I don't have that much of a career for it to be 'stalled,' as you say. I'm just a former dirty-neck newspaper guy who stumbled into writing about murder. Number two, the human race being what it is, there is never any shortage of material to write about. I don't have to go looking for killings. They're everywhere . . . and number three, you truly are dumber than ape shit."

He shifted in his seat, as if he might be ready to leave. "Just the same, Weaver, I'd like to know where you were, say, four days ago when this unfortunate girl disappeared. I want to know for sure you weren't personally around here."

I practically came across the table into his face, my voice

a hoarse whisper. "Listen, you puffed-up son of a bitch, I wasn't 'personally'—or impersonally—around here when that girl disappeared. Now get away from me and if you're lucky I'll pretend this conversation never happened."

"That a threat? Are you threatening me?"

"No threat. It's just that I don't like to remember stupid things—like what you said—and you, personally."

The waitress approached. "Are you having anything else, Mr. Schweikert?"

"No, he's just leaving," I said.

She looked bewildered, then nodded quickly and left.

Schweikert rose. He smoothed his tie down on his starched white shirt. "Okay," he said, "it may sound far-fetched, but just the same I'm keeping an eye on you."

I turned toward the window until he left. The waitress came and stood by the table expectantly. My appetite was gone. But I ordered a cup of the seafood chowder, bread, and sweetened iced tea. My mouth was dry. I handed her the closed menu.

When the soup came I ate slowly, trying to think about the bright sunny day just outside the window. One pleasant lunch ruined.

The waitress came back with her pitcher of sweetened iced tea. "Everything all right?" She nodded at my half-full cup of chowder.

"No, it's fine, really."

I took another big swallow of the tea. I wanted to get the bitter taste of Schweikert out of my gut. The conversation had stirred vague memories that tugged me to the edge of sadness.

I paid, took my book, and strolled outside, determined to enjoy the sunshine, sit on one of the benches at the Manteo Waterfront, watch the boats and the people come and go.

The sun sparkled off the water. A small boat with a man and two women aboard left the docks and headed slowly toward the sound, its engine barely audible. The light breeze clinked metal fittings against the masts of the sailboats docked a few yards from me. As I took in the gently swaying boats and the soft music of the fittings, I saw out of the corner of my eye two women strolling toward me. A flicker of familiarity made me turn to look at them.

The pretty woman from the courthouse and her companion ate frozen yogurt cones from the shop next to the restaurant. In the sunshine, the wind blowing gently against her dress, she looked even prettier than she had in the old courthouse.

I stood as they approached. She smiled, but rather shyly, and the two of them stopped. "Well, our mystery writer. Welcome to the Manteo Waterfront."

Up close, both of us standing, she was shorter than I had thought. Tucked under one arm nestled a section of newspaper folded to the crossword. A ballpoint pen was clipped to the page.

"Mabel didn't introduce us. I'm Harrison Weaver, and—"

"Oh, I know who you are, Mr. Weaver."

"Please, no *Mister*."

"Well then, Harrison."

Not many people call me by my first name. They call me Weaver or Weav. A few try to shorten Harrison to Harry but I hate that and make no bones about it. When she said Harrison, it sounded good to me.

She said, "I'm Ellen . . . Ellen Gray Pedersen. Most people call me Elly." I caught a trace of the native Outer Banks accent in her voice.

She introduced the other woman, Linda Shackleford. She said, "They don't call me anything but Linda. They better not." She was stocky and tanned, with a wide grin, showing big white teeth strong enough to bite through rawhide.

We talked briefly of boats and the dock and the water, of how the waterfront had been improved, benches and all. I kept glancing at Elly. They both worked at eating their cones and talking at the same time, not letting the yogurt melt.

I mentioned the crossword tucked under Elly's arm.

Linda said, "She works 'em every day."

"Well, not every day. Sometimes I can't get all of the clues."

"Yes, she can," Linda said. "Crosswords and ancient history. She can tell you all about the Punic Wars. Wanna hear about the Punic Wars?"

Elly laughed. "I'm not that bad." Maybe embarrassed to have the conversation center on her, she glanced at a sailboat being prepared to shove off.

Then Linda spoke up: "So you're here to write about our latest murder, huh?"

"Oh, no. I mean, I didn't *come* here to write about it. I didn't even know there *was* a murder until last night."

"Aw, come on now, Mr. Weaver." Linda grinned broadly. "You just happened to arrive when there's a big murder story?"

"Really."

"Linda works for *The Coastland Times*."

"Yeah, but I'm in the office. Not a reporter. I hear you may have a good idea of who did it." She eyed me as if she thought I might blurt out the culprit's name.

I was taken aback. I tried to smile. "Where in the hel . . . heck . . . would you hear that?"

"Sammy Foster. Deputy Sheriff Sammy Foster."

"We grew up with Sammy," Elly said.

"Deputy Foster knows I just got in town. Believe me, there's nothing to that." I resolved to have a talk with Deputy Sammy Foster.

Elly glanced at her watch. "Come on, Linda, leave the man alone. I've got to get back to the courthouse." She had eaten most of her yogurt cone, and disposed of the rest of it in the trashcan just beyond the bench.

"Okay," Linda said. "It's just that not every day you get the real lowdown on a murder." She popped the last of her cone into her mouth.

I got my grin back. "Wish I could help."

"Good to meet you," Elly said. "I ought to tell you,

Mabel had awfully nice things to say about you." While Elly
was friendly and appeared open in her manner, there was
still a certain formality in her bearing that I couldn't help but
notice. I got the impression she kept a protective shield of
reserve about her.

I said, "Mabel is a dear. She is always so helpful." Then,
"I'm sure I'll see you back at the courthouse . . . and Linda,
you'll be the first to know if I do find out who the murderer
is."

"Yeah. Sure I will," Linda said.

I smiled at them and watched as they left. In just that
moment, I felt the all-too-familiar tug of vague guilt as I
admired Elly. It had been ten months since Keely died but I
still didn't feel it quite right to look with a certain longing at
another woman. Since Keely's death there had been no one
else except for a drunken, fumbling episode in Richmond
with a woman friend of years back. While I knew, too, that
when I spoke of Keely I didn't use euphemistic terms like
"passed away." But to say simply that she "died," in itself,
was skirting the issue. I knew that.

I forced my thoughts to the Stick book. I read randomly
of North Carolina's role in the Revolutionary War, efforts
for statehood, the conflicting sentiments here on the Outer
Banks about the Civil War, and the Wright Brothers, who
launched the first powered flying machine only a few miles
from where I sat in the sun.

I shut the book. My thoughts skittered around. Even
Schweikert popped back up in my mind. I knew I should say
something to Balls about the confrontation with Schweikert
in the restaurant.

I smiled wryly. Unlike a few not-too-distant periods in
my life, I'd have no difficulty establishing my whereabouts
during the past week. Most of the time I'd been in Danville,
Virginia, working with detectives on another murder story.
I'd had to force interest in the piece because I was so sick of
writing about murder, and couldn't wait to return to the
Outer Banks.

I stood up from the bench, stretched, and started walking back to the courthouse. I headed around the side of the parking garage that ran under the Manteo Waterfront complex. The garage was open on the sides so you could take a short-cut through it to the courthouse side. Instead, I went the long way, staying in the sun.

I'm ashamed to admit that I felt a touch of smugness at having the word out that I knew who the killer was.

That was stupid.

# Chapter Seven

I knew Balls would still be questioning the Carlyle kid, so I planned to leave word with Mabel at the courthouse that I could meet him later for dinner. I figured I'd walk the few blocks back to the motel and take a nap.

As I came out of the courthouse front door, Deputy Sammy Foster ambled up the steps.

"Sammy, let's chat a bit, okay?"

"Sure, Mr. Weaver." He smiled shyly. With others not around, he seemed slightly more at ease. "Deputy Creech show you what he found?" he asked.

"Yes. Real interesting."

Sammy nodded. "You got any ideas?"

"Hell, Sammy, you know I just got here. And that's what I want to talk to you about. I'm not psychic or anything."

I could tell he was forming the words in his mind before he spoke. "Some of the people around here seem to think maybe you are. Psychic or something." He was looking at me. He smiled rather sheepishly, then looked away again.

I was sure I was getting his drift, but I wanted him to play it out. "What do you mean?"

"Oh, you know. Courthouse crowd, folks at the restaurant. They know who you are. They know Agent Ballsford Twiddy, too. They think something's about to break and that's why you showed up."

"I've been planning to come here for weeks."

A slight smiled played on his lips. "Folks don't know that, though." Then he put his hand in his pocket and rattled his change. "Mr. Weaver, I know I'm not in charge of this investigation or anything like that and I reckon there are plenty of lawmen who know more about this sort of thing than me, but . . . it just sort of occurred to me that maybe it's best that way."

I was less than truthful when I said, "I don't know what you're talking about when you say 'maybe it's best that way.' What way? The fact that some of the townspeople think I know more than I do?"

He looked at me and didn't glance away when our eyes met. "Yep." He took his hand from his pocket and folded his arms. "Maybe it won't hurt at all if the word sort of gets out that this investigation is farther along than it is, that you and Agent Twiddy and the sheriff know more than you're letting on."

I knew his answer before I asked. "Why?"

"Just might make somebody nervous. Flush 'em out."

"You got anybody in mind?"

He smiled, hand back in his pocket. There went the jangling change again. "Nope."

I thought about it a moment. I didn't like it. I'm not much for games.

He squirmed to make his exit. "I'd better get on back upstairs."

I remained on the porch a minute or so after he left. I would talk to Balls about this, also. I was going to keep Balls' ear busy.

With my book tucked under my arm, I strolled along one of the side streets toward the motel. I had to watch my step in a few places because ancient live oak tree roots buckled the shaded sidewalk. Neat white frame houses lined the street. Geraniums in white and red pots proved the flower of choice. A few hanging baskets of petunias broke the pattern. An elderly woman in a faded blue housedress puttered around near a birdbath in her front yard. She smiled a greeting.

The quiet time, with virtually no car traffic, gave me a chance to reflect on my encounter with the officious county prosecutor. The confrontation with Schweikert bothered me more than I liked to admit, leaving me with a tinge of depression. I had told Schweikert that as a newspaper reporter I'd stumbled into writing about murder. True, in that I had never *planned* to write about murder.

Early one morning, when as a young reporter still in my twenties, a radio news broadcaster and I had sped to a parking area behind a shopping center where two police officers had been found shot dead. I knew what we were going to see and I was nervous. My mouth was dry. I had never seen violent death before.

I rolled down the window of the car we were riding in and took slow, deliberate breaths of fresh air, while the broadcaster told me how he monitored the police radio dispatcher's call for officers to go to the scene. A guy in a bread truck had discovered the bodies and called police headquarters.

We got there minutes before the back-up officers arrived. We stopped in the rear of the shopping center, twenty yards from a black and white police cruiser that sat eerily silent there in the early morning light, its engine off. As we drove close to the cruiser and stopped, I could see one of the officers slumped behind the steering wheel, his head tilted forward as if asleep. The passenger door was open.

We got out of the car and I tried to lick my lips but my tongue felt like sandpaper. I held my reporter's notebook and pen in front of me, shield-like, as if I were going to take notes. But everything I saw stood out so sharply I knew I would never forget any of it. That was when I discovered I could flick a switch in my brain and become someone else, outside my real self, and look at horror in sharp detail as if a harsh spotlight illuminated the scene.

Still holding the notebook and pen, but not writing a word, I walked around to the passenger side of the cruiser.

Partially hidden by the open door, the other officer was sprawled out on his back. A pool of dark blood stained the asphalt around his hips and head. He'd probably been shot in the lower back as he got out of the cruiser. I stood there, my switch turned on, and stared at him. In my mind I could see him falling on his back, struggling to get up, the killer standing over him pumping bullets into his face. The bullets had pushed his features out of shape as if his face were made of flesh-colored putty that an unskilled sculptor had tried to fashion into something human-like.

I stepped carefully around the body and walked to the front of the car to the driver's window, which was down. I stood close to the door, not touching it, and saw the way the officer's head was slumped forward on his chest. I couldn't see where he was shot, but blood had flowed down behind his seat and pooled on the rear floormat.

The other police cars came screaming to the scene, and I stepped out of their way. I turned my gaze to the sky, which was getting bright and blue and beautiful. And I kept taking breaths of fresh air.

The switch had let me look at those bodies and the strangely misshapen face and the black pool of blood as if I was reading a textbook. Later at the newsroom I wrote about it clearly and accurately.

But at times the switch didn't work. If I couldn't turn it on, the process of writing about murder became too painful, too real. In recreating the horrors in my mind as I knew they happened, the images would come before me so vividly my breathing would almost stop, as if an invisible hand clutched my throat. I could feel the panic, the absolute terror of the victim moments before death came. I could see the bullet, feel the brain explode. And know darkness.

Whenever that happened, I knew it was time to back off. Get away from it. Maybe never go back to writing about murder again, ever.

As I continued walking along the quiet side street in Manteo, I felt a cool breeze across my face and I realized I'd been perspiring. I passed a big white house on the corner that had been converted to a bed and breakfast establishment, and the pots of red geraniums sitting on the porch were a welcome sight. The vague sense of depression began to dissipate. I felt good about my decision to come to the Outer Banks. My spirits became buoyed by walking in the sunshine and breathing in the fresh coastal air.

Just the slightest cloud shadowed my mood as I pictured the murdered Sally Jean Pearson.

But it was such a pretty day.

# Chapter Eight

Janey chirped happily when I opened the door to the motel room.

"Hello, Janey, pretty bird."

She bobbed her head up and down in a dance she does when she's in a good mood. Other days she can be sulky, especially when she is molting. They say female parakeets don't talk or mimic sounds like the males. Just the same, I always talked to her in hopes that someday she would repeat sounds. Besides, you should always talk to a pet. Makes them feel special.

I saw marks on the floor where housekeeping had vacuumed around my bass, without moving it. Good. The bass is too valuable to be handled by those who don't know what they are doing.

I stripped off my damp shirt and stretched out on the bed. The air conditioning felt great, sweeping a coolness over me. My mind kept bouncing around, from wanting to see what the ocean looked like today to what progress was being made on getting my little house ready to move in to the next day, Saturday. I couldn't lie still. I went in the bathroom, splashed water on my face, slipped on another golf shirt.

I left Manteo and drove toward the beach. It was the same route I had taken at breakfast, but I was thrilled anew in the sunlight on the bridge above the sparkling waters of Roanoke Sound, looking toward the ocean.

This time of year as many out-of-state vehicles as local ones are on the Outer Banks roads. Two sedans, one with North Carolina tags, the other with Virginia tags, passed me on the crest of the bridge. Ahead of me, a car drove at my speed, and two vehicles stayed behind me, one a dark-colored SUV.

Once across the bridge, I drove the older Beach Road, as Highway 12 is mostly referred to by the locals. It runs north and south parallel to the 158 Bypass. Years ago, motels, shops, and sturdy old cottages with juniper siding sprouted along the narrow Beach Road, where they remain today. Here and there the ocean is less than a football field away. With high tide and an occasional northeaster, the ocean comes a whole lot closer, washing across the highway, depositing sand and debris and brownish foam against the pilings that keep houses raised ten feet and more above the sand.

When I thought about high tide, I imagined how native Outer Banker Elly Pedersen would say it, with that soft accent of hers. It would come out faintly sounding like "hoigh toide."

Driving the Beach Road, I watched for tired and sunburned pedestrians. They have a tendency to wander across the road zombie-like, their hair matted with saltwater and windblown, dragging blankets and beach paraphernalia, a red and squalling youngster in tow.

Near Mile Post 8, I pulled into a public ocean access area and parked. I took the wooden walkway to the dunes that edge the beach. The west wind flattened out the ocean, but it never completely quiets the powerful *shush-shushing* of the surf. A young man and woman in bathing suits, sand cling-ing to their legs, came from the beach and walked past me, nodding shyly. Down the beach to the south, away from most of the sunbathers, two people fished, wading out a few yards to cast, then backing up on the beach, waiting. I watched them a moment, then I closed my eyes and breathed in deeply, the wind gently on the back of my neck. I realized

I was smiling.

After a while, enjoying the calmness the ocean always gives me, I drove from the Beach Road to the Bypass. After waiting for a break in the traffic, I turned onto the Bypass, headed toward the Wright Brothers Memorial. In the rear view mirror I saw a dark SUV pull out onto the Bypass, forcing two cars to shift lanes.

Hell, don't start getting paranoid. The world is filled with dark-colored SUVs, and many of them hog the road.

Another mile and a half and I was at Wright Shores subdivision, an older development, with mostly small, moderately priced houses. I got in the middle turn-lane and waited to make a left. The SUV had stopped at the light behind me. I made my turn, slowed, and watched in my mirror as the SUV continued on the Bypass. I smiled at my jumpiness.

The cottage I was about to occupy nestled among scrubby pine trees on a cul-de-sac. A vacant lot on each side and a growth of brush and water willows behind made the cottage secluded and quiet. The cottage sat on pilings, creating a carport underneath. A porch or deck extended across the front of the house and wrapped around to the side door at the top of the stairs. Two bedrooms, a living room with a sliding glass door that opened to the deck, a large kitchen and bath. Central air and heat. A great place.

Pulling into the cul-de-sac, I parked behind the work-van used by Jerry, who maintains a number of nearby cottages, with assistance from his wife, Betty.

Jerry stood by the open back door of his van, retrieving cleaning supplies. We chatted for a minute or two and he insisted I come in to see the house and speak to Betty.

As we started up the flight of steps to the side door, a dark SUV with tinted windows drove slowly past the entrance to the cul-de-sac. Had the SUV gone beyond my street, made a left, circled back?

Jerry said, "What's the matter? Come on in."

We found Betty on her knees in front of the opened oven. She got to her feet and took off a rubber glove to greet me.

The place smelled good.

For a house at the beach, it was nicely furnished: rattan furniture upholstered with light-colored fabrics—what Keely would have called dusty rose and sea mist green—that gave the place a cheerful, airy look. Cable TV and telephone hook-ups. I would switch the utilities to my name next week. I jotted down the telephone number to give to Balls. The people who owned the house, long-time friends of mine, used the cottage themselves part of the year and occasionally rented it. This summer they had rented it to a retired couple who needed a temporary place while their new house was being completed. My friend had said that this fall he was going to make an offer to sell me the house that I wouldn't be able to refuse.

While Jerry and Betty talked, I stole glances out the window.

Jerry gave me a set of keys to the place and offered to help me move in the next day.

When I drove away, I checked for that SUV. Not seeing it, I chalked up my sense of apprehension to an overactive imagination.


The telephone message light in my motel room was blinking. The voice of the woman at the front desk told me, "Mr. Twiddy called, said he was tied up with some folks and he would see you at Queen Anne's Revenge at seven-thirty. Call the sheriff, the sheriff's office, if you can't make it."

"Anything else?"

"No, that's all he said. He sounded like he was in a hurry. Didn't have the time of day, you know what I mean. But he was nice and all, I don't mean that. Was just that he sounded. . . ."

"I understand. He was just busy. Thank you very much."

Queen Anne's Revenge is a nice restaurant tucked away at Wanchese. I guess ol' Balls was out to impress me.

Couple of hours before I had to leave. I sat on the bed,

still feeling edgy. I looked at my bass fiddle. Practicing a few scales and an exercise I had been working on always seemed to calm me. At worst, it got me so frustrated as I tried for proper intonations and bowing that I shifted my concerns.

I tuned one string to the harmonics of another. I bowed softly, first a two-octave F-major scale, then G-major, B-flat major, and C. The high C was off. I practiced that again and again, muttering "shit" every time I missed it. I do a lot of cussing when I practice. Then I tried the passage from Mozart's "Requiem" that I use as an exercise. The section requires crossing the bow from string to string. Maddening. I shook my head. "A bitch."

I heard chirping and the tingling bell in Janey's cage. She liked activity, and wanted attention. I laid the bass down, checked her water and seed supply, and told her, "Okay, pretty bird. You'll be in your new house tomorrow with lots of sunshine. You'll like it." She bobbed her head.

I went back to the bass.

Shadows from the tall pine trees at the back of the motel began to lengthen. I set the alarm for six o'clock, stripped, and stretched out under the sheets. I was just drifting off when the phone made me jump.

"Hello?"

The line was dead.

I called the front desk. The woman said, "No, I didn't get his name. He just asked to speak to Harrison Weaver in room 218. I told him that was the wrong room, that you were in 108. And you were the only Harrison Weaver we had." She paused for a moment. "He sounded like he had a cold or something."

I thanked her, hung up, and sat looking at the phone, as if it could tell me who had placed that call.

I drove the winding road to Wanchese in the growing dusk, bore off to the right to Queen Anne's Revenge, and got there

at seven-thirty on the dot. Balls was already seated at a table
off to one side where he could keep an eye on the front door.

He grinned at me and glanced at his watch. "Oversleep?"

"You're full of crap, Balls."

The waitress came to our table. Probably forty, she was
tall and regal, her hair done neatly in a loose bun. Balls
ordered a beer, then changed his mind. "Make it iced tea."

"Same," I said. "Sweetened." I remembered we were in
the South, where presweetened tea was available.

I knew Balls well enough to recognize that his cheer-
fulness was mostly an act. "Hard day at the office?"

The woman brought the iced tea. I ordered the grouper
and Balls got fried shrimp, as I figured he would.

He kept putting sugar in his iced tea and staring at it.

"That's already sweetened," I said.

"I don't like this case. Something about it."

"Like what?"

"I don't know. That's just it." Absently stirring the tea. "I
don't think we're even close."

"The Carlyle kid?" I asked.

"No, he doesn't have anything to do with it. Hell, the gal
could have out-wrestled him. Put a noose around *his* neck if
she'd wanted to." A quarter of an inch of sugar settled at the
bottom of his glass. He took a sip, set the glass down, and
stirred again. The restaurant lighting etched the lines deeper
on his face, giving him a look of weariness that wasn't there
this morning. I could practically see his investigator's mind
clicking, but getting zeroes.

He said, "What we've been doing this afternoon, after
talking with the Carlyle kid, is getting names of people in
the Green Dolphin that night. Creech has been doing that.
Nothing. Around in circles. Exercises in futility. We've got
to get the whole list of players and stagehands and others out
at the theater. And we've checked for a list of any stalkers or
sex offenders on file here in the county."

He chuckled. "You know what we came up with? A file
on one tourist, last year, an old geezer from New Jersey,

took his pecker out at the movie house on the Bypass and two little girls told their mommies. That's our Dare County sex offender file!"

"No leads at all?"

"We're not even lukewarm. It's one of those things you can sort of feel or not feel. And I don't feel anything." He glanced around the restaurant again to make sure we remained far enough away from other diners not to be overheard. The restaurant was nearly full, but quieter than the places along the beach. "It wasn't sex. I mean it wasn't sex in the sense of rape. It was still sexual, as so many of them are." I waited for him to mentally play out his thoughts before I mentioned what was on my mind.

Idly rubbing condensation off his tea glass, he said, "No enemies. Young girl like that. Hell, everybody loved her. Maybe whoever it was, was just mad at the world, mad at the women in the world. Maybe it wasn't personal at all."

He sat frowning at the table, toying with his thoughts. The waitress, her carriage erect and the slightest smile softening her patrician features brought the pitcher and refilled our glasses. Balls glared at his tea, as if it offended him. I knew he would start the sweetening process again.

"Crap. That's not what I think at all. She was picked for a specific reason." He sighed. "I just don't know what it is."

We stopped talking as Her Majesty brought our food.

I decided to broach the subject that no one seemed willing to talk about. "The two *are* linked, aren't they? The two murders. Four years apart, but they're linked, right?"

Without answering me, Balls said, "The Pearsons, the girl's parents, went home this afternoon. I went to the motel to speak to them. God, that was a sad sight."

He saw me looking at his shrimp. "Try one. They're good."

I gave him half of my baked potato. The broiled grouper was good and it was prepared nicely, but I wished I had ordered the fried shrimp.

"Okay," I said, "you going to freeze me out of this or tell

me what you think?"

"You tell me. Want to see how good you're getting. Whether you're good enough to tag along with me. Hell, you're supposed to be my lucky charm."

"Some of it appears obvious. Both murders done by the same person . . . not Bobby Ford, of course, who's dead, and not the Carlyle boy who was hardly into puberty four years ago. But done by the same person. Number one, both girls *look* alike. Same coloring, same build. Number two, both girls are in *The Lost Colony*. Number three, they are both killed the same way, maybe even with the same type cord. Number four, both girls get their blouses and bras ripped the same way and maybe even the same kind of bruise on their left breasts.

"And five, it appears that neither one of these girls wore lipstick that made them look, to use your words, like 1940s movie stars. The killer must have smeared that bright color on both girls." I stared at Balls. "Now, by God, tell me I'm wrong."

"You're not wrong." He spoke quietly, leaning forward and looking directly into my eyes. "I think the same thing and so does Albright. He just doesn't want to admit it. But let's not lock ourselves into that theory too tightly. Might not be right at all. You can always get fooled."

"Copycat?"

"Not out of the question. Trying to keep the details confidential in a small town like this is all but impossible. So, still comes back to who? Someone who has been connected with the play for four years? Maybe a couple dozen people fall into that category. Someone in the town who only murders every four years? A tourist who comes back and does a couple of murders to keep from getting bored on his vacation?"

He signaled for another refill on his iced tea. The waitress, that faint smile on her lips, poured the tea regally, offering no idle chatter.

When she walked away from the table, Balls said, "You

know, a woman like that, all high and mighty acting, makes you want to take 'em out and get 'em all hot and flustered. Get their hair mussed up. Get 'em panting a little bit. You know, you think maybe it'd be good for them." He grinned at me.

I shook my head in mock disapproval of what he said. I knew the real T. Ballsford Twiddy. He might try to play the part of the rounder, but underneath he was as straight an arrow as they come, an elder in his Presbyterian church and a devoted husband and family man. He liked role-playing, though, just to get a reaction.

Sucking the meat out of the tail of a shrimp he held between his index finger and thumb, he turned his sly grin on me. "I saw you eyeing that Pedersen gal today."

"I wasn't *eyeing* her, as you so delicately put it."

"Lusting after her." He wiped his hands, that big smirk still on his face. "She *is* good looking."

Trying to be noncommittal, I said, "I ran into her at lunch and introduced myself. None of you clowns would introduce me."

"We're trying to keep our women safe."

"What do you mean, 'our women'? Since when did you become a father of the community?"

"When they found that body."

I nodded. A moment later I said, "She *is* attractive. Married or anything?"

"I figured."

"You figured what?"

"You know, staking out what's available. Looking over the crop."

I smiled, really sort of enjoying his game. "You're disgusting. You know that?"

He speared another shrimp. "Just honest." He looked at my plate. "Don't you like your food?"

"It's fine. It's great."

"No, she's not married. Was, though, and has a little kid. Boy about three or four. She's from around here. One of the 'hoigh toide' natives. Says 'doime' for 'dime' and all that. Love to hear her talk. Married a guy from Raleigh she met years back when she was in school there, a musician, classical stuff mostly."

He winked. "Hey, maybe she's got a thing for musicians, bass fiddle players, perhaps." Abruptly his face clouded, and I knew he wished he hadn't made that last statement. He must have made the connection with Keely, who had been a singer with a band I played with at times.

He continued, a tad less jovial. "I don't know what kind of a marriage it was. Didn't last long. Fact is, she never changed her name. She still goes by Pedersen. Maybe her kid does too. Not sure. Anyway, her husband was real sickly. Sick all the time. I don't think it was drugs or nothing. And then he just up and died a year or two after they were married. I think it was some kind of viral pneumonia. You know, like that guy Jim-something that came up with the Muppets."

"How do you know all this stuff?"

"That's my business to know stuff. I know stuff here and all the way down to Stumpy Point, and I know stuff in Elizabeth City, Ahoskie, Edenton, Rocky Mount, Little Washington, all over Eastern North Carolina. Now you, you know stuff in Washington, *Dee Cee*. But I know stuff in Eastern North Carolina."

His face got more serious. "And she's a real straight gal."

I felt a flicker of guilt because right then Keely's death seemed so far away, like I was trying to forget it, to give it less significance than it deserved.

The waitress came within a few feet of the table, one eyebrow arched inquisitively. I signaled that we were fine. To Balls I said, "What's Sammy Foster doing in all of this?"

"Huh? Sammy?" Balls stopped eating. "What about Sammy?"

"What's he doing in the investigation?"

"He's nosing around town. Why?"

"Well, apparently while he's just sort of nosing around

town he's dropping broad hints that maybe I know who the killer is, like it's just a matter of time before I'm going to break the whole damn case."

"Where'd you hear that?"

"I heard it from Linda, Elly's . . . the Pedersen woman's friend. And I heard it more or less from Sammy. At least that's what I think I heard from Sammy."

"He's sort of a peculiar one. Got a good head on him, though. He may have ideas he's not talking about. But he shouldn't be spreading word like that."

"Says it might flush the guy out."

"Right—or flush you out to sea. I'll speak to him."

I knew what he was talking about. It probably showed on my face. I started to tell him about the SUV, but it seemed like too much of a stretch.

Instead I said, "Another thing. About Schweikert." I told Balls about the encounter at lunch and the man's veiled accusations.

Balls said, "Don't worry. Schweikert tried to run his mouth off to me this afternoon about where you were and all that crap. When he got through, I jotted down the name of Detective Tom Childress in Danville, and the phone number. 'Call him,' I said. 'Weaver was with him last week.' You could see Schweikert deflate. I let the air out of his balloon."

Balls nodded at his plate. "You want this last shrimp?"


As we left Queen Anne's Revenge, I told Balls to go ahead. I didn't want to try to keep up with him as he headed back to his motel on the west side of Manteo. He planned to leave early in the morning so he could spend most of Saturday and Sunday at home with his wife and two teenagers.

We agreed that I would come to the courthouse Monday morning and get a fill-in on what, if anything, had developed in the meantime.

I followed Balls' taillights, but they soon disappeared ahead of me. Traffic was almost non-existent until I got on the main highway, US 64, into Manteo.

When I arrived back at King's Motel it was nearly nine-thirty. I waved toward the office and drove around to my room at the back. Business had increased for the weekend, but there was still room for a half dozen more cars. Two outside fixtures created a weak pool of light along the edge of the sidewalk and parking area.

I parked in front of my room, got out, and opened the back door to get my jacket. I had laid it across the boxes and other stuff piled high in the back seat.

As I reached in for my jacket, I saw through the rear window a movement in the dark pine trees about twenty yards away at the far edge of the lot. A form, a person, stepped quickly behind one of the trees.

Pretending to be searching for something in the car, I kept stealing a look through the rear window. I saw it again, as if the figure had stuck his head and upper body out from the tree, then ducked back. No question about it.

I felt chilled. I got my coat, locked the car, and went into my room, bolting the door. I had left the bathroom light on. I turned it off and went to the window. I heard Janey shift in her cage.

Slowly, I lifted a slat in the Venetian blind. I couldn't see nearly as clearly as I had from inside my car. The window reflected the outside light and the salt air had left its smudgy imprint. But I could make out the pine trees. I thought I saw a shadow move away from the trees toward the side street.

A moment later I heard a vehicle start and pull away from the curb on the side street. Whoever it was didn't turn his lights on, but he did touch the brakes once. The taillights lit, spaced high and wide apart, as on a pickup truck or an SUV.

I sat on the bed and turned the light on. Though I knew the door was locked and bolted, I still glanced at it. Get hold of yourself. Probably a guy out there taking a leak. Hell, maybe a peeping Tom and I interrupted his show.

But somebody was out there.

# Chapter Nine

I woke before my clock went off at seven. No attacks during the night. I glanced out the window at my car. All intact, tires not slashed. No intruders lurking in the sunshine. I smiled.

Time to get moving. I showered and dressed in thirty minutes.

Mr. King's tall, pudgy son was on duty in the motel office. He looked sleepy, wrinkled and pale, the same as the night I arrived. I told him I was able to move into my house today.

I packed my car, adding the bass and Janey last. Then I strolled to the trees at the edge of the parking lot. Trampled pine needles at the base of one of the trees told me someone had stood there for a period of time.

Okay, I'm getting jumpy. A dark SUV with tinted windows—just like in the movies—appears to follow me. The phone rings and no one is there, and a mysterious stranger stands by a pine tree behind my motel. Boy, talk about letting my imagination connect the dots.

Even so, Deputy Sammy Foster's broad hints that I knew who committed these murders could be putting me in danger. No doubt about that. Balls will speak to Sammy. Get Sammy to do a reverse spin on what he's been saying.

When I got to the house in Wright Shores, I began unloading my car, starting with Janey and then the bass fiddle.

I stopped every so often to jot down another item on the list of things I needed to get from the grocery store or from Ace Hardware.

When I had lugged my box of prized books into the house, sweat drenched my shirt. I shut the door, checked the air conditioning again, and sat down on the couch, feeling satisfied. Setting up housekeeping. The place was mine. Well, practically mine.

Yes, setting up housekeeping, but without Keely. Doing it alone. Then, unexpected, unbidden, a feeling of deep sadness swept over me. Keely would have loved this spirit of adventure, this starting out anew. That was before she slipped into a depression where no one could reach her. November would be one year since I found her curled in a fetal position in our bed. All the pills gone. A note pad by the bed with nothing written on it, as if she had nothing left she could explain.

I stood and went to the sliding glass door. Looking at the clear blue sky of the summer day, I was unable to stop the sadness and the tears that came.


Monday morning I was up by seven, did my daily push-ups and stomach crunches, then started a slow jog out of the cul-de-sac toward Kitty Hawk Bay. At the bay, I turned and jogged eastward along a parallel road to the convenience store at the Bypass. I bought a copy of *The Virginian-Pilot* from one of the machines and carried it under one arm as I continued my jog back to the house. The ocean was less than a half mile from me. Even when the ocean was not visible, I always sensed its presence, a force that overlay everything at the Outer Banks. It was there from the be-ginning, like God.

Despite my original intention to become immersed in the peacefulness of the Outer Banks, I was once again in the midst of a murder investigation. I should accept that writing about true crime was important to me, not just for the income but because of something deeper. The chase? The puzzle? An adrenalin rush? I don't know. But I was sure I could still manage to get away from the stench of killings when it became necessary. And once this case was over. . . .

Yeah, right.

No suspicious vehicles followed me when I drove to the courthouse. I parked in the street-level garage underneath the Manteo Waterfront complex and walked across the street to the courthouse. Upstairs, I found Sheriff Albright standing at the files talking with Mabel. He cast a glance at me and jerked his head toward his office. "Agent Twiddy's in there," he said, with an uncharacteristic curtness of tone. He went back to Mabel. I had a big smile on my face that got left hanging there.

Balls slouched in the chair near Albright's desk.

"God, what time you leave home?" I asked.

"Four-thirty." He motioned for me to step closer and dropped his voice to a whisper. "Sheriff's feeling a bit antsy about you being here. He's not ready to shut you out but stay as low-key as you can."

Sheriff Albright came in, several sheets of paper in his hand. "That Doc Mordecai is good. She faxed me the preliminary autopsy report this morning. She's still got tests to run but this is pretty much it." He gave a few pages to Balls.

The two of them read in silence. I saw Balls scanning down the pages. "Nothing much new here," he said. "Doesn't tell us a lot more than we already knew, or figured. Death by asphyxia . . . before she went in the water." As if talking to himself, Balls muttered, ". . . no sign of rape . . . trauma to the nipple . . . and the lipstick business." I knew he was summarizing for my benefit.

Albright continued reading. He lay the faxed pages down. "Doesn't add a whole lot to the case, at this point, does it?"

Balls stifled a yawn. He said, "I been up since real early this morning. Let's go downstairs to Diane's, get some coffee."

I looked questioningly at Balls.

"Come on, join us," he said.

Albright led the way, saying nothing.

Many of the regulars already sat at their customary places in the restaurant. I shook hands with Ross Haynes, an official at the Manteo Post Office where I had done a lot of mailing.

"Oh, simply delighted to see you again," he gushed. "Got any of those nifty manuscripts for me to mail?"

We took a table toward the back. After we had settled at the table, Balls said, "Sheriff, rumors have got started, thanks to our good Deputy Sammy Foster, that Weav here practically knows who the killer is. We don't want folks to get too curious about how much ol' Weav knows—especially if that someone happens to be the type what does folks in."

Albright turned toward me. More of the usual benevolence registered in his eyes. "I understand," he said. "We need to squelch that."

Since the subject of my possible safety had come up, I then told Balls and the sheriff about someone ducking behind a pine tree at the motel. I tried to make it sound like no big deal.

I could tell Albright didn't put much stock in the incident.

The three of us looked up as Charlie Ferguson and his son-in-law, Dixon Nance, approached our table. I remembered Nance used to coach the high school's successful basketball team and then went to work for Ferguson. He was married to Ferguson's daughter, Sandra.

Ferguson smiled broadly, his silver hair swooped back along both temples. "Gentlemen, pardon the intrusion but I would like to extend an invitation. Sheriff, I'd like for you and your bride and these two gentlemen to join a number of us Friday night for good North Carolina barbecue over at the hall next to my place. Several of us in the community decided it was time to get together, show that life goes on, celebrate the end of another season. Eat a pile of barbecue, drink a little beer, tell a few lies."

Taking Balls and me in with the sweep of his eyes, he said, "We all get so carried away with business, and the recent unpleasantness, we get in danger of letting the good times, the fellowship, just slip away."

"Sounds like a good idea, Charlie," the sheriff said.

Balls and I thanked him for the invitation.

Nance said, "You don't have to bring anything. It'll all be there. Beer and everything." He smiled, and then glanced at his watch. I figured Ferguson caught the signal because he said his goodbyes. I got the impression that Nance had moved steadily up the Ferguson business ladder. I remembered him from four years earlier as basically the husky, ruddy-faced typical jock, and one who might put away a goodly amount of beer. He definitely appeared more businesslike now.

After they had moved away from our table, Balls turned to the sheriff. "*The Lost Colony* this morning? Talk with some of the kids, check with the business staff?"

I figured now was a good time to try to wedge myself into going with them. "I've known Ken Cavanaugh, the general manager at *The Lost Colony*, since he was in Virginia as the executive vice president of a community symphony I played with. I feel like he'll remember me."

Albright didn't answer immediately, and when he did, he spoke to Balls. "Instead of going over there right now, I'd like you to do me another favor."

Balls nodded.

"Two young brothers down in Wanchese, fishermen. I know their daddy and mama. They're having a real tough time financially. And what I'm hearing and what I'm afraid of is they're getting mighty tempted to try to run dope in here along the coast. Meet somebody out in the Gulf Stream, come back in here after dark, drop it off anywhere from here to Stumpy Point to Swan Quarter, anywhere."

He permitted himself a hint of a smile. "They know the

coast like you and I know the backs of our hands. Later, they'd stash the dope inside one of the fish in a shipment being trucked to the New York market. They think they'll pick up fast money. Swear to themselves they're not going to do it ever again. They're not bad boys, just a bit desperate right now."

"You got a good tip on this?"

"Yeah. I figure that if you and me go out there, pay a call, and they see you, a state guy, they're going to know this is serious business. We'll just tell them we're checking around because of rumors, that some folks in the community might be tempted to do something foolish and we know for a fact that the Coast Guard and the DEA and God knows who all is really on the lookout for this sort of thing."

The waitress approached with the coffee pot for refills. Albright shook his head. "Tell the boys that we'd sure appreciate it if they hear of anything or anybody about to do something foolish that they let us know. That way we scare them out of it before they go and mess around with it."

"Happy to oblige," Balls said.

"And anyway," the sheriff said, "I want to step back from this murder case for a tad. Refocus on it later. I don't know, I don't really feel good about it. We're not getting any-where." He stopped talking and glanced at me. "Weaver, since this is a delicate semi-official call that Agent Twiddy and I will be making . . ."

"I understand completely, Sheriff. Believe me, I ap-preciate being permitted to . . ." I started to say more, but let it drop.

"Besides," Balls said, "he'd probably like to hang around your office in hopes of seeing that Pedersen woman."

A smile brushed across the sheriff's face. "Ellen Pedersen? Elly? Fine young woman. Her mother, too. Went to school with her mother. Daddy's dead. He was from up north somewhere."

"That's Balls running his mouth, Sheriff. I only spoke to her yesterday. I don't even know where she works."

"But you're just set to find out," Balls said.

"Register of Deeds office," Albright said. "And from time to time she helps Mabel out. She started out in my office. We're a small family here."

Balls tapped me on the chest with one of his big fingers and winked. "Register of Deeds office. Downstairs. First door on the left if you come in the front of the courthouse." To Albright he said, "Oh, this may be a mistake, Sheriff. I think we should lock up all the women for safekeeping."

I knew the joshing was Balls' way of urging me to get on with life. He still hadn't talked about Keely and her death.

# Chapter Ten

To tell the truth, I did think about stopping by the first door on the left downstairs, but I felt it'd be a wee bit adolescent to go hanging around in hopes of seeing a pretty girl.

What I really wanted to do—overriding even an itch to swing by the Register of Deeds' office—was to bypass the sheriff and Balls and scoot over to *The Lost Colony* theater and talk to Ken Cavanaugh. I wanted to get on with the investigation, check out the cast members and others at the theater. But talk about a move that would piss Balls off, that would be it. Not to mention the sheriff. Balls made it possible for me to tag along on this case. I had better sense than to screw that up.

So I took a deep breath and went upstairs to finish reading the files on the older case.

I'm glad I did. Mabel and Elly stood talking in the hall outside the sheriff's office. "I don't know why they brought it here, anyway," Mabel said, handing Elly several pieces of mail. "Looks like they don't pay attention at all anymore."

Mabel's face brightened. "Well, good morning! Back to dig into those files again?"

"Gotta keep at it." I couldn't help but look at Elly. She wore a pale yellow cotton dress that buttoned close to the throat. Her hair was pulled back again, showing a delicate and appealing neck.

We stood making idle chatter, and for lack of anything

else to say I asked them both to lunch. At first Mabel declined, said she had brought leftover chicken from home. Then she changed her mind and encouraged Elly to accept. We set it for noon.

I used the same office as on Friday. Reading through the files methodically, I was aware of my urge to not only write an article but also to play detective. Why else would I be studying them, absorbing anew all of the facts, comparing them with what I knew about the current case?

One of the old news clips contained a three-column picture of the late Sheriff Claxton briefing several reporters and a gathering of residents in the courthouse. The picture, taken from slightly behind the sheriff, showed him in three-quarter profile, with the audience as the main focus. I concentrated on the faces. Indistinct but unmistakable was the silver-haired Charlie Ferguson. A couple of others I recognized, including Dixon Nance, and Ross Haynes from the post office. Mabel stood against the back wall, and near her the scowling face of Jules Hinson appeared.

While I scanned other old news clips, Mabel shuffled into the office on those black, sneaker-like shoes, and quietly laid a folder on the desk. The folder contained news clips on the new case, plus two reports of interviews and data on the Pearson woman signed by Creech and Sammy Foster.

From long years as a reporter, I always carry one of the skinny spiral notebooks that fit either in a jacket pocket or, in this case, the back pocket of a pair of khakis. As I read from both files, I listed the similarities in my notebook. One thing I had not paid attention to before, both young women lived in rented rooms in the central part of town, only two blocks from each other. Each would have walked virtually the same route from the center of Manteo to get home. A notation based on an SBI report was inserted in the new file to the effect that no other young women of a similar age from the area were reported missing. However, the brief report did note that a year earlier the slaying of a young woman—strangled with a cord and thrown into a pond in Raleigh, less than a four-hour drive from Manteo—remained unsolved.

Bodies of both of the young women from *The Lost Colony* were found in the Croatan Sound on the northwest side of Roanoke Island where the play is performed. Sheriff Claxton had surmised that the killer drove to the top of the old bridge over Croatan Sound to a pullover spot for bridge maintenance. From that point, a person could see almost a mile and a half each way. Late at night, the killer could make sure no one was coming and haul the body out and drop it over the side.

I kept reading through the old case file, parts of it more than once, until I heard Mabel moving around in the hall. It was close to noon.

We got Elly and headed out of the courthouse. We passed two young women co-workers, who smiled knowingly at Elly. Without turning her head or breaking stride, Elly raised a hand and wiggled her fingers goodbye at them.

We drove in my car to Sugar Creek's on the causeway at Whalebone Junction. The restaurant sits high on wooden pilings. About halfway up the long wooden walkway, I noticed Mabel's breathing was labored and she moved more slowly.

I stopped and commented on the ducks and Canada geese playing around at the edge of the water. We stood watching the water fowl for a few moments. When we started walking again, Elly held Mabel's hand.

We got seats on the glassed-in side porch overlooking the water, and all three of us ordered flounder filet luncheon specials. Elly set her small purse on the window's ledge. The folded top of a crossword puzzle poked out from the purse.

I tilted my head toward her purse. "Carry a crossword everywhere?"

She smiled. "Just about."

Mabel said, "She's a crossword addict."

"Be surprised at how many useful things you can learn," Elly said, a trace of a sly twinkle evident. "I mean, just think about how many times in ordinary conversation you can manage to mention the middle name of Walt Disney—that was one of the clues today—or what an ornamental needles case is called."

The meal was brought quickly by a waitress who addressed us as "you guys."

As soon as we started eating, Elly leveled her gaze at me. "You think they'll solve this murder, or will it be like the other one?"

"I really don't know."

Mabel said, "It makes a lot of the young girls, older ones too, uneasy. Nobody wants to be walking around town at night, not unless there are two or three of us together."

Elly said, "I don't think they'll solve this one either. There'll probably have to be more deaths before they catch whoever is doing it, if they ever catch him." Her voice had an edge of bitterness.

A moment later she smiled and pointed down at the water. "Look, there's a granddaddy turtle."

I saw him. A round, dark shadow, the size of a dishpan, swimming slowly from under the walkway among small fish.

When we got up to leave, Elly's hand darted out and snatched two rolls from the uncleared table next to us. "For the fish," she announced, head thrown back, leading the way.

We stopped on the walkway and dropped small pieces of bread in the water. The fish swirled the water and made sucking sounds as they gulped the crumbs. The ducks and geese, seeing the action, paddled closer, but they were too late.

I parked just beyond the sheriff's reserved space, and got out to help Mabel.

She thanked me again for the lunch. "I'm going on in," she said. "It's hot out here."

I asked her to tell Agent Twiddy I'd be back at my place this afternoon and that I'd call him.

Elly said, "I'm coming in just a minute." I had sensed for the past mile or so there was something she wanted to say. We stood by the car.

She said, "When we talked the other day," she inclined her head toward the Manteo Waterfront, "Linda mentioned that Sammy, Deputy Sheriff Sammy Foster, said you were about to solve the case."

A noncommittal, "Yes?" I wanted to draw her out.

"I've known Sammy since the first grade. I know he's quiet and all but he doesn't do anything without a reason. When he said that about you knowing more than you do, he had a reason for it."

"I know what he was thinking, and I don't really approve." I gave a short, mirthless chuckle. "And I just hope this ploy of his doesn't, you know, backfire."

"No . . . Sammy would never want that to happen." She squinted in the sun, looking at me. The sunshine seemed to create tiny flecks of gold in the hazel part of her eyes. "He hasn't talked to me but I got to thinking. He wants somebody to think you know something so maybe they'll act different and he can spot it."

I nodded.

She shielded her eyes with one hand. I shifted so she wasn't looking directly into the sun. One strand of her hair had come loose from the way she had it done up in the back and fluttered at her neck.

"And here's the thing. Sammy's got to think it's somebody here in town. One of the townspeople. Maybe somebody we see every day. Sammy's got to think it's somebody who knows who you are and maybe somebody who has known who you are for years. It couldn't be just a tourist, a stranger."

Elly had to be right about Sammy's thinking. Whether *he*

was correct in his thinking was another matter. But I didn't want to get into what-ifs, and I learned over the years to keep my mouth shut at such times, let things play out. So I nodded again and said, "I know."

She appeared to study my face. I stared deeply into her eyes, and that seemed to embarrass her. She pushed the strand of hair away from her neck. "I better go in."

She turned, then looked back at me with a slight smile. "Elias."

"Huh?"

"Elias. That's Walt Disney's middle name."

She held up one hand and wiggled her fingers goodbye.

# Chapter Eleven

I drove back toward the beach and my house thinking about Sammy Foster and the rumor he'd started. I know that as a reporter it can be an asset to have people think you know more than you do. Deep down, though, I knew the reason I had not called Sammy off had to do with ego—I enjoyed being viewed as strutting around town just waiting to break the big news. But that illusion was not something to be proud of.

At the house, I resolved to get myself in gear. I needed to talk with one of my editors in New York and set a later time for delivering the Danville murder story that I was supposed to be writing. But I also needed to establish a checking account with a local bank and take care of some personal finances. I could probably think of other things to delay getting to work.

For what I really wanted to do was poke my nose into the Pearson murder case, but I knew that if I tried to go solo on this I'd screw my chances of having access to the investigation. Only through Balls did I have a tenuous connection for being a part of it. Piss him off, and I could kiss that access goodbye. I had to cool it, a behavior I was doing my best to learn.

After a quick trip to a local bank and to Food Lion to pick up food, bug spray, and a fly swatter, I spent the rest of the afternoon enjoying my house. I took the bass out of its cover and put it on the stand in the corner of the living room. Its beautiful carved spruce top gave off a rich, warm glow in the afternoon light. I set Janey's cage on a low table near the sliding glass door, giving her a view to the outside. I moved my laptop and printer from the back bedroom to the dinette table so I could watch the late summer sun traverse its east-to-west course in the southern sky.

The domestic chores brought back images of Keely. In the beginning, she would watch with a bemused smile as I puttered around the house or in the kitchen. Later, when the depression began to take hold, I might enter the kitchen to find her standing immobile, staring blankly at unwashed dishes piled in the sink. I would speak to her and she would turn slowly to face me, studying my face as if I were a stranger to her.

I sat down in the chair by the phone and stared out the glass door. I liked the way the late afternoon sun made the needles of the pine tree in the front yard give off a dull glow. Janey cocked her head and chirped at me.

I was tired of feeling guilty about Keely's death. I had done enough of that. Just the same, I had to remind myself repeatedly that I had done everything I could to help her, help that she managed invariably to negate, turn to naught.

After she died, I spent weeks drinking too much, something I usually did in moderation. One Saturday morning I woke up not remembering where I had been since Thursday night. That's when I put the cap on the bottle and decided to get away from Washington, change my life, do my writing full time.

But I found out I wasn't through with the drinking. A few weeks later I was working on a murder story in Richmond and staying in a motel there. I called a woman I knew from years earlier. She said she was thrilled to hear from me and yes, it would be a marvelous idea to get together at my motel for a drink for old time's sake, especially since she was more or less on the verge of getting a divorce.

I saw her coming into the lobby. She was still thin, and I

felt her back and hipbones when we hugged in greeting. I could smell her perfume, one of those musky scents and too strong.

We went into the bar portion of the restaurant and ordered drinks. I already had a head start. She drank white wine. I had another whiskey shot with a beer chaser and then just beer to maintain the glow. I was charming as all get-out, and had her laughing and drinking along with me.

Her hair was tinted a reddish brown. She had quick, jerky movements and bobbed her head when she laughed. I had forgotten that she did that, and now it seemed more exaggerated than it used to. She still smoked, stretching her chin forward as she sucked on the cigarette so that the ligaments stood out on her throat.

The waitress brought us club sandwiches, which we only nibbled at. We leaned our heads together and laughed aloud when I told her a joke. I was getting used to her perfume.

She took my hand at one point, and later we started toward my room, laughing as we bumped down the hall with our arms around each other, and I threatened to squirt her with the fire extinguisher that hung on the wall because she was such a hot number.

In the room we kissed standing up and I tried to put feeling into it. I unbuttoned her blouse part of the way. She wanted one more cigarette, or just a drag or two, if I didn't mind, and I watched her fingers shaking as she lit the cigarette. She sucked hard on the cigarette and I turned away from watching her neck.

Her body surprised me that it looked so good. Her tiny, compact breasts did not sag. The elastic and seam of her pantyhose had left indentations in the soft white flesh around her waist and faintly down the front like a scar. There was something curiously intimate and vulnerable about seeing evidence of where her underwear had been. I could tell by the way she watched my face that she was apprehensive, and hoped her body would pass. I thought that was a little sad. Who the hell was I to judge?

Then as we fumbled toward having sex, I tried to concentrate to make it work, which it did, after a fashion. She said it was her fault that it took her so long. Afterwards, we laughed about how clumsy we acted.

I ordered a bottle of white wine and four beers from room service but she said she could only take a sip. She said she was going to have to leave before long. I said why not live it up. She said she knew it was awful to sort of eat and run, and we laughed about that. She really and truly did have to leave, she said. No sense in jeopardizing her chances for a good, clean divorce. We both agreed that was a good idea. I wanted to walk her to her car but she insisted that would be silly. I promised to call her because that seemed like the polite thing to say.

After she left, her perfume lingered on my shoulders and hands. I called room service and ordered another bottle of wine just to be sure there would be enough. I thought about Keely and poured more wine. Late that night I called two of my friends in Washington. They wanted to know what was the matter with me. The next morning I told the maid not to worry about the room, that I was working. But for two days I did not work. I did nothing but drink and stare at the television with the sound off.

I was supposed to be finishing a magazine article. Under the circumstances, writing was no more possible than flapping my arms and flying to the moon. The missed deadline could be extended, I knew, but I felt bad about it. I phoned the editor but hung up before she came on the line.

At one point I got dressed and drove very slowly to a nearby ABC store and bought a pint of whiskey. I wrapped it in a newspaper and strolled through the motel lobby as if all was right with the world. The desk clerk kept looking at me.

At mid-morning on the third day, I checked out of the motel, and went to a McDonald's next door. I drank a milkshake, and felt like people stared at me, but it was probably my imagination.

I started driving toward Asheville and kept driving until well after dark. I stopped at a motel with a restaurant next door where I got tomato soup and a ham sandwich and went back to the room. I slept about ten hours and woke up knowing I was getting better. But I was scared and depressed and feared I had crossed an invisible line. I didn't want to get back on the other side again.

Here in the sunlight at the Outer Banks, the motel in Richmond seemed a long way off.

I heard Janey softly chirping. From the corner of my eye I saw her doing her head-bobbing dance. I put my hand in the cage and let her nibble my finger. "Okay, pretty bird. No sense in being morbid, right? And you want attention, don't you?" I took her out of the cage, cupped her gently in my hand, and held her up close to my mouth so I could talk to her softly.


Later I got a call from Balls.

"That business with the two brothers down in Wanchese took longer than we thought it would," he said. "I dropped the sheriff off when we got back and then did a little nosing around on my own."

It would do me no good to ask him what kind of nosing around he did.

He said, "Right now I'm bushed. Ready to crash early tonight. Get a hamburger, bring it to the room."

"Tomorrow?"

"I want to pay a visit to *The Lost Colony*. You say you're acquainted with Cavanaugh, the manager? Can use you on that. Friendly visit. People I want to check on."

"I'd like to go," I said.

"I'll call him. Tell him you and I are coming to get his help."

I sensed Balls had something else to say. "The sheriff won't be going. He says he's got other things he needs to tend to." His conversation hung there a moment. Then,

"Actually, as I said this morning, he doesn't want to be seen with you too often. Doesn't want to appear too chummy with you. Reasons include Schweikert and the local press people. Showing favorites, you know."

That didn't bother me. I felt I could do better on my own, with just Balls, than having the sheriff around, anyway.

We agreed to meet at ten the next morning at a coffee shop near King's Motel.

Balls was my friend, and I know he enjoyed our Sherlock-to-Watson relationship, but I also knew that he figured the article resulting from this case—or maybe TV script or even a book—would feature him prominently and wouldn't do his career any harm. Nothing wrong with that. It served both of us.

Just before dark, I stepped out on the deck. The fading sky was all pastels, pink and yellow, with a band of rose near the sound. A gentle wind came from the southwest, brushing my face, as warm and humid as a lover's breath. I breathed in deeply.


That night I dreamed of an overbearing, unfriendly official questioning me about finding Keely's body curled up on our bed. At one point Keely was standing in my room listening, and I knew in the dream that she couldn't be standing there because she was dead. I woke and thought the air conditioning had gone out, but I had wrapped myself so tightly in the sheet and bedspread that I was sweating.

I got up, splashed water on my face and massaged the back of my neck with my damp hands.

Restless, I went into the living room. Moonlight gave a soft glow to the room. Through the glass door I stared at the night sky and the infinite scattering of stars.

As I turned to go back to bed I caught sight of a vehicle parked at the end of the cul-de-sac. Although I couldn't see it clearly in the dark, I could tell it was large, like a pickup or SUV. There was no reason to stop there. No houses lay at that end of the cul-de-sac or at that point on the east-west road.

I eased open the sliding glass door and listened for any sound. Quiet as death.

Then I heard the crunch of gravel and fading footsteps moving rapidly away from the house and toward the main road.

Quickly I reached my hand behind me inside the door and flipped the two light switches, throwing a flood of light in the carport beneath me and over the outside stairway.

But I couldn't see anyone.

The vehicle door opened and immediately shut, permitting just a flicker of the dome light. An instant later I heard the engine turn over and saw the taillights come on briefly. Whoever it was drove away—without lights.

I stepped back inside the door, picked up the three-foot-long steel rod I use to secure the sliding door and hurried to a kitchen drawer to get my heavy-duty flashlight. I slipped my feet in boat shoes I'd parked by the side door.

I was determined to find out whether there was another son of a bitch out there, or whether this one had done something to my house. An incendiary device? A bomb?

I edged down the stairs to the carport, playing the flashlight beam. In my other hand I held the steel rod, ready to whack anything that moved. The carport was flooded with light and I didn't see any damage to my car. Its doors remained locked, nothing foreign underneath. I went all the way around the house, shining the flashlight up and down, left and right. The heavier foliage in the back of the house gave off a woodsy smell. I jumped at the sound of a small animal, maybe a chipmunk, as it scurried away in the underbrush. I walked to the end of the drive. Everything looked okay.

I went back upstairs, closed the sliding glass door, and dropped the iron security rod in place. I left the drape eased back half way. I checked the bolt on the side door. Janey stirred in her covered cage. "Not time to get up yet, Janey," I said. "Go back to sleep," as if she'd understand.

I lay in bed staring at the ceiling, thinking that a gun wouldn't be a bad thing to have. When Keely and I got married, a cousin had given me an ancient .32 caliber revolver that had been in the family. The gun made Keely nervous, and as her depression increased, I decided to get rid of it, and gave it back to my cousin. Now, maybe it's time for another one.

Tonight's events were not my imagination. Too damn many strange things to be ignored. Someone is checking me out. Maybe getting up nerve to make a hit? Let the bastard try.

# Chapter Twelve

Early the next morning, I walked around my house again to make sure no mischief had been done. I saw no signs that anyone had even been on or near the property. Still . . .

The lurker in the pine trees behind the motel, the SUV that appeared to follow me, and last night's visit to or near my house—maybe even the phone call at the motel with no one there—if they involved the same person, what was he waiting for? If these events *were* linked and not figments of my admittedly active imagination and suspicious nature, they added credence to the theory—mine and Elly's—that Deputy Sammy Foster was spreading the word about me in hopes of flushing someone out in the open. And, as Elly said, it would have to be a person who knows who I am, a townsperson.

These were all "ifs" of course. Just the same, I was already mentally cataloging "people of interest," as the police so delicately put it. My next step would be to begin a more concrete list in my ever-present reporter's notebook.


Before I left to meet Balls, I kept a promise to myself to practice the bass at least a few minutes every day. I was forever making promises to myself and doing only a so-so job of keeping them. But playing the bass wasn't a chore, because wrestling with that big instrument to get a good sound always took my mind off everything else.

I tightened the bow, ran it eight times over the rosin, and prepared to tune up. By watching the needle on a palm-sized electronic tuner, I tuned only the A string. The other three strings I tuned harmonically by ear in relation to the A. Good practice for pitch.

I did major scales and a couple of my least favorite minor ones. After an exercise to pick up speed, I tackled that Mozart section again. God, he must have hated bass players. I was convinced that a lot of the composers hated bass players.

I kept at it, stopping every few measures or so to curse anew, using a well-worn four-letter word.

Janey liked the commotion. She chirped and bobbed, even when I stopped to study the music and mark a new fingering to try.

Janey kept up her soft muttering sound. Then at one point I could swear she said "Shit." She said it softly but clear as a bell. I stared at her. She was busy bobbing her head and making her usual low sounds. Maybe a female parakeet *can* talk. But after all this time, is that the first and only word she'll say?

I ran through the section of Mozart once again, using the new fingering. It helped. I watched my language. Janey had no comment, but she did bob her head when a missed bowing caused the bass to emit a sound like a cat in distress.


When I left to go meet Balls, I swung over to the Beach Road to glimpse the ocean again. With a flattening wind from the west and the tide out, the swells and surf were minimal. But I knew how quickly the sea could change. It wasn't without reason that the waters off the Outer Banks got the nickname "Graveyard of the Atlantic."

Well past the French Fry Alley section, I switched to the Bypass and was able to make close to the posted fifty miles an hour. The giant sand dune known as Jockey's Ridge was crowded with hang-glider enthusiasts, kite-flyers, and hikers. At the top of the dune, the climbers looked like toy soldiers silhouetted against the sky.

I arrived at the coffee shop a couple of minutes before ten and ordered a regular coffee, black. Balls came in moments later and joined me at the small booth. He waved the waitress away. His unbuttoned cotton sport coat didn't quite cover the holstered 9mm handgun.

"You've been busy," I said.

"Yeah, I did some checking yesterday and again early this morning. Getting a line on *The Lost Colony* crowd. Got a feeling we might have us an interesting time out there today."

I left my Saab parked out of the way at the coffee shop and we started out 64 heading west toward the amphitheater.

Balls said, "I asked Albright to send one of his deputies ahead and park in the lot near the administration building. When we pull up, we'll chat with him a moment so anybody who's around sees we're in tight, part of the team. Have him hang out with us a bit."

We passed a state marker notifying motorists that Murphy, NC, is a mere 543 miles to the west. A bit of droll North Carolina humor. Manteo is the farthest east of any county seat in the state, and Murphy is the most western. Its county, Cherokee, lies smack along the Tennessee border.

A mile before the bridge to the mainland over Croatan Sound, we turned into the entrance of Fort Raleigh, the restored earthenworks believed to be where the ill-fated colonists tried to make their start in the New World. Also on the grounds are the manicured Elizabethan Gardens, the National Park Service buildings, and the office for *The Lost Colony*. Everything is nestled among tall pine and hardwood trees and all are reached via gently curving paved roads and walkways.

A group of young people, apparently from the cast, played a pick-up game of touch football on an expanse of lawn-like grass as we drove up. One of the young women caught a lateral but was tagged with both hands by a grinning, shirtless young man in ragged cutoffs. Sunlight glistened off bare arms and faces. All were trim, like dancers.

We parked beside a Dare County Sheriff's car. Balls and I got out. Balls smiled and nodded a greeting to the deputy, a tall black man in uniform, who stood beside his cruiser. We shook hands. His name badge read "O. Wright." He saw me looking at it.

He tapped the badge with a finger and grinned. "I'm one of the Wright Brothers."

Serious again, he said to Balls, "You want me to tag along, Agent Twiddy? Go in with you? Sheriff said follow your instructions."

Balls said, "I think it's good we stand here and talk 'officially' for a minute or two. Then maybe you stroll in with us." He inclined his head toward the young people. "We're already noticed."

The football game had stopped. The cast members watched us in silence.

We started toward the office.

The shirtless young man in cutoffs walked toward us, tossing the football idly from hand to hand, never taking his eyes off us. Several others followed. As he got closer, he tossed the football over his head without looking. One of his buddies caught it, tucked it loosely under his arm.

"Detective? Officer? We're wondering if you're any closer to getting a break in this case, in who murdered Sally Jean?" Cutoffs pushed his dark hair, wet with perspiration, back from his face. He flashed a practiced smile. A young Tom Cruise look-alike.

We stopped.

Balls said, "The investigation is continuing."

"Well, that's really good news," said a redheaded member of the group, a rather sarcastic grin on his face. He glanced around for assurance from the group. A few snickers.

With what I know was a phony tone of patience, Balls said, "We're taking every step to—"

"All due respect, Detective, but we're not really interested in 'steps.' We want to know about an arrest." Cutoffs stood close, that theatrical smile planted on his face. I could smell the salt and moisture on his lightly tanned skin.

Balls waited several seconds before responding. His phony patience had vamoosed. He took a long step that put them toe-to-toe and breathed right in the guy's face. "What's your name, pal?"

Cutoffs didn't back away, but I noticed a slight droop of his shoulders. "Eric. Eric Denny." He swallowed, jutted his chin back up and said, "What's yours?"

Had to hand it to the guy.

Balls' barrel chest inched closer. Denny was forced to take a step back. "It's Special Agent T. Ballsford Twiddy, State Bureau of Investigation. They call me Balls—because I got 'em. And let me tell you something, pal. If you and your friends here got something that can help, you know anything at all, you come talk to me or the sheriff."

Balls let his gaze sweep over the rest of the group. "But until you know anything that's going to help—or that I come talk to you about—you and your buddies stay out of my face. You understand what I'm saying to you, Denny?"

One of the girls spoke up. "No sense in getting all huffy about it. All we want to know is what's going on. Sally Jean was a friend of ours."

Deputy Wright stood tall and still like a sentinel, his face blank.

The door to *The Lost Colony* office building opened and Ken Cavanaugh came out, making patting motions with his hands as if quieting children. "Okay, okay, guys. Let's get back to your football game. The officers have an appointment with me to talk over matters that may assist in the overall effort of the investigation."

Like he had practiced his speech.

I could see the resolve go out of the group. The one with

the football flipped it from hand to hand, ready to get back with the game.

Balls wasn't quite through. Eric Denny started to turn. Balls said, "Mr. Denny, I'll be back to talk with you and your buddies."

Denny looked at Balls, his dark eyes not wavering. "Sure. Be happy to see you . . . pal." His smile really was remarkable.

Balls' face broke slowly into a grin. He pointed a finger at Eric Denny, thumb up like a pistol, in a good-natured gesture, like Balls admired Denny's guts. Takes balls to know balls.

Cavanaugh's glasses took on a grayish tint in the sunlight. Then he obviously recognized me from the symphony days when I played with the orchestra and when I also wrote a couple of magazine pieces about community orchestras, with much of the focus on our own orchestra. He held out his hand, saying he was glad to see me again, and this was a pleasant surprise. He appeared to accept my being here with Balls and the deputy, just part of my job as a writer. Quickly extending his hand to Balls and to Deputy Wright, Cavanaugh introduced himself as the general manager of *The Lost Colony*.

He said, "The most difficult thing for the kids to do is to carry on as if nothing has happened. But you can just imagine the trauma this tragedy has caused among the cast. Everyone working here. It's simply devastating. It really is."

He enunciated his words clearly, as if he were teaching a college drama class. Training had all but obliterated a trace of Southside Virginia accent. "But I've been so proud of the young people, and older ones, too, at how they have carried on their performances." He cast a rather sad smile at us, and then continued: "As a matter of fact, this Saturday night, which would not normally be a performance night, we are putting on the final show of the season and dedicating it to Sally Jean." He swallowed. "It will be quite moving."

As we walked toward the office, he added quietly, "Quite

frankly, if we can't put this thing behind us we may have difficulty with auditions for the new cast in February. I mean, this has received wide, wide publicity." He glanced at me, as if his last remark might have offended me. "Young people, or their parents, may not see this as, as the most wonderful opportunity in the world to get good solid theatrical experience."

He opened the door for us to enter. "You know this is where the actor Andy Griffith got his start. Right here. Playing Sir Walter Raleigh."

I had heard that many times. Andy Griffith acted here several summers before and after graduating from the University of North Carolina at Chapel Hill, and for years had maintained a home on Roanoke Island.

A large square room, the size of a basketball court, formed the center of the building. A piano was pushed against the far wall. "We do casting calls and rehearsal in here," Cavanaugh said, a tinge of weariness in his voice.

Smaller rooms could be reached by going through this main room. We filed into his office, and he motioned for us to sit down. Balls and I took canvas-back chairs near his desk, which was cluttered with programs, papers, a folder of fabric samples, newspapers. Deputy Wright sat ramrod straight in one of the metal chairs against the wall.

"Here's a list of all the permanent employees," Cavanaugh said, "like myself and the secretary, the public relations person, maintenance, grounds, and so forth, with addresses. There are nine of us."

Balls produced a pair of reading glasses he perched on his nose as he took the list.

Cavanaugh handed Balls another sheet. "Here's the cast and stage crew list you wanted, and I've highlighted in yellow the seven cast members—most of them townspeople—who were also here four years ago . . . when that other tragedy occurred."

Cavanaugh patted his hair down with one hand while Balls studied the documents.

Balls glanced up at Cavanaugh, whose distress at the whole process appeared to weigh down the flesh on his face. "I see you've been here only two years."

Cavanaugh nodded, a spark back in his manner. "Yes, I was in Northern Virginia, executive director of a symphony." He flashed a quick smile toward me. "That's where I met Mr. Weaver."

Balls stood. "Appreciate your cooperation on this, Mr. Cavanaugh. I've been doing a little asking around, as you know, and I think I'd like to start today with questions for your maintenance man, Pernell Hunnicutt. He's been here six years and I understand he was friendly with both young women—the deceased."

I might have known this was the sort of thing Balls was checking up on when he told me he had been "sort of nosing around." This was exactly the same type information I had wanted to get from Cavanaugh on my own—before I discarded the idea.

When the time was right, I would tease Balls with the same words he had used on me: "You're getting right good at this detective stuff."

Cavanaugh said, "That can certainly be arranged. Pernell's here on the grounds this morning." He glanced at his watch. "They've been getting the theater ready for tonight. We've not cancelled any performances, even when Miss Pearson's body . . ."

He cleared his throat and continued. "Mr. Hunnicutt's up at the theater. I know there was a problem with one of the water fountains and a stopped-up toilet in the ladies restroom."

"We'll also want to talk to a few of the cast members." Balls' glasses pushed down comically to the tip of his nose and rumpled cotton sport coat made him look like a dressed up bear. "I see here that Eric Denny, the young man we met outside, was in the cast four years ago?"

"Yes. He was here for that season. One of the dancers. An Indian . . . Native American. Then he was in Upstate

New York, teaching and doing community theater work, and joined us again this season. We're glad to have him." Cavanaugh handed Balls a program. "As you can see, he has a more substantial role this year. A very good dancer. He plays the part of the Indian Uppowoc. Also, he works with the cast as a fight choreographer."

"A what?"

"Fight choreographer. He teaches stage combat technique classes for the company. There're scenes with Indians attacking, sword fights, that sort of thing. It takes skill to do that properly, so it's authentic looking, without getting the kids hurt."

Balls nodded, his face perfectly blank.

# Chapter Thirteen

We got up from the canvas-back chairs, and Cavanaugh volunteered to walk to the Waterside Theater with us to find Pernell Hunnicutt. Balls shook his head. "No sense in doing that, Mr. Cavanaugh. Pretty day. The walk'll be good for us."

Cavanaugh appeared relieved, clearly buoyed, to be getting rid of us. He followed us into the large rehearsal room, chatting about living at the Outer Banks. I told him I was looking forward to it. Smiling, he said, "Have you found a musical group to play with here at the Outer Banks?"

"Not yet. Just getting settled."

"Well, you will. Lots of musicians here. Your wife's a musician, too, isn't she?"

"She was. Voice and guitar. But she died last year."

"Oh, I'm so sorry, so very sorry." He stopped, his face stricken.

Outside, I had to squint against the bright sunshine. Deputy Wright's sunglasses hid his eyes, like one of those threatening lawmen in the movies. To Balls he said, "You tell me, sir, when you want me to cut out. I'm with you until you do."

"Come on with us, Odell. See Mr. Pernell Hunnicutt, our friendly maintenance man."

So the "O" on Wright's nametag didn't stand for Orville,

as I had begun to believe.

Balls stuffed the lists Cavanaugh gave him into his jacket. "Also want to talk to our new friend, Eric Denny, the kung-fu expert."

On the walkway, two elderly women tourists approached and smiled shyly. They offered a weak hello sound as we stepped aside to let them pass. A dozen other tourists milled about, several with small children.

Historical markers along the path told of Sir Walter Raleigh's ill-fated colony. To our right the reconstructed earthen Fort Raleigh looked as if it could accommodate maybe seventy-five people, huddled together in terror. I tried to imagine what it must have been like at night for those people four hundred years ago, so far from the Mother Country, here in the utter darkness of the Outer Banks.

Wooden stockade fencing fronts the outdoor Waterside Theater where *The Lost Colony* drama is performed. A two-story structure just inside the entrance to the amphitheater houses the lighting controls and sound equipment. From the back where we stood, we could look down at the stage. Beyond the stage and its backdrop, the sun-sparkled waters of Roanoke Sound glistened at us.

In front of us, three sections of wooden benches slope down the sides of the bowl-like theater toward the stage. Permanently on center stage stand a chapel with an A-roof, flanked by a pair of structures that resemble mangers from a nativity scene. Proscenium wings to the right and left lead to entrances and exits.

Deputy Wright nudged Balls and nodded toward a shed to our left.

A tall, raw-boned man of about fifty came out of one of the restroom doors carrying a large pair of pliers and other tools. At a water fountain near the doors, he dropped to one knee, spread out his tools, and began to work.

As we approached him, he looked at us, focused on each of our faces in turn, then went back to his work. A new water fountain handle lay on the ground with the tools.

Balls said, "Pernell Hunnicutt?"

For a moment, he stared up at Balls, said, "Yeah?" and turned back to his work on the water fountain. His face appeared permanently wind-burned. He had not shaved today. His dark hair, damp with perspiration and oil, stuck out from around the stained edges of a worn, billed cap.

"I'm Agent Balls Twiddy of the SBI. This is Deputy Wright . . . and Mr. Weaver. We'd like to talk to you."

"I figured that." With huge hands, the man fitted the new handle on the fountain.

"We want to see if you can help us any." Balls was being Mr. Nice Guy.

Pernell Hunnicutt glanced at Balls, gave a barely audible snort, and again turned back to his work. He made a tightening twist to the water fountain handle, turned the pressure on, and tried it. Water spurted too high and missed the drain basin. "Shit," Hunnicutt muttered. He made another adjustment. He tried the fountain again. This time water arched up from the spigot and fell on target back into the basin. He gave a final tightening to the handle, gathered up his tools, and stood. He was an inch or so taller than Balls.

Balls said, "We're trying to find out something about that poor young woman from *The Lost Colony* who got killed."

Hunnicutt said, "That first girl or the new one?"

Was there a trace of a sardonic smile hiding among the perspiration and wrinkles?

Hunnicutt settled by resting his buttocks on the back of the last row of seats, feet extended and crossed in front of him. He stared at Balls. "I get off at three."

"I know. We'll just take a few minutes of your time, Pernell. But we need to talk now."

Hunnicutt's eyes narrowed. "Okay."

"Where were you the night Sally Jean Pearson disappeared? That was Monday night."

"Home."

"By yourself?"

"Sure."

"What were you doing, Pernell?"

"Where?"

"At home. By yourself."

"Nothing."

"Nothing?"

"Naw. Oh, you know, drinking beer. Trying to watch television, but it warn't even working. I called Jules Hinson to come fix it again but he said he was busy. So, nothing. That's what I was doing. Nothing."

I could see the muscles in Balls' jaw working overtime. I knew Mr. Nice Guy was about to take a powder.

Balls leaned his face closer to Hunnicutt. "I hear you were trying to come on to Sally Jean Pearson, Pernell. That right?"

Hunnicutt's gray eyes narrowed. "What you mean?"

"Oh, you know. Doing little things for her. Kind of taken with her. You sort of had the hots for her."

Hunnicutt stared hard at Balls, his eyes not wavering. "Let me tell you another thing, mister. You listen to me. I didn't hurt that girl. And there ain't nothin' else to say about it."

Mr. Nice Guy again, quick as that. "Now, Pernell, nobody's accusing you of doing anything to that girl, but we got to do our job and check out folks who might know something."

Making himself more comfortable, Hunnicutt took the pliers from his back pocket, held them loosely in one hand. He nodded at Balls, but I could see he didn't buy into what Balls had just said.

"What about that first girl, Pernell? Joyce Brendle. Four years ago. You knew her, too, didn't you? Weren't you sort of sweet on her too?" Balls got that grin like actor Gene Hackman. "Seems like these young women you get sweet on end up getting killed."

"I already told Sheriff Claxton long time ago what I knew about that girl."

"Unfortunately, Sheriff Claxton is dead and so we got to

ask you all over again. So I'm asking you, weren't you sort
of sweet on Joyce Brendle? And weren't you sort of sweet
on this Sally Jean Pearson, too?"

"Mister, you listen to me—"

Uh-oh. That was a mistake.

"No, Pernell, you listen to me. Your big, brave Joe Cool
act doesn't do a thing for me. It doesn't impress me worth a
hoot. Now if you want to talk with us and be nice, we'll talk.
If you don't want to be nice, well, we'll still talk. It'll just be
under different circumstances and it might not be out here in
the open with this beautiful view all around us, with this
nice breeze." Balls leaned forward, but Hunnicutt didn't
budge. "What's it gonna be, Pernell?"

Like two bulls staring at each other.

"I said I'd talk to you fellows. But first I want to say
something. Naw, I want to say two things."

"Sure, Pernell. We're happy to hear what you got to say."

"First off, I did know both of those girls, like I know a lot
of other young'uns in the show. But most of them are sorta
stuck on themselves. Think they're hot stuff and don't even
know you're around. That first girl, Joyce Brendle, was nice
and I didn't mind doing things for her. She did makeup and
needed more lights in both of the dressing rooms by the
mirrors and I helped her with that and she really appreciated
it, and always spoke to me by name. She was a friend of
mine. I wouldn't have hurt her."

He looked down at his big hands, then stuck the pliers in
a side pocket. "The girl last week, Sally Jean. I didn't know
her as good, but she was nice, too, and friendly and always
spoke to me. She needed extra hooks to hang stuff on
backstage and I done that for her."

Balls listened, and then looked off across the sound as if
his mind was a hundred miles away. "What kind of vehicle
you drive, Pernell?"

"Huh?"

"Vehicle. Car. What do you drive?"

"I don't have a car. I have a van. An old Dodge van."

"What do you keep in it?"

"What you mean, what do I keep in it? Stuff. You know, tools, fishing gear. Stuff."

"Got a mattress in there?"

"Naw. Got me a sleeping bag in there case I want to go fishing late or something."

"You ever get any girls in there in the sleeping bag with you?"

"Not'n a long time." He almost smiled.

Balls said, "You were telling us that 'First of all . . .'"

"I've already told you first of all. Both of those girls was nice to me. They wasn't stuck up. And I didn't hurt neither one of them. That's the first thing."

Balls pursed his lips, put his hands in the pockets of his jacket, before he said, "And two? You said there were two things."

"Yeah," Hunnicutt said, nodding his head, just the trace of a smile beginning at the corner of his mouth. He slowly raised one hand and pointed his fingers toward Balls' chest, not touching him, but aiming at him. "Two is that, mister, I think you're a real sure enough flat-out asshole."

# Chapter Fourteen

When Hunnicutt said that to Balls, Deputy Wright shifted his stance and stared out toward the stage. I could tell he stifled a chuckle, and although I couldn't make out his eyes behind those dark glasses, I felt he winked at me.

Slowly, Balls began to get that grin on his face. He leaned toward Hunnicutt. "Pernell, I'm gratified that you have determined my true nature. When I'm dealing with assholes, I become one. Never fails. Sort of a built-in asshole detector turns on every time I get close." That grin disappeared as fast as a computer screen going black. "You think I'm getting close?"

"I told you I didn't hurt that girl. Neither one a them."

Balls stood back, hands in pockets, his cotton jacket pushed back, the holstered 9mm visible. Two small perspiration circles spotted the front of his shirt. "Tell you what, Pernell. How about letting us have one of our guys look over your van?"

"Why?"

"Just to see what they can find."

Hunnicutt studied Balls several seconds before answering. "What you mean, look it over? What'm I supposed to drive while they looking over my van?"

"Oh, it won't take them long. There's a unit over in Elizabeth City. I can get them to come on down here this afternoon. Take a look. You could have your van back in the morning. Maybe even tonight."

"How'm I supposed to get home? Get to the store and back in the morning?"

"We'll run you home. Take you by the Red Apple, pick up a six pack. You drink Bud Light, don't you?"

Warily, "That's good as any."

"No problem then."

"Why can't I just drive myself home and they come look at the van there?"

"We'd like for you to leave it right where it is, if you don't mind. Now, I want you to know I'm not threatening you or anything like that. That's not the way we do it. We want to keep it legal. So what do you say?"

Hunnicutt still didn't move. He continued to study Balls, then Deputy Wright and me, and back to Balls, who had this phony pleasant look on his face.

"After you look at my van, then you leave me alone?"

"Well, I sure hope so, Pernell." Then, as if an afterthought, Balls said, "What I'd really appreciate you doing is take a polygraph. Polygraph test?" Balls rubbed his chin, awaiting a reaction.

"You mean lie detector test?"

"That's what some folks call it."

"Nope."

"Why not?"

"'Cause that's your machine, not mine. If it's your machine, you can make it do what you want it to do. Same's I can make my machines do what I want them to do."

Balls nodded, conceding. He had the van. He wasn't going to push further. "Pernell, I'll check with Mr. Cavanaugh. I'm sure he'll let you take off a little early today. You can ride with Deputy Wright here, we'll follow in my car. If you'll just show us where the van is, lend us the keys."

"I don't want them ripping up my van or anything like they do in the movies."

• • •

As we followed Deputy Wright, I could see Pernell Hunnicutt sitting ramrod straight in the passenger seat, staring straight ahead.

Balls said, "Want to see where Hunnicutt lives, case I need to come back here right quick."

Wright slowed as he approached the Red Apple and I saw Hunnicutt shake his head. They drove on, turned onto a side road, then went down two more lanes to a faded blue house trailer at the end of a long sandy drive. The trailer had a rickety shed built onto the back at one end. The yard was littered with rusty crab cages, a rotting wooden boat on saw horses, and broken parts of God-knows-what. An ancient light-brown mixed-breed dog, as lanky as Hunnicutt, lay at the base of one of the tall pine trees. The dog got up stiffly, considered us a moment, then lay down again.

Balls said, "I'll send someone over to pick you up at seven-fifteen in the morning. That okay?"

Hunnicutt nodded, got out, and leaned his big hands on the sill of Balls' open window. "Get my van back tomorrow?"

"Sure."

Hunnicutt turned and walked toward the trailer. The dog got up and followed him.

Balls thanked Deputy Wright, said he could go back to the courthouse.

As we drove away from Hunnicutt's, I said, "Will the lab guys rip up his van?"

Balls seemed distracted. "Huh? Oh, no. They're good, though. When they get through, we'll know all we need to know about that van and what Mr. Pernell Hunnicutt's been doing in there. Those lab guys are so good, we'll know if Pernell even had lustful *thoughts* about Sally Jean Pearson while he was in the van."

We were out on the main road to Manteo. I said, "What's your assessment of Hunnicutt?" I had my own opinion. He was on the mental list of suspects I was compiling, but not right at the top.

Balls chuckled. "Don't know. Didn't rattle worth a damn, did he? Like many of them out here, from a long line of watermen. Independent lot. Used to being on their own, hard times, asking nothing and getting nothing. And, lordy, did you get a load of those arms and hands. I got the feeling he could have picked up any one of us and pitched us half way down toward the stage."

When we got to my car at the coffee shop, Balls said, "Funny thing that Hunnicutt mentioned Jules Hinson, the TV repair guy. He's one of the people on my list to do a little checking with. Pretty heavy into porn. I wonder if he's also into S-and-M. I understand he's got a few weird preferences."

As I started to get out of the T-bird, Balls grinned. "At least you didn't cause any trouble today—even though you just about busted a gut trying not to laugh when old Pernell Hunnicutt called me an asshole."

"He's got your number," I said.

He held up a finger for me to wait a moment. "Listen, I've got a plan for tonight. You might want to go, see the fun. Make the rounds at Saber's over on the Bypass about ten-thirty or eleven. That's where much of the cast from *The Lost Colony* goes to party after the show."

"Sure," I said. I wanted to stay as close to the investigation as I could, and it was not as if I had a heavy social calendar.

Balls said, "I want to go there just in case I might run into my friend Eric Denny, the Actor and Martial Arts Instructor. Lean on him. Let him know everybody else may think he looks like Mr. Movie Star, but to me he looks like a possible suspect."

# Chapter Fifteen

Traffic was heavy on the Bypass. I looked forward to the lull in tourism at the Outer Banks that would occur next month after Labor Day. The number of vehicles would fall off considerably then, even though the area was becoming more of a year-round vacation place for people from Northern Virginia, Maryland, Pennsylvania, and New Jersey.

On fall weekends, promises of bountiful fishing on the Outer Banks brought flocks of Jeeps, pickup trucks, and SUVs with four or five nine-foot rods sticking straight up from racks on the front bumpers. These vehicles would race up and down the Outer Banks like giant beetles in heat, chasing after rumors of where the birds might be working, signaling a feeding frenzy of bluefish. Up into winter, in the sloughs along the shore, surf-casters could catch keeper trout and thirty-pound striped bass, even heavier, as well as huge puppy drum.

As I pulled into my cul-de-sac, I thought, heck, I ought to be out there trying to catch a summer flounder or two. Instead, I went in my house.

As soon as I opened the door to my house, Janey chirped at me, eager for attention. But immediately I headed for the dinette table where I had my computer and office stuff. Even though I kept in the background when tagging along with Balls, my mind was always in the foreground, sifting through what I learned, analyzing the people I ran across.

I removed the slender reporter's notepad from my back pocket and flipped to a clean page. Somewhat randomly, I wrote names of people who could have any possible connection with the case, one, because they were here when both killings occurred, and two, because they—well, because I thought they showed an unusual interest in the case or there was anything about them that made me suspicious of them.

At the top of the list I wrote Pernell Hunnicutt. Next I listed Eric Denny, who had to have known both young women and who had martial arts training. Porno king Jules Hinson got his name entered. I didn't stop there. I listed our Town Father, Charles Ferguson, and his sidekick son-in-law Dixon Nance, mainly because Ferguson and Nance showed a strong interest in the case. But, in all honesty, every damn person in town showed a strong interest in the case. I listed Mr. King's son who worked at the motel and was the first one to tell me about finding the body. I added a few more names, knowing full well I was stretching. More names would be added in time, and names would be eliminated about as fast as I entered them. I was heavy on names, but light on anything concrete to connect them to the murders.

If the killings were carried out by a tourist, this was a total waste of time.

The Carlyle kid, Sally Jean Pearson's date that night, got listed, and just as quickly crossed off. Number one, he wasn't around when the first killing occurred. Two, Sally Jean could have out-wrestled him. And three, he was on foot and had no transportation. Someone had transported Sally Jean from where she was picked up in downtown Manteo to the bridge where her body was likely dumped into the sound.

Then I made another entry: Vehicle, and a question mark. Mystery SUV, van, or pick-up truck. I had to believe there was a connection between the three incidents with vehicles that aroused my suspicion of someone scoping me out. The vehicle parked behind my motel my second night in town was large enough to be either of those types, even though I saw only its taillights when the driver pulled away. So was the vehicle waiting at the end of my cul-de-sac in the middle of the night. And I couldn't I dismiss the SUV that appeared to be following me when I came to the house the first time. Whoever murdered those two young women had access to a vehicle. That was a given.

Later in the afternoon I called one of my editors and talked with her about the new case. She practically salivated. The murder had all the elements she loved. I promised to keep her up to date. With what was almost an afterthought she asked when I would deliver the Danville murder story. In two or three more days, I promised. When we hung up, I did try working on the article. I plodded mechanically through a few paragraphs but my mind kept shifting to the murders of Sally Jean Pearson and Joyce Brendle.


Balls arrived shortly after nine-thirty that night. Standing near the dinette table, he surveyed my quarters. "Looks like you've hunkered down real good." Two table lamps were on in the living room, giving a soft glow to the room. "Right homey, Weav." He looked back at me. "You doing okay?" I knew he referred to Keely's death.

"Yeah, settling in."

He hung his sports coat on the back of one of the dinette chairs. He had taken his holster off.

He accepted the glass of iced tea. "I don't mean to butt in, Weav, but the final ruling was accidental, wasn't it? Keely?"

"Yeah, that was the official ruling. But I know it wasn't accidental. It was deliberate. I should have seen it coming."

He nodded. "Can't beat up on yourself. Once they head that way."

"I just couldn't reach her, Balls. I couldn't reach her. It was like she had vanished—the Keely I knew—had vanished, weeks and weeks before she. . . ."

"Nothing you could have done."

"Yes, I know. But I can't help wondering."

Balls held his glass out. "You got anymore iced tea?"

I welcomed a different subject. Keely's suicide was too painful. But the nagging sense of guilt that everyone said was a natural burden for the person closest to a suicide victim had gradually begun to lift over the months. Every now and then, though, it bubbled to the surface.

I handed Balls his iced tea. "If the cast of *The Lost Colony* goes to Saber's, they won't be there until, hell, late, right?"

"Drifting in a little after eleven, when the show ends," he said.

I glanced at my watch.

"Don't worry. We'll grab a table before the grease-paint bunch gets there. Watch the crowd."


We drove toward Saber's in silence. I felt subdued and quiet. Our talk about Keely made me remember how I'd found her, lying on her side in our bed, knowing she was dead even before I put my hand on her shoulder. It was as if my fingers pushed against an ungiving mound I had never touched before.

I chased the image from my mind and broke the silence by telling Balls about the SUV I thought was following me. I also described someone's nighttime visit to my house and the vehicle's rapid getaway.

Balls listened without saying anything. He glanced at me and back at the road.

"Could be coincidences," he said quietly.

"Bullshit. I've made a career out of being suspicious. I know when things aren't right. I've got a sixth sense about it. These aren't coincidences."

We stopped at a traffic light in the Bypass' French Fry Alley. I watched the bustling traffic in and out of the fast food places.

When the light changed and we started again, I said, "Someone's got me in their sights. The problem is, I don't know what they plan. Is someone trying to get up nerve to strike? Or just spook me? What?"

"Deputy Sammy Foster," Balls said. "He stirred this up."

"Goddamn right. That was my first thought. But then I got to thinking, that's putting an awful lot of faith in Sammy Foster's ability to flush out a suspect by starting a rumor that I know more than I do."

"But why else would anyone be scoping you out?" Balls said.

I shook my head. "I don't know."

After we passed Jockey's Ridge, Balls moved to the inside lane, ready to make a left turn. "You still got that old .32 revolver?" he asked.

I shook my head. "No."

"Something you may want to think about."


Saber's Seafood Bar & Restaurant is located on the east side of the Bypass, south of Jockey's Ridge. The concrete-block construction, together with its wood-frame additions at the side and back, is painted bright pink. Even at night the pink stands out. At the entrance sit two large rusted buoys and a dilapidated wooden boat. Decorations.

Balls backed into a parking space off to one side. We started toward Saber's entrance. A young woman in skimpy shorts and a tank top got out of a car and began looking on the ground. Apparently she had dropped her keys. She reached down to pick them up, dropped them again and said, "Shit." She held on to them this time, straightened up, gave us a surly look, and walked ahead of us to Saber's front door.

Impossible not to watch her rear as she walked. Grinning, Balls nudged me and whispered, "Two kittens playing under a blanket."

Miss Surly Bitch of the Week swung her hips in ahead of

us and didn't bother to keep the door from closing in our faces. In the instant the door was open, I could smell the place. We went from the soft breeze coming in off the ocean to the strong scent of raw fish and shrimp for sale in the shop to the left of the front door, combined with that of flat beer, cigarette smoke, and the stale odor of countless sunburned and sweaty bodies.

We were greeted by a tall young woman, who could have fit nicely as a high-hurdles runner. "Hi, you guys want the bar or," she glanced around, "a table? Booth?"

"That table back there," Balls said. "Okay?"

From there we'd have a view of much of the place, especially the front door.

She seemed to do some mental calculations for a moment, as if there might be some other place she'd rather stash us. But then she said, "Sure. Come on." She picked up a couple of menus and glanced back over her shoulder. "You want anything to eat, or just drink?"

"Both."

She smiled. Her face had a cleanly chiseled look to it that didn't seem harsh. She was really quite pretty, I realized.

I saw the young woman from the parking lot at a table near the front wall with two other women. All three were outdoing each other with looks of sullenness. Who told them sullen is sexy?

We got a big pile of boiled spiced shrimp and crackers. Balls told the waitress that she might as well bring more crackers and more napkins. He ordered a beer and I got a Coke that I didn't really want.

I was busy looking around the place—an entertainment all of its own. Near our table, bolted to the floor, was an old-fashioned barber chair with a male mannequin dressed in a Coast Guard uniform.

Balls saw me looking around. "Quite a place, huh?"

Every wall was covered with a mishmash of items—flags of the USA, the old USSR, the skeletal mouth of a huge shark, harpoons, signs, and pictures of sea scenes. Near the

front hung a huge mounted marlin in colors more psyche-
delic than natural, neon blues and unworldly oranges and
reds.

A half-barrel contained live lobsters, and a dust-en-
crusted aquarium held three large salt-water fish, which
swam slowly back and forth in their cramped space.

Affixed over the front door was a damaged wooden
airplane propeller with a plaque underneath it reading,
"Birds fly. Men drink." I knew that to be the motto of the
Man Will Never Fly Memorial Society International. It
meets in Kill Devil Hills every December 16, the day before
the anniversary of what the skeptics—tongue planted in
cheek—call the "alleged flight" by the Wright brothers. The
society was started years ago as a prank by a local doctor
and a bored journalist who had to come to the barren Outer
Banks to cover the anniversary of the Wright Brothers'
flight.

One year the Man Will Never Fly Society meeting was
held in conjunction with the National Association for the
Preservation of Gravity. Literature on the joint meeting said
the members were concerned that too much gravity was
being expended by such things as space launchings and pop-
up toasters.

I glanced at Balls and smiled, shaking my head.

He plopped a peeled shrimp in his mouth, fingers stained
from the shrimp's Old Bay seasoning. He jerked his head
toward the far right corner of the room near the end of the
long, curved bar. "Sign over the doorway."

A big sign read, "Casino Ballroom Upstairs." I cocked a
questioning eyebrow.

"Ain't no upstairs to this place," he said.

He motioned to the waitress, and pointed to the shrimp
bowl and his beer. She nodded.

"They're starting to come in now," Balls said, his eyes
narrowing to watch them. Two college-age women and a
man entered, laughing. They called a greeting to the young
blond fellow tending bar. They spoke to the tall hostess.

Another couple came in behind them.

The waitress brought us another bowl of shrimp and set it between us, looked at my small discard pile. "You better eat faster," she said.

A moment later, I saw a smile creep over Balls' face. I followed his gaze. Just inside the front door, Eric Denny stood with an arm draped loosely around the waist of a young woman. He seemed to be giving instructions to another young man who had come in with them. Above the general noise I heard the word "beer" and the phrase "over to the table." At the same time, Denny let his eyes sweep the room, checking out who was here. He saw. The smile vanished and his body appeared to tense, a change in mood as if a curtain had fallen.

Balls raised his chin in a nod of greeting.

Denny glared, turned with the girl, and headed toward a table at the other side of the room. The friend followed with three beers. Denny took one and drank straight from the bottle, head thrown back and throat working, downing probably two-thirds of the beer before he took a breath. He looked back at Balls, who continued to have that shit-eating smile on his face.

Balls peeled another shrimp, dipped it into the cocktail sauce, and chewed slowly. "Our actor friend will be over here to see us once he's had a coupla beers."

Less than twenty minutes later, while I was watching a spirited discussion between two women and the bartender, Balls bumped my knee. Eric Denny was walking toward our table carrying a bottle of beer. He moved with the assured arrogance of a dancer, or a boxer. His table companions watched.

# Chapter Sixteen

"Well, Eric Denny, our actor friend. Have a seat."

Denny took one of the chairs at our table. "I get the feeling it's not a total surprise that I'm here."

"Not really."

"I get the feeling that you might be trying to hassle me. That right, Mr. Twiddy?"

"It's Agent Twiddy. Special Agent Twiddy, State Bureau of Investigation."

"Okay, *Agent* Twiddy."

"Did want to see you in your natural habitat." Balls waved a hand around, taking in the room.

Denny glanced at me with disinterest, then back at Balls.

Balls nodded toward me. "This is Harrison Weav . . ."

"I know who he is. Your buddy the crotch writer. You tie up the cases and he types them up. You got yourself a good arrangement."

I started to light into the smartass son of a bitch, but Balls bumped my knee hard.

Denny didn't take his eyes off Balls. "Look, if you want to talk to me, why don't you just do it? I know you've asked around about me. So isn't this, this lurking around sort of so much bull?"

"Maybe we should talk, Mr. Denny. After all, you did know Sally Jean Pearson, even went out with her yourself on one or more occasions, I understand. And, Mr. Denny, I understand you knew the other one, too. Four years ago.

Joyce Brendle."

Denny stared evenly at Balls, kept his mouth shut.

"Only a few people with *The Lost Colony* were with the show four years ago, same as you."

Denny leaned forward, his dark eyes searing into Balls' face. "Yeah. Sure. But what about your townspeople? Don't you want to think about that? How many of them were around four years ago, for God's sake? Don't want to face the fact that it could be one of your goody-good, holier-than-thou assholes in the town?" Denny blew out a puff of air. "You talk about weirdos. This county's got them. Within shouting distance of that old courthouse you got more freaks than a fucking sideshow."

"You got anybody specific in mind?"

"That's your job."

Balls shrugged. "That's what I'm doing, Mr. Denny. My job. Checking folks out. Getting a feel for the way they think."

"Maybe I can save you time because I can tell you right up front how I think."

"How's that, Mr. Denny?"

"I think you don't have crap to go on in this case. You're fishing, hoping to come up with something. But you got to do better than this." Denny's smile came back, perfect teeth and all. "This ain't the right pond for you, Agent Twiddy."

"Maybe not, pal. But I want you to come up with an explanation as to where you were the night Sally Jean disappeared. I know something about where you were, where you ate, that sort of thing. But I want to hear it from you. I want you to tell me where you went after you ate at Darrell's—and left by yourself, I might add—and where you were, say, from about eleven o'clock to one in the morning."

Jesus, Balls never ceased to amaze me.

For a moment, a trace of uneasiness shadowed Denny's face. His voice had a pitch to it that I knew he would not want his friends to hear. "Is this some sort of official questioning?"

Balls kept smiling at him.

Denny got a trace of his bravado back. "Where'd I go? That's what you want to know?"

"Yep."

"I rode around."

"Your friends said you were kind of depressed, kind of quiet that night. Not like you. What was on your mind, Mr. Denny?"

"I just get quiet every now and then. Didn't feel like talking to these guys and gals." He jerked his head at the table behind him. "With them day and night. I was tired of them. Bored."

"Looking for a little more excitement?"

The glare was back full force. "Not the kind of excitement you're talking about."

"Where did you ride around?"

"I went down to Coquina Beach."

"I thought you wanted to get away from the guys and gals in the show. Isn't that where all of you go? Coquina Beach?"

Coquina Beach is south on Highway 12 toward Oregon Inlet. From the wide beach of coarse sand at Coquina, with its picnic tables and large bathhouse, the white and black lighthouse for Bodie Island is visible. On display in the parking lot at Coquina Beach are the skeletal remains of a large wooden ship that was sunk at the beginning of the twentieth century. Vandals have tried from time to time to burn the heavy beams of the ship.

"There weren't that many people around."

"That's sort of late at night to go swimming, isn't it?"

"I didn't go swimming. I just went down there. Parked the car and walked out to watch the ocean awhile."

"Anybody see you down there watching the ocean?"

Denny's rage began to show, almost as if he realized he was on stage for his friends back at the table. "Yeah. God did. Go ask Him about it." Denny pushed back from the table.

"Just a minute, pal. I want you to think about something." Balls stared dead-level into Denny's face. Denny eased back into his chair. "Now you can go around and act tough-ass all you want to for your admiring friends over there. But let me give you some advice. I've butted up against the biggest tough-asses in the business, and you ain't in that league. You understand me? You ain't even close. So, I want you to remember that I'm doing an investigation and I'm going to be asking a lot of people—not just you— where they were when this Sally Jean Pearson girl disappeared. And they better come up with good answers because if they don't, I'm going to be all over them like stink on shit."

Denny raised one finger and opened his mouth to start to speak.

Balls was right back at him before Denny got the first word out. "You just listen to me. You understand me? You just listen to me. When I'm through talking to you, you can go back over there and rejoin your thespian buddies and tell them what a tough guy you are. But unless you can get God to come down here and personally vouch for your whereabouts on that night, you better get somebody else to cover your ass. And, frankly, I got a feeling God ain't that interested in covering your ass."

Denny's mouth worked to come up with something.

But again, Balls spoke first. "So, I'm through talking to you now, pal. Get on back to your table."

Denny stood up, stared silently at Balls, who had gone back to the shrimp, and walked back to his table. He picked up a beer and started drinking from it before he sat down.

A short time later I saw them settle their bill and get up to leave. Denny glared once more at Balls, who was eating the last shrimp.

Balls dipped his fingers in his water glass and wiped them on his napkin. Once Denny and his party went out the front door, Balls grinned at me. "How'd I do?"

"You got him nervous, all right."

Balls stared at the table. "Gives him something to think about," he said quietly. The grin was gone.

I waited a minute before I said anything else. "Is he really a suspect? I mean, in your mind, honestly, is he a suspect?"

"Sure."

"Sure?"

"Look. Out at *The Lost Colony*, we've got two people we know of who were around during that time and knew both of the girls. Pernell Hunnicutt and Eric Denny. So we got to look carefully at them. Check if Pernell's van tells us anything."

"Aside from them?"

"Aside from them, we've got exactly what Eric Denny said."

He saw the look on my face.

"Yeah. We've got all of the townspeople. We've got the whole fucking county. And don't forget the tourists. Like a hundred thousand of them." He motioned for the waitress. "Let's get out of here. This place gets on my nerves."

Outside I took several deep breaths of ocean air. My shirt smelled like Saber's.

"I'll give you a ride up to your place, then I'm going back to the motel. Crash. Start again tomorrow."

As we approached Balls' car, one of the patrol cars from the Dare County Sheriff's Department swung into Saber's, spotted us, and drove over quickly, spewing bits of gravel.

The patrol car had hardly stopped when Deputy John Creech jumped out. "Sheriff said you were here. The crime lab guys went to *The Lost Colony* to pick up Pernell Hunnicutt's van and it wasn't there."

"What?"

"It wasn't there. They called me and we went high-tailing over to Pernell's place, and there's the goddamn van in his front yard. He's in the trailer, sittin' on his ass drinking beer and watching that flickering, crappy TV set of his."

Balls put his hand on his forehead. "Jesus."

"I said to Pernell, 'What the hell's your van doing here? It's supposed to be at *The Lost Colony* so the evidence crime lab guys can go over it. You trying to tamper with state's evidence or something?' And Pernell just looks at me real slow and says, 'I ain't tampered with nothing. My friend Boody come by and give me a ride back up to the *Colony* and I got a extra set of keys and picked up my van because I decided that, yes, I believe I do want me some more beer. Ain't no law against drinking beer, is it?' I said to him, 'That's not the point, Pernell—'"

Balls held his hand up to stop Creech. "Never mind. Have the lab people got the van now?"

"Yes, sir."

"Did it look like Pernell had tried to clean his van up?"

"No, sir. I looked inside. It looked just as trashy as ever."

"Even if he did try to clean it up, the lab people could tell that, too, and that would tell us something. Are they working on it now?"

"They secured it at the Elizabethan Motel where they're staying. They're going to get on it in the morning."

"I'm going to go talk to them before they get to sleep."

"They may already be asleep."

"They won't be asleep long. I'll see to that. Look, would you mind giving Weav, here, a ride back to his place? Wright Shores. I dragged him out here tonight."

"No problem at all. Get in. Just make me look good when you write all this up."

Balls was out of the parking lot before we got turned around.

I only half-listened as Creech chattered about the case. "I've got a theory that there's more sex motive in this thing than the sheriff or anybody thinks. I believe it's something about those left tits and lipstick and stuff."

"Might be."

When we parked in my cul-de-sac, I was glad I'd left the lights on.

I thanked Creech for the lift, and as I opened the door to

get out, he said, "Probably see you Friday night, if not around the courthouse before then."

"Friday night?"

"The fish-fry, barbecue thing that old man Ferguson is throwing."

"Oh, yeah."

"Can't forget that, Mr. Weaver. Anytime Ferguson decides to spend that much money, it's a night to remember."

# Chapter Seventeen

The next morning, Wednesday, I got up early and worked on the Danville crime article, as promised.

The Danville story dealt with a young, married guy, wimpy-looking sort, who had been in and out of minor trouble with the law until he raped and murdered a seventy-two-year-old woman who lived in his neighborhood. He stuffed her body into a black plastic yard bag. Then he put that bag into another yard bag and bound the whole package with duct tape. He transported the gruesome cargo in his van and dumped it in the Dan River, where a fisherman found it four days later.

But Mr. Wimp was a recycler of plastic bags. A receipt was found in one of the bags from a local hardware store for mulch and other items. The detective I interviewed traced the purchases and nailed the guy.

My writing moved along well. As usual I started work before I showered and got dressed. When I began to day-dream, I figured it was time to exercise, shower, and dress, then get back to the writing again.

Every so often I took a break to play the bass. As a change of musical pace today, I worked on passages in Beethoven's "Ninth Symphony." I tried to stop saying "shit" every time I messed up. Instead, I would sigh, mutter under my breath, and look toward Janey's cage. Didn't want her to pick up any more of my language. I could tell she was listening intently. Okay, I did keep calling Beethoven "sonabitch" or a variation of that. I couldn't practice without venting. She'd have to get used to it.

By early afternoon I thought I would have heard from Balls, so I called the sheriff's office and asked for him. Shortly, Mabel came on the line. She said Balls told her to tell me if I called that "the van was clean," and I would know what that meant. She said he had to go back to Elizabeth City. "They're running him ragged, you ask me," she said. "Have him trying to work on two or three cases at once. Course none of my business, but just the same. . . ." I said I agreed with her.

For the rest of the afternoon I plugged away at the Danville article, stopping at a point where I could see the end. Before fixing a dinner salad with ham and cheese as my evening meal, I took a glass of iced tea and sat for a long time on the deck watching the day evolve into evening.

Thursday morning I wound up the article, printed a hardcopy and another for my files, and wrote captions for the eight photos I packaged with the manuscript. The magazine paid extra for pictures. I always took several pictures, including shots of the detective who solved the case. The police were good about letting a crime scene photo or two "fall on the floor" during an interview. I included these with the article.

Not quite noon I decided to treat myself. Head to the Kitty Hawk Post Office to mail the manuscript, then stop at Capt'n Franks for a foot-long hotdog with light chili and mustard, a small order of cheese fries, and a Coke. Might as well mainline cholesterol, I figured. I'd take my surf-casting rod and gear with me, pick up a handful of bait shrimp at TW's, and go to the beach at Mile Post 6 in Kill Devil Hills where there was supposed to be a slough offshore. Surf action opened and closed the fishing holes frequently. Whether I caught a fish wasn't that important. Getting out on the beach was what mattered.

I put on a pair of old shorts, a faded T-shirt, and slipped

my feet into scruffy sneakers. Dressed for the Outer Banks.

The beach wasn't as crowded as I thought it would be. I walked south a hundred yards, carrying my surf-casting rod and white plastic bucket. I used a bottom rig, with two hooks baited with shrimp, and a two-ounce weight. I waded into the surf, felt its pull and tug, the powerful swooshing of the ocean driving out any other sounds.

Early afternoon, I wasn't that optimistic about catching anything. Just after the first cast, though, I felt a sharp tug and I jerked back to set the hook. I reeled in a ten-inch croaker. I didn't want him and released him into the surf. Fished for maybe thirty more minutes with no strikes.

Standing at the ocean's edge, the surf pulling gently at my feet, a sense of peace slowly came over me. That good feeling happens to all of us from time to time, I believe, and there's nothing to put a finger on as to what causes it. It just happens, and it's a most pleasant feeling, like God bends down and breathes on us, making us glow with a blush of happiness.

With that unexpected gift of well-being, I felt that I was beginning to accept my role, or my life, or whatever I wanted to call it. I was a crime writer, and that wasn't a bad profession. If I got sick of it once in a while, so what. I had a good life, enough money, and damn it, Keely's death grieved me and continues to sadden me, but my own life must go on. And I realized it *was* going on. It was going on right this moment, here at the ocean's edge, with the sun warming my skin, the fresh salt air, and looking out at the ocean as far as I could see. I felt as if I'd turned a corner. A corner of acceptance.

A man and woman in their twenties stopped their stroll down the beach to ask me if I was having any luck. I smiled and told them about the croaker, and I tried to do no more than steal a glance at her skimpy bikini.

I reeled in, waded out a bit, cast again. It wasn't long before my mind inched closer and closer to *The Lost Colony* murders of Joyce Brendle and Sally Jean Pearson. Pernell

Hunnicutt didn't fit my mental picture of the type who would do both killings. Hunnicutt was too direct, too straightforward. The person who did this hid a twisted kinkiness that I didn't see in the big, raw-boned maintenance man. Our actor, Eric Denny, fit the profile only slightly better. Hell, there was no way I could be sure.

Deputy Sammy Foster has more in mind that he's admitted. Just as Elly said, Sammy Foster doesn't do anything without a reason. At the sheriff's office with Balls and me, Sammy went into that narrative about the late Bobby Ford's last visit to Manteo because he apparently figured it had more significance than Balls attached to it.

As for my knowing more than I do, Sammy wasn't randomly spreading that rumor. No, he was doing it among townspeople, among those few who know who I am. He was targeting someone.

I wanted to know who was in his sights. I decided that tomorrow morning I would show up at the courthouse, act as though I were there to chat with Mabel or Elly, just "happen" to run into Deputy Sammy Foster, and squeeze him until he tells me what he's up to. Handled that way, it can't piss off Balls or make the sheriff think I'm sticking my nose in where it doesn't belong.

As I reeled in through the surf, I got another strike. A pompano, larger than my hand. A good fish, easy to clean. I put him in my bucket with the ice. Shortly after, I caught another pompano. Again, he struck in the roiling edge of the surf. Dinner for tonight.

I fried them in olive oil, heated to the point that a thumb-sized piece of bread danced with bubbles around it when dropped into the skillet. Fresh coleslaw, a small baked potato, and I was fixed.

At the courthouse Friday morning I didn't see Elly but I ran into Mabel. She said if I was looking for Agent Twiddy, he had gone back to Elizabeth City. I told her I'd like to visit with Deputy Foster.

She shook her head. "You'll have to hitch a ride on a

boat. Sammy's day off and he and Bobby Midgett out'n the Gulf Stream trying to catch a tuna or something."

So much for that. I went back to my place.

Later that afternoon, I thought about Elly, and wondered if she would be at the Ferguson party. There was no law of God or man that says I couldn't pick up the telephone and call her at the Register of Deeds' office, and ask.

I dialed the number.

She is one of those people who sound on the telephone exactly like they do in person.

I mumbled about getting settled in, then asked about the get-together.

"I haven't decided," she said. With a playfulness in her voice, she asked, "And what about you? You going if you get all of your curtains hung or whatever it is you're doing?"

"Yeah, I'm going. Thought it'd be nice if you were there."

I could see her smiling as she said, "I'll be there. You've helped me *maike* up my *moind*." There it was again, that trace of soft Outer Banks accent. Appealing.

When I hung up, I felt buoyed. I stood in the middle of the living room, hands in pockets, looking out the double windows and whistling softly to myself. I decided to put on a driving, bouncy Mannheim Steamroller CD. The drums of Chip Davis would help define my spirits.

# Chapter Eighteen

That evening I parked underneath the shops at the Manteo Waterfront in the visitors' section. I locked the Saab, and strolled across the street to a large one-story structure where the Ferguson party was being held. As I approached the hall, I could hear country music that was more pop than nasal hillbilly. In addition to the taped music, Ferguson even had outdoor lights strung on poles along the grassy area. I smiled a greeting to several guests who stood near the front door chatting and drinking.

Inside, a number of people were already eating, sitting on folding metal chairs at makeshift tables. Two long tables covered with white butcher paper were used as the serving line. A man and three women with J&K Catering printed on their aprons dished out pork barbecue, hushpuppies, baked beans and slaw, along with smiles and banter with those in line.

Two tables from the doorway, Mabel sat talking to another woman about her age, but much trimmer. Mabel had a paper plate of food on her lap.

When I took Mabel's hand and bent over to give her a hug, she introduced me to the other woman, Margaret Pedersen, Elly's mother.

I glanced around the hall.

"Ellen'll be here in a bit," Mrs. Pedersen said. Her eyes crinkled when she smiled. "Her friend Linda was coming around to pick her up."

Mabel said, "You better get something to eat. Good North Carolina barbecue, either chopped or pulled." She referred to the choice between pork cut into small pieces, minced, or pulled in larger chunks from the barbecued pig.

Balls stood near the center of the room talking with Ferguson and a thin, bird-like woman I assumed was Ferguson's wife. Balls waved me over. I exchanged pleasantries with the Fergusons, then they moved on to mingle with others.

"Feed time," Balls said to me. Sheriff Albright had just turned from speaking to one of the guests. Balls said, "Join us, Sheriff?"

"Not just yet, thanks. I'll be getting something in a minute."

We started toward the serving line when Dixon Nance spoke to us, beer in hand. His face was ruddy, either from the golf course or an early start on the beer.

"Maybe you don't remember," he said to me, "but I'd met you before—before the other day at Diane's Cafe. The first time when you were here doing that other story, with Sheriff Claxton."

"Oh, yes, I remember." Only vaguely, though. I recalled that he was coaching part-time at the high school. Though growing fleshier, he still looked athletic.

Dixon turned to the woman who stood silently and unsmiling beside him. "This is my wife, Sandy."

She managed a smile as she was introduced. In stature and looks, she took after her father, Charlie Ferguson. She was tall, with nearly shoulder-length ash-blond hair that she parted in the middle and gathered loosely at the back. I was fairly sure I had not met her before, yet there was something vaguely familiar about her.

Dixon took a swallow of his beer. "How's the investigation going?"

"For God's sake, Dixon," Sandy said, "let's let that drop for a while."

He put his hand on her arm, as if gently touching her, but I saw her stiffen. "Honey, here are the guys who can tell us. Give us the low-down."

"Just plugging away," Balls said with a smile, and made a move toward the serving line.

Sandy, her mouth firmly set, glared at her husband. I felt as if we were in the midst of a family fight that had started earlier.

In the serving line, I realized we were right behind Jules Hinson.

Balls said, "Nice party, huh, Jules?"

"Ferguson can afford it," Hinson said.

A really gracious son of a bitch.

We inched up a step in the line. Balls said, "Jules, we were all just speculating earlier about what type person would do that awful thing to a young woman from *The Lost Colony*. You know, speculating about different personality types, so to speak, that would commit such a crime. What do you think? What's your guess as to what type guy it was did it?"

Hinson turned to Balls, an expressionless stare, calculating. "Ain't it your job to figure out that sort of thing?"

"Oh, sure. But you know, I like to hear what other folks think. Especially folks who've been around here in town for many years."

"I'd say it'd be a boyfriend. Somebody who'd been bang-ing her, maybe. Somebody in the show with her, you want my opinion."

"Well, that's interesting," Balls said, as if it had never occurred to him before. "That's an interesting theory." He patted Hinson on the shoulder, a phony show of appreciation. Then he added, "We're also looking into the theory that it might be somebody who didn't know her real well but, you know, had sort of a thing for nice-looking young women, liked to look at 'em, view 'em, so to speak. You know what I mean?"

Hinson picked up one of the paper plates. He glared over

his shoulder at Balls. That cold, expressionless stare. He turned toward the serving line.

"Chopped or pulled?" asked the smiling woman serving barbecue.

Hinson moved on, stepping around one woman who couldn't make up her mind about the baked beans.

I got the pulled barbecue and asked for extra vinegar-based sauce. I whispered to Balls, "That's number three I know of that you've got pissed off at you—Pernell Hunnicutt, Eric Denny, and now Jules Hinson."

We took an end table where we could view the entire hall.

Jules Hinson sat alone near the end of another table, not looking up from his plate. A tall, muscular man wearing rimless glasses and carrying a bottle of beer, sauntered over to Hinson, bent down, and whispered close to his ear. Hinson half-smiled and nodded, continuing to chew a mouthful of barbecue.

I nudged Ball's elbow. "Who's that? Talking to Hinson."

"Earl Tyler. Accountant. CPA. Doesn't look the part, does he? Except for the glasses."

His hair was cropped short, like a military cut, and his sport shirt stretched tightly across his shoulders.

Balls said, "He moved here from Raleigh five or six years ago. I think he may do work for Ferguson." Balls frowned slightly, mentally sifting through the catalog of facts about people stored in his brain. "I heard he got into some sort of business trouble, I think it was, in Raleigh, made him decide to leave."

Earl Tyler patted Hinson on the shoulder, glanced around the hall, his gaze stopping for a moment on Balls and me. He took a swig of his beer, and strolled toward the serving line, moving with the self-assurance of a natural athlete.

I would put him on my list. Someone I wanted to find out more about.

I had just taken a big bite of barbecue, leaning forward to keep from dripping sauce on my shirt, when I saw Elly come in the front door with Linda. After speaking to her mother and Mabel, Elly saw me, smiled, and waved. She headed for us, Linda following.

I stood and slid a chair out for her. As far as I was concerned, Elly brightened the whole damn hall in her smartly creased white slacks and peach-colored pullover shirt. I realized I was paying more attention to her figure than previously.

I started to get a chair for Linda but she beat me to it. Grinning, she said, "Not to worry. I can snatch a chair at a standing-room-only concert."

Balls hunched forward as he ate. "Pedersen . . . Pedersen. Scandinavian. What's a good Scandinavian like you doing among all these English and Scot-Irish at the Outer Banks?"

"That's my father's doing. He was from Minnesota. Came down here in the Coast Guard and never left." She glanced at me and back at Balls. "Daddy died when I was six. So that's how I got here, along with two older brothers."

"Come on, let's get something to eat," Linda said.

Balls watched them get in line and wiped his mouth with a crumpled paper towel. "Now, don't go falling all over yourself trying to impress that young gal. You heard the part about two older brothers, didn't you? Those tough Outer Bankers probably wouldn't take kindly at all to some slick, middle-age yuppie type in a Lands' End shirt trying to romance baby sister."

Under my breath I muttered, "Screw you, Balls."

When Elly and Linda came back with their food, we chatted about the Outer Banks' changeable weather—always a favorite topic—and the summer's winding down.

"Yep," Linda said. "You know it's getting to the end of summer because tomorrow night's the season's last performance of *The Lost Colony*."

Balls said, "I'm going to be there, see the show." I knew he wasn't doing that for entertainment. "Why don't you take these ladies and all three of you go tomorrow night?"

Linda spoke up. "I'd love to. But I'm going to Wilson

tomorrow, right after I get off work."

I turned to Elly, who nibbled at a cinnamon and sugar-coated piece of yam. "I'd love to go," she said. "It's been three years since I've been."

We agreed I would pick Elly up at seven. She gave me her address and directions, a neighborhood near the Manteo Airport.

Balls said, "You folks excuse me. I've got to catch up with the sheriff about something. Then I'm going back to the motel and turn in."

While we ate desserts, I noticed Jules Hinson, a cigarette in his mouth, heading toward the door. He walked past Balls, who said something to him but Hinson kept walking. Mr. King's son lumbered away from the dessert line carrying a plate piled high, and stood shoveling in the goodies before heading to the exit. Sandy Nance spoke briefly to her father, and also walked toward the door. Dixon took a last big swallow of his beer and followed her.

"You like to people watch?" Elly said.

"Yeah. I'm guilty of that."

Elly's mother and Mabel prepared to leave and stopped at our table. Mrs. Pedersen mentioned picking up Martin, Elly's three-year-old son. To me, Elly said, "Martin had an upset stomach today. I decided best to leave him next door, where he's been spending a lot of time anyway."

Linda broke in, "Okay, boys and girls, the world of journalism won't come tumbling down if I'm late for work tomorrow morning, but I've got to be there early and. . . ."

After they left, I sought the men's room. When I came out I saw that even more people had left. I paid my respects to Charlie Ferguson, who was talking with a woman I recognized as the owner of one of the large motels. At a table near the door, an older man sat with his cane between his legs, both hands resting on the head of the cane. He cocked his head at me. "Get enough to eat?"

I patted my stomach appreciatively.

"Me, too. Now gonna go sleep it off—I hope. If

Maudeen ever gets outta that ladies' room there."

Outside, the breeze from the east was soft and light. I breathed in the freshness from the ocean and gazed up at the heavens, convinced anew that stars sparkle more brightly here than anywhere else on earth. I decided to stroll over to the Manteo Waterfront, take a walk along the dock and enjoy the solitude and peacefulness of the evening.

I crossed the street to the steps leading to the atrium level of the Waterfront complex. The complex is above the ground-level parking garage where I left my car. From both sides of the Manteo Waterfront complex—the street side and the dock side—the interior of the garage is visible through the lattice work. One or more of the lights in the garage must have been burned out because it was darker than usual.

The shops on the atrium level were closed, and business appeared to be winding down at the restaurant.

I strolled toward the back steps that lead down from the atrium level to a walkway along the docks.

Feeble light from the lamp posts spaced along the dock reflected on the water, four feet below the walkway. In the semi-darkness, the water looked dark purple, heavy, gelatinous in consistency. Thin puffs of grayish clouds moved slowly, like magic, across the sky.

I felt the wind gently against my shirt and on my neck and face. The breeze made the faintest tinkling of the fittings atop the masts of three sailboats at the dock.

Hands in pockets, I continued leisurely along the walkway toward the end of the complex and the garage. Taking my time, enjoying the night.

I stopped near a post to look out over the water. The light on the post was out, too. I imagined the darkness of this place four hundred years ago and how lonely it must have seemed for the settlers of Sir Walter Raleigh's colony.

I thought I heard a shuffling noise and glanced to my right, thinking someone might be coming down the walkway from the restaurant.

The pain was sudden.

A blow crashed against the right side of my head. Not a fist, more like an object swung at me.

My head snapped to one side. My eyes shut and I felt my knees bend as if I was getting ready to kneel. Then something else—a knee or a kick in the small of my back and I tumbled forward into the dark, purple water.

# Chapter Nineteen

I was going down, down, and I didn't do anything to try to stop it. It was as if I wanted to rest, and the water was cool and dark. Still going down, I slowly began to come back to myself. Fear and panic took over. I tried to swim, but I wasn't sure whether I was going up or farther down. I groped with my hands and by luck felt a piling. I was turned around and swimming under water beneath the walkway. I used the piling to propel myself farther under the walkway. Then, holding to a second piling that my head bumped lightly against, I eased around to the far side of it and came to the surface, my eyes open. I was under the walkway, a good ten feet back from the outer edge of the dock.

I had enough presence of mind to force myself not to gasp for air. It would make too much noise. I was shivering. Not that it was cold but I was shivering from shock or something. I tried to will myself to stop because I was afraid whoever attacked me would hear me.

A step sounded directly above me. Whoever it was must have moved toward the edge of the walkway. I imagined him peering at the purple water to see if I'd surfaced. I clung to the piling, hiding behind it, my face barely above water.

I heard no movement for what must have been two minutes. Then the beam of a small flashlight played about the water where I had gone in. The beam searched along the edge of the walkway. I scarcely breathed. No way could he see me unless he lay down and shone the light under the dock. Even then I would be virtually invisible, I thought. The flashlight clicked off.

I was shivering again and I clenched my teeth to keep them quiet. My neck was so tight that my head began to shake. I touched my fingers lightly to the side of my head. I couldn't tell whether I was bleeding, but my head felt tender and a hell of a lump was forming.

I heard steps, quickly back and forth, searching. The flash-light flicked on a moment, then off. The footsteps stopped. After several seconds, I heard hurried footsteps away from the edge, and nothing more. I assumed he left. Still I waited, clinging to the piling. Soon I heard a vehicle engine start. A big, powerful engine, like a pickup or a van. It drove away.

I clung to the piling for another minute, maybe two. I heard voices. Three or four people, men and women, probably from the restaurant, had walked down to the docks. They laughed and talked loudly. One of the women giggled and said something I couldn't understand. Then their voices faded as if they walked back toward the restaurant.

Pushing myself to the next piling, I slowly worked my way to the outer edge of the walkway. I waited again. No sounds. I inched along the walkway to the nearest dock that jutted out into the water. In the corner formed by the walkway meeting the dock, I eased my fingers over the edge and pulled myself up slowly so I could see.

The walkway was deserted. Using the piling and hoisting myself with my arms, I clambered up on the dock and crouched, staying in the shadows of one of the boats.

No one was around.

I stood, wobbled, and almost collapsed to my knees. So I crouched again and took deep breaths. I couldn't stop shivering. I felt the right side of my head. It was sore and swollen but I was sure it wasn't bleeding. I kept thinking about a cake of soap in a sock, something I had heard about years ago. A way of knocking out a person without leaving cut marks.

I stood again, my clothes soggy and heavy. I thought about my wallet and how everything in it was wet. Maybe I was still dazed because I didn't know what to do next. My car was in the garage, not far away. But I wasn't sure I wanted to go into the garage.

I would be safer where there were people. I was pretty sure the person who had hit me had left. But would he come back? Hell, I didn't know.

I would call Balls. Damn right. That's what I'd do. He'd be back at his motel. I stood straight, took a steadying breath of the night air, and started walking toward the restaurant. My clothes and shoes sloshed as I walked, and I left a watery trail along the walkway. I shifted to walking on the grass. I had a notion it would throw off anyone following.

I knew there was a public phone near the restrooms on the atrium level. I didn't want to go into the restaurant to call, have to explain.

The alcove for the phone was in shadows, and I glanced around me before I reached for the receiver.

I couldn't remember the number. I wrestled with the phone book in the gloomy light, then saw an advertisement on a glassed-in bulletin board. It listed several motels. I could hardly get my hand in my wet pocket to retrieve change for the call.

The phone rang four times before the night clerk answered.

"Ring Ballsford Twiddy," I said. My voice sounded strange to me.

"I can't hardly hear you," he said.

I realized I was whispering. "Mr. Twiddy, please. Ballsford Twiddy."

"Mr. Twiddy doesn't like to be disturbed after nine o'clock."

I squeezed the handset like I was throttling the guy on the other end. I hissed, "This is an emergency. Get Twiddy on the phone. Now!"

"Yes, sir."

I heard the connection.

"Yeah?"

"Balls, I'm in trouble. Somebody tried to kill me."

That brought him around real quick. "You okay now? Where are you?"

I told him I was okay but my head was hurt, and where I was calling from.

"Didn't see him?"

"No . . . I think he thinks he . . . he killed me."

"Listen to me, now. Get away from that public phone. I know where it is. It's dark. Get over to the restaurant. You don't have to go inside but stay right there near the front door in the light where everyone can see you. Don't move from there. Anybody gets near you, start yelling and raising hell. I'll be there in four minutes."

I stood near the front entrance to the restaurant, close against the wall in the light. Two young women came out of the restaurant and hardly glanced at me. I don't think they even realized I was standing there soaking wet.

In minutes I heard Balls' powerful Thunderbird roar up in front of the Manteo Waterfront and brake harshly. The door slammed and Balls came bounding up the steps, two at a time.

I was never so damn glad to see anybody in my life.

# Chapter Twenty

Balls had thrown on a light windbreaker over a pullover golf shirt. I knew he had his fat Glock 9mm under the windbreaker.

We took a few steps away from the door, keeping our backs to the buildings, facing the open section. Balls stood beside me, eyes roving over me and over the area.

"Tell me." His voice was steady, flat, and his gaze concentrated on my eyes.

When I got to the part about something smacking the hell out of the side of my head, Balls took a look.

". . . and I felt my knees giving way. I think maybe I had turned just a fraction so the full blow didn't get me. But enough did. It hurt like a son of a bitch. I think about those guys in the movies getting whacked around like it doesn't really hurt. It hurts. And as soon as I started going down, my knees giving way, he hit me in the back with his knee or kicked me and I went into the water."

"You didn't see him?"

"Not a glimpse. Had to be a man, though. No woman could hit like that."

"Don't count on it," he said. "But it isn't a woman's style."

I told him about coming up under the walkway and hiding there, and about hearing a truck or van start up. "I figured it was his, but of course I don't know for sure."

Balls looked me over again. "Want to see a doctor?"

"I'm okay. Still scared. Head's sore. But don't need to see a doctor."

Balls nodded in the direction of the docks. "Show me."

My clothes clung wet and cold and I fought to keep from shivering again. We took the steps to the walkway and retraced my route.

Standing at the lamp post where I was hit, Balls looked around, then we walked less than a dozen paces to the darkened corner of the garage. We entered a side door I hadn't known about. Someone could have hidden there, waiting for me to get my car, parked in that corner of the garage.

Balls nudged me and nodded up at the overhead light fixture. A bulb had been smashed practically over my car. Shards of glass from the bulb lay on the garage floor, and three or four pieces glistened on the hood of my Saab. Another bulb was smashed near the lattice work closest to the docks.

We stood beside my car. "He may have waited for you here. But you made it easier for him by standing out by the water. I've got a feeling he wanted it to look like an accident. Knock you out, throw you in the water. Otherwise, why not stab you or bust open your head with a crowbar."

I reached my hand toward the door of my car. Balls stopped me. "Just in case," he said, and began to look the car over with a small, powerful flashlight he took from his pocket. He crouched and shined his light under the car. He examined the hood. It showed no signs of being jimmied. The locked doors and trunk appeared okay. He nodded and I fished my keys out of my wet trousers and unlocked the driver's side. He looked inside. Then we popped the hood and he checked with a steady sweep of the flashlight.

"Start it up and if it doesn't blow up we're doing fine."

I started it and let the engine idle. "What do we do next?"

"Get you on home."

"Do we need to report this to, you know, the sheriff or

anybody?"

"You've reported it to me. I'll tell the sheriff in the morning. Think you can drive?"

"Yeah."

"No, wait. Let's leave your car here just in case he cruises back this way to make sure. We may want him to think he succeeded in doing you in."

"Damn near did."

"I'm going to be your house guest tonight."

I was glad to hear him say that.

He studied me again. "Any theories?"

"Sure, I've got a theory. So do you." Despite the warm summer night, I felt cold again. "Thanks to Deputy Sammy Foster, somebody thinks I know something about the murder. Murders."

Balls said nothing. Then, for the first time, he permitted a hint of a grin. "Looks like Sammy's done a pretty good job of it."

We walked to Balls' Thunderbird.

"Sorry about the wet clothes," I said.

"Got me leather upholstery just so's I could haul wet-ass reporters around."

He pulled onto the road to the beach, and when he saw me shivering he turned off the air conditioning.

Instead of driving straight into my driveway, Balls did a circle in the cul-de-sac and backed in quickly and expertly.

I had left a couple of lights on upstairs. I thought I had left the carport light on, too. We got out of the T-bird, and just as I glanced up at the light fixture, I stepped on something crunchy. I knew without looking what it was.

Balls examined the light fixture, flashlight in hand. "Bulb smashed," he said.

He whipped out his Glock with his other hand and played the flashlight around the carport. He quickly stepped to each corner of the house, the flashlight beam darting and searching. He motioned to me to get behind him and follow him up the steps to the side door.

The plastic light fixture at the top of the stairs had been crushed.

The house was far from burglar proof. But I had locked the door tonight, for whatever good that did. The top half of the door was glass panels. A panel near the doorknob had been knocked out.

Balls whispered, "Where's the other door?"

"Sliding glass door in front."

"Step over there." He was so close to me I could feel his breath. "If nobody comes running out as I go in, come in behind me."

The lights were on in the living room and somewhere in the back of the house.

He opened the door quickly and stepped into the kitchen, sweeping the area with his 9mm. I could hear him moving about the house in fits and starts. To the hall, to the bathroom. Slammed open the back bedroom door.

No one came running out, so I hurried into the kitchen behind him. I could hear him in the main bedroom, checking the closet.

I took one look at the dinette area and said, "Damn!"

My computer monitor lay on the floor, smashed. The laptop I use to hook into the monitor had been thrown to the floor, a big dent in its top, as if hit with a hammer. Papers, notes and CDs covered the floor and were strewn about the table. The two drawers on my new wooden file cabinet had been jerked open. What few papers had been in there were scattered about.

My bass was okay, where I had left it after practicing. Janey was not harmed, although a few small feathers lay on the floor near her cage. Something had upset her, made her flutter about. She doesn't take to strangers.

What a hell of a night this was. First, a damn-near successful attempt to kill me, and now this violation of my home, my work, my entire nest away from the world. My haven did not exist anymore. It was gone. Just like that. The Outer Banks had taken on an ugly, harsh edge. And I hated that. Anger and depression from that fact were building in me, swelling in the pit of my stomach, making me physically ill, hurting more than the lump on my head.

Balls came back into the living room. "A few things knocked around back there. Just to make it look good. But I'll lay you eight-to-five nothing's missing. Did a number on your computer, didn't he?"

I picked up the laptop, still connected to the busted monitor and keyboard. I nodded. The movement made me realize my head hurt. I'd put ice on it just as soon as I checked one thing.

Balls said, "Try not to touch any more than you have to. We're not going to find any prints, but we'll get the lab guys to go over this anyway."

I closed the drapes across the sliding glass door and at my work table, I reached carefully behind the file cabinet. My fingers closed upon a dog-eared brown nine-by-twelve envelope that I'd marked "Old Files" with a blunt felt-tip pen. The envelope contained three CDs. "I back up everything onto CDs frequently. Did it this morning. He didn't bother with this."

"He was looking for 'New Files,' not old ones," Balls said.

"I get a feeling he doesn't know much about computers."

I went to the refrigerator with a dish towel and wrapped three ice cubes in it, pressed the coldness against my head.

Balls sat down heavily in the rattan chair by the phone. His big frame dwarfed the chair. "I'm calling the sheriff's office. Report it. Just for your insurance if nothing else. They don't need to come out tonight. Same thing with Kill Devil Hills police. Let them come out in the morning. You can make a full report tomorrow."

I nodded, then said, "I'm taking these wet clothes off."

"Uh-huh." He was thinking.

I changed into baggy khaki pants with an elastic waist and a faded pullover shirt. I examined my head in the mirror. Swollen and discolored, but not looking nearly as bad as I'd imagined. When I came back in the room, Balls was sitting in the same position.

I held the iced towel against my head. "Want a Coke, iced tea or something? I don't have any beer or booze."

"Coke." Then in the same breath, "Rule Number One, never assume. Rule Number Two, don't hesitate to break Rule Number One, as long as you know you are breaking it."

I gave him the canned Coke, no glass, and poured myself a tall glass of iced tea. I sat on the couch and realized how tired I was. The towel was getting soggy. I laid it on the glass-topped coffee table.

"Okay," Balls said, "let's skip right to Rule Number Two and start assuming. Let's assume that these two incidents have been perpetrated by the same individual."

He reverted to police talk, describing these outrages as "incidents." I felt my jaw muscles tighten.

"Of course it's possible that the guy who tried to do you in—and probably thinks he succeeded—is not the same guy who broke in here and trashed your computer. But that's unlikely and we both know that. Too much coincidence. It's the same clown."

Balls hadn't bothered to take his windbreaker off. He went on talking, a monologue, as if I were not around. "This guy was real nervous. He was convinced that you knew something and were about to spill the beans, which is crap of course. The whole damn theory is farfetched." His eyes focused on me. "No offense to you. But the idea that here's this goddamn mystery writer who knows all and is just waiting for the proper moment to give the word is all bullshit. But, hell, it looks like this guy believes it. Unless there's somebody else you've royally pissed off."

I shook my head. "Not to that extent, anyway." The movement prompted me to put the soggy towel against my head again.

Balls slipped back into his monologue mode: "Okay, what do we do now? In the beginning, the guy thought he had done you in. And he may be convinced of it if he cruised back by the garage. He'll wait for things to develop. Wait for the word to get out tomorrow that you're missing, or your body floats up at the dock."

"Pleasant thought."

"It's possible he came here first. But I don't think so. I think he had you in his sights and wanted to make sure he had an opportunity to do you in before he came back here. Getting you was number one priority."

"Jesus. In his sights?"

"Well, so to speak."

Balls looked at his watch. I'd already checked the wall clock against my wrist watch, which had survived the dunking, so far. It was ten minutes after midnight.

"It was just before eleven when you got clobbered, wasn't it?"

"I think so."

"The show was over."

"Huh?"

"*The Lost Colony*. The show was over. There would have been time, maybe, to get from the show to the Manteo Waterfront, but just barely." Balls made a face as if he didn't care for his own reasoning.

I knew what he was thinking. Whoever did it knew where I was, where I had parked. That didn't sound like someone from *The Lost Colony*. Sounded more like someone who knew I was at the Ferguson party.

I said, "Speaking of the show and the whole business of life goes on, just what do I do next? Pretend I'm dead? Go around with a bodyguard? Move? Just what do I do next?" My voice was loud, had an edge to it.

Balls didn't answer. He sat staring straight ahead, his big hands folded on his belly like the Buddha. "First, take you out of as much danger as possible. We're going to get Deputy Sammy Foster to call off the dogs, damn quick. Let him get the word back out that you don't know ape shit from apple butter about who the murderer is. Next, we take the official reaction that somebody tried to mug you."

"Mug me? In Manteo? Nobody's ever been mugged in Manteo."

"How do you know? People get mugged all the time. Everywhere. But if we let it be known that somebody tried to mug you, and Sammy gets the word out that you don't know anything, you'll be, well, you'll be better off."

"You mean I might stand a better chance of not getting killed." My throat tightened. "You think he'll try again?"

Balls shook his head. "Don't think so. I think the whole thing was a stupid act on his part. Panic. We'll take away the cause of the panic." He was silent a moment, obviously turning ideas over in his head. "The fact that he is displaying signs of panic, though, may actually be good for us. May show he's beginning to crack, that he'll do other stupid things, acting out of panic."

He stood up and stretched, walked toward the kitchen, saw the trash container and deposited his empty Coke can. "Our 'official line' is this: You've had bad luck tonight. Not only did somebody try to mug you in downtown Manteo but teenagers broke into your house and vandalized it while you were out."

"Who's going to buy that, and why?"

"We don't care. What I *am* gonna do tomorrow, though, is watch closely to see who looks surprised to see you alive."

I shook my head again, disbelief at the whole bizarre situation. I touched the tips of my fingers to the lump on my head. "I'm taking a couple of aspirin."

I went to the bathroom for the aspirin. When I came back into the living room, Balls said, "No matter what we say, the guy is going to be nervous. He already is. And I'll be on a lookout for a real nervous guy."

He strode to the phone, punched in a number that I assumed was the sheriff's department. After a terse exchange with the dispatcher, in which Balls said he didn't give a crap what time it was, Balls got Sammy Foster's mother's number and called him there. He told Sammy what had happened to me and—yes, I was all right—and waste no time tomorrow spreading the word that Weaver doesn't know pea-turkey, and not to say anything at all about what happened tonight.

Balls listened for a moment, then broke in on Sammy and said, "Okay, then you go back to all those Misters Nobody-In-Particular and tell them that he's just a dumb-ass writer and doesn't know any more than the rest of us."

Balls hung up. "Sammy says tell you he's real sorry." Balls rubbed his face and blew out a puff of air from between his lips. "I got a feeling Sammy's not telling us everything that might be going through that head of his. That bothers me."

I took the last swallow of my tea. "I'm tired. You can take the other bedroom. I've got sheets in the closet."

"I'm going to sleep right there," Balls said, pointing to the couch, "with my shoes on, ready to chase anybody." He wedged one of the dinette chairs under the doorknob of the side door and checked the iron bar I used for the sliding glass door.

I tossed him an afghan and a pillow and put one of those toothbrush travel kits I had on the coffee table. When I flopped into bed I thought I was too tired and wired to sleep. But it didn't take long.

I slept like the dead.

# Chapter Twenty-One

I woke with a start when I heard Balls stirring.

The sun was up. I slipped on a pair of shorts, and examined my head in the dresser mirror. The lump was not nearly as bad as I thought it would be, but a lump it was, the bruise turning yellowish.

I went in the kitchen and got the coffee going.

"Great day," Balls said, coming out of the bathroom. He unhooked the chair from the door and stepped onto the deck. He looked at the door, and called back to me. "You're going to have to get that fixed. But I'm getting the crime scene guys over here first."

I followed him onto the deck.

He breathed in the fresh morning air there in the sunshine. His slept-in clothes weren't wrinkled too badly. "Good day to go fishing. Wanna go fishing?"

"Yeah, sure, Balls. Let's go fishing. Christ! I haven't been fishing but once since I've been here. And I know you're not about to go fishing. Not with all this stuff going on."

I went in and stared at the coffee pot.

Balls came back inside. "You'll feel better once you've had some coffee—and go an hour or two without having threats made on your life."

"What do we do now?"

"You got any cream?"

Feeling dejected, I sat down on the dinette chair Balls had moved away from the door. "There's skim milk in there I use for cereal."

"Skim milk? Blue-john. Man, you've sure slipped over to the other side."

He toyed with his coffee cup, stirring it absently. "Okay, here's the drill. See what you think about this. I'm going to the sheriff's office and check on a few things there. You're going with me. We'll take another look at your car. Then during the morning I'm going to do some follow-up questioning of Pernell Hunnicutt, our friendly *Lost Colony* maintenance man. See how he reacts when he sees you. See if he acts surprised. Determine where he was last night.

"Also, we're going to run out to *The Lost Colony*, have a quick talk with Eric Denny, and note his reaction when he sees you.

"Then if we've got time we may try to rent a dirty video from Jules Hinson. See what *he* did last night after he left the party."

Then, with a grin, the "smart-ass Balls" came back on center stage. "Hey, you got a VCR or DVD player? Man, we could get us some popcorn and sit here investigating Jules Hinson's dirty videos. No, you don't have a VCR. Might a known it. TV's probably permanently set on PBS."

I thought about last night. "I got the impression the guy who hit me was bigger than Jules Hinson."

"You don't know. A blow side the head can change your perspective real quick." He turned to face me. "How's your head?"

"Huh? Oh, it's okay. Hurts if I shake my head, or touch it. But okay. Better than I thought it'd be. How's it look?"

"Not bad. Little yellow. Your hairline hides it. You were lucky. Didn't get the full blow."

"It was enough. But no nausea, headache, sleepiness."

I poured more coffee. "What about tonight?" I referred to my plans to take Elly to *The Lost Colony*.

He didn't seem to be listening. "You ought to call somebody to get that door fixed first thing."

A Kill Devil Hills police cruiser pulled up. Two officers, one in plain clothes, came up the stairs to the door. The older one knew Balls. While they worked at dusting for prints, which all of us knew was a waste, I showered quickly and dressed.

The officers were about to finish up. Balls said he filled them in on the break-in and asked them to inquire among the neighbors.

After they left, Balls stood in front of the refrigerator with the door open, checking out the food.

"You want cereal? A bagel?" I asked.

"Naw, we'll get something at Diane's at the courthouse. She's open Saturdays." He closed the refrigerator door. "Now, back to you," he said. "About tonight? *The Lost Colony*? I think you should take her. We'll keep an eye on you."

"I want to talk to her first, though. Give her the option."

"I'll bet she'll go. Wouldn't want to miss it. Her man in danger, all that sort of thing."

Before we left, I called my maintenance guy, Jerry. I knew the owners had a policy with State Farm, but I doubted if the door repair would be enough to make a claim. Just the same, I resolved to call them, report the door and my computer loss. Heck, this was a time to upgrade my business set-up.

The traffic was already heavy, a lot of it heading in the opposite direction, north, back home to Virginia, Maryland, Pennsylvania.

Driving with one hand, Balls retrieved an electric razor from his glove compartment, plugged its charger cord into the dash, and went about shaving, careful of his mustache.

I glanced at the ocean. Paying it homage. Recognizing it, respecting it.

The morning sun was behind us as we crested the bridge over Roanoke Sound. A speeding power boat trailed a white, bubbly wake off to our left, and sunlight made sparklers around the boat. Off the bridge, the greenish-gray marsh grass on both sides of the road ahead looked as thick as fur on a sleeping, half-submerged giant animal.

We parked on Budleigh Street in one of the official courthouse spots and walked into Diane's together. I could sense Balls' eyes sweeping the place, which, since it was a Saturday, was devoid of the usual courthouse crowd and town businessmen. Tourists at three tables were having breakfast. I recognized a couple of local people but didn't know their names.

We ordered from a waitress I had not seen before. Jules Hinson came slouching in, the inevitable cigarette between his thin lips, squinting against the smoke. He took a table near the front, a couple of tables away from us.

I nudged Balls, who was already watching.

Hinson scowled in our direction before he picked up the plastic-backed menu on the table and appeared to be studying it.

I said, "If he thinks he's seen a ghost, he didn't show it."

"How can you tell? He's the sourest-looking sumbitch I've ever seen." Then Balls spoke up loudly, "How you doing, Jules?"

Hinson glanced in our direction, made a half-hearted acknowledgment with one hand, and went back to the menu.

Balls kept eyeing Hinson to make sure he ordered something, which he did. When our food came, Balls ate faster than usual. He finished when I was only about half through.

"I think I'll stroll over there to speak to Joy-Boy."

He dragged out a chair at Hinson's table and sat down. Hinson jabbed out his cigarette and glared at Balls, who had a big grin on his face. The waitress brought Hinson's breakfast, and I saw Balls peer at it and make a comment. Hinson hunched over his plate while Balls carried on a mostly one-sided conversation. At one point, Balls jerked his head in my direction and said something. Hinson peered at me briefly and went back to eating.

Near the front of the restaurant I heard a familiar voice.

Charlie Ferguson was speaking to the hostess. A moment later, his daughter, Sandra Nance, came in. They passed by my table and Ferguson spoke, smiling his usual award-winning smile, but it didn't manage to light up his face very long. Sandra looked at me. There was a slight hesitation in her pace that made me think she might stop and speak. Instead, she nodded seriously and kept on walking. No smile, but then she hadn't been exactly giggly-girl last night.

Ferguson held up two fingers to the waitress to indicate they wanted coffee. He and Sandra immediately leaned toward each other across the table and became quietly engaged in conversation.

The waitress took our plates away and poured me more coffee. Balls got up from Hinson's table, made a final comment to him, then turned to Ferguson's table and said, "Great party last night."

Ferguson looked up with a smile, waved, and said, "So glad you could come."

Balls slid into his seat, glancing back at Hinson, obviously still thinking about him. "I wish I had something on that little bastard. He's a surly slime bag."

"I take it you didn't get anywhere."

"If he's the one tried to do you in, boy, he sure hides it good." Balls shook his head. "That doesn't mean I'm taking him completely off my list. There's a meanness in that guy, plus some dark sexual undertones or something. I can't quite put my finger on it. But I don't think we're through with our Porn King."

Hinson stood, counted out a few coins for a tip, and left. Balls stared after him.

I whispered, "Looks like heavy conversation over there between father and daughter."

"Huh? Oh, yeah." Balls picked up the check and sighed. "She's probably bitching to him about Dixon. Drinking too much. But he runs the businesses, doing a good job."

"I thought he also did some coaching or something with the high school?"

"He did. On the side. Part-time. For the fun of it and the school was short a basketball coach. He'd done it for several years. But they gave it to another, full-time teacher. Been some complaints, too, about Dixon driving the boys too hard, you know, losing his temper and all." He chuckled. "A regular Bobby Knight."

We were outside when Balls said, "Shall we mosey on out to *The Lost Colony* thee-AT-trical production?" But before we reached his car, as if he'd just thought of something. "First, need to go upstairs, fill Albright in on what's happened. Be right back. Stay outta trouble." He gave a quick grin. "Be ready to run." Then, just like that, he was serious again. "It was a sneak attack. I don't think you're in danger of a repeat. Daylight and all." He ducked into the courthouse.

Ferguson and Sandra Nance came out, talking quietly. This time she did smile a bit. An attractive woman.

Something so familiar about her, but I still couldn't place what it was.

# Chapter Twenty-Two

Before going out to *The Lost Colony*, Balls and I checked on my car at the Manteo Waterfront complex. Everything was as we had left it last night. We decided to move it to the Elizabethan Motel where Balls was staying, which was on the way to *The Lost Colony*.

At the motel, Balls made a quick trip to his room to call his wife, let her know his schedule. I knew that when things eased up, Balls would be able to spend several days at home. Staying at home had to be an unusual treat for him, but one that I knew he thoroughly enjoyed.

We turned into the Fort Raleigh historical site and swung to the left toward the office. The sky was clear, the wind light from the northwest. Despite the breeze, the day was going to be hot, and I could already smell the heat on the tall pines and the grass.

As we neared the parking area, Balls pointed a finger at a big, lanky man walking toward a van. "Bingo."

Pernell Hunnicutt carried a saw and other tools. Balls maneuvered to park near Hunnicutt's van.

Hunnicutt didn't bother to look at us until we approached him. He peered at Balls, who had that big grin on his face.

"Hi there, Pernell Hunnicutt. How you doing?"

Hunnicutt didn't acknowledge my presence but walked straight to Balls. The tools in his right hand were a large flat-head screwdriver and a heavy rubber mallet. Looking at the mallet, I involuntarily touched my right temple, then quickly lowered my hand and kept it by my side.

"I finally got my van back from those knuckleheads and I'm thinking serious on suing the state government, the way they messed up my van."

"What you mean, messed it up, Pernell?"

"The back of it? Inside? They messed up everything. They got my fishing stuff so tangled up I had to throw out a whole bunch of it. Looked like rats been playing in it."

"Well, Pernell, I'm real sorry about that. Now understand, Pernell, I don't mean any offense, but I took a look in that van of yours, and it didn't exactly look neat as a pin before the crime lab boys started work on it."

"It suited me and I knowed where everything was and wasn't none of that fishing gear all messed up."

"Okay, Pernell, you been a real patient fellow. A good citizen. Tell you what I'll do. I'll speak to those crime lab boys—of course, I do want to know what they found, if anything—and see if they can't spring for a few fishing rigs and stuff. So if they messed it up, I might replace it for you myself. First, though, as I say, I want to find out what they found out."

Pernell said, "They didn't find out shit and you know it 'cause there weren't nothing *to* find out." He started to turn away.

"Ah, just a minute there, Pernell." Balls stepped closer. "How about telling me where you were last night about the time the show was ready to close?"

"I was right here."

"At the theater? At the show? I thought you got off about three in the afternoon, Pernell."

"I do. Unless something goes wrong. Like last night. The cord to the main tower light by the stage shorted out just before show time and they called me to come help them."

"What about the staff electrician?"

"He was sick, throwing up, like about three or four of the young folks in the play. His helper was here, for what good he was. I stayed with them through the whole show and then we fixed it more permanent once the show was over. We didn't finish up until about twelve or one o'clock. Then they expect me back here first thing in the morning. I took my own damn sweet time this morning, I can tell you that."

"Can't say as I blame you," Balls said, his voice quieter, the grin gone.

Hunnicutt continued to his van.

Balls sighed. "Let's go inside and find out where Eric Denny lives."

Ken Cavanaugh was talking to an attractive brunette who held several press clippings in her hand. I heard her say something about responding to a reporter. Cavanaugh said, "Go ahead, Elizabeth. You handle it. . . ."

"We're here because we'd like just a word or two with . . ." Balls began, then stopped to refer to a folded up piece of paper he pulled from his pocket, as if he needed a reminder of whom he wanted to see. "Here it is, Eric Denny, one of your actors."

Cavanaugh got that pained expression on his face.

"Just want to check something with him. About last night. What he might have been doing."

The young woman with the news clips spoke up. "He was probably throwing up."

Startled, Cavanaugh looked at her.

"Sorry," she said. "I was just leaving."

Cavanaugh turned back to us. He brushed at his sandy colored hair with one hand. "She's referring to the fact that Eric was very ill last night. Stomach flu. It hit five or six of the cast yesterday. Eric had to miss the performance last night for the first time in, oh, golly, first time ever, I guess."

"Where was he?"

"In his apartment, in bed, I'm sure. He was really quite ill."

"His apartment?"

"Yes, he lives in the Morrison Grove Apartments. Apartments for the cast. Quite nice, and subsidized somewhat so they can afford them. There's a sign on the highway back toward Manteo. Let me look up what apartment he's in and I'll go with you, if you don't mind."

In the parking lot, I noticed Cavanaugh studied the side of my head, too polite to ask.

"Bumped it," I said. "Really hard."

"That's bad. Sorry." Cavanaugh folded himself up in the Thunderbird's cramped back seat. We chatted about how pleasant the weather had been for August. Hot but not too humid. He said, "The weather looks like it'll be fine for tonight's performance. Our last of the season, you know. I dare say, this has been some season! But the kids have held up marvelously well. They are a remarkable bunch of young people. And talented, too. Turn left here."

The apartments were tucked down among woods and rolling sand dunes with vegetation. The gentle hills surrounding the site made it seem more like the Piedmont section of the state than the coast. The wood frame apartments blended in with the trees.

"Nice," Balls said.

"Yes, and it helps keep the kids together. They can live elsewhere if they want to—like, like the poor Pearson girl did—but these apartments are good deals for them and quite popular. There's even a guard out front to keep an eye on things when the show is going on."

We followed Cavanaugh up a set of wooden steps. "Eric is here in B-4."

We stepped onto a tiny porch that contained a wicker table and three ratty lawn chairs. The theater manager knocked on the screen door. "Eric? It's Ken Cavanaugh, and two gentlemen to see you. A Mr. Twiddy and—"

The door opened quickly. "Jesus Christ!" Denny said. He stood holding the screen door open, glaring at us. "I'm sorry, Ken. But I'm not pleased to see these two guys—Dick Tracy and Dick Tracy's personal Boswell."

I started to blurt out something but Balls nudged me sharply in the ribs.

Cavanaugh held his palms toward Denny in a sort of patting motion. "Oh, my goodness," he said. "I know you don't feel well, Eric, but Mr. Twiddy said it would take just a minute."

"Whether it takes just a minute or a few hours depends entirely on whether Mr. Denny wants to cooperate or not," Balls said. That old shit-eating grin was on his face. I couldn't blame Eric Denny for wanting to hit him. That grin was enough to make me want to hit him.

Eric stepped out on the porch, letting the screen door slam. His hair tousled, circles under his eyes. He wore only a pair of cut-off jeans, low around his hips. No shoes. Muscles rippled across his abdomen. I caught myself holding my stomach in, squaring my shoulders and trying to stand a little straighter.

"Okay, what is it?"

"Understand you missed the performance last night?"

"Yeah, what do you want, your money back?"

"Oh, dear," Cavanaugh said. "Eric, please. They just want to ask you a—"

"I don't talk to the press," he said, nodding toward me.

Balls had taken as much as he was going to. He stepped forward, practically in Denny's face, standing there belly-to-belly. "Listen, pal. I don't like talking to you anyway and especially standing out here in the heat in these goddamn woods and I'd just as soon do it downtown, where I know you're going to be a lot more respectful. Now you think you've had the runs the past twenty-four hours, you don't know what the runs are until you get it scared out of you back at the station. I'll keep talking to you and talking to you until you'll think that having the stomach flu is a piece of cake. Let me tell you something else, pal, you don't want to get any more on the wrong side of me than you already are. You understand that? Huh?"

"Oh, my," Cavanaugh wailed softly.

Denny's steely dark eyes didn't waver. "What do you want to know?"

Balls stepped back slightly. "Let's start with where you were last night—all of last night."

"I was right here, alternately wishing I were out on stage or dead."

"Who can vouch for the fact that you were here all night?"

"Well, I know he was too sick to perform and that had to be really sick—"

"All due respect, Mr. Cavanaugh. I want to know who actually saw Mr. Denny here all night."

"Jim Waters, the head electrician, was sick, too, right in the next bedroom," Denny said.

"Was he here all night?"

"Yeah . . . no. Actually, no. He got to feeling better and after the show he went over to the theater for a few minutes where they were working on one of the light towers or something."

"Then there's no one who can vouch for the fact that you stayed here all night?"

The screen door opened and a young woman with short red hair and the biggest green eyes I've ever seen stepped out on the porch. "Yes there is," she said. "I can vouch for it." She wore shorts and a T-shirt from Awful Arthur's Oyster Bar, no bra.

"I see," Balls said. He got her name and wrote it down on the piece of paper he pulled from his shirt pocket. Denny's aggressiveness came back. "What difference does it make? There's no new law is there that says I have to stay here all night?" Then his face took on a pained look, a look of growing anguish. "Oh, my God. There wasn't another murder last night was there?" He spun to face Cavanaugh. "Is everyone all right?" The girl with the green eyes stood close to him and took his hand.

"Yes, yes. Everyone's all right," Cavanaugh said. "I think this has to do with something else."

Balls turned to leave. With his back to Denny, Balls said, "Thank you for your time, Mr. Denny." He stopped and turned slowly back to Denny. "This is the last night of the show. Will you be leaving town, Mr. Denny?"

"In a few days."

"I may want to get in touch."

"The office will have his home address," Cavanaugh said.

Cavanaugh followed us down the wooden steps to the car. The heat and the sun made beads of perspiration run down my back.

One thing was sure, neither Pernell Hunnicutt nor Eric Denny acted like they'd seen a ghost when they saw me.

# Chapter Twenty-Three

We dropped Cavanaugh off at *The Lost Colony* office and headed toward downtown Manteo and Balls' motel.

Balls was quiet the first mile or two. Then he said, "Pernell Hunnicutt's got damn-near a foolproof alibi. Denny doesn't, though. That little gal's hot enough for our Tom Cruise to swear he was in church with her if that's what she thought he wanted her to say."

"Yeah, but he didn't act like he was surprised to see me raised from the dead."

"He was probably at the window watching us come up the stairs. He had time to get himself together."

"Okay, but he really did look upset when he thought we might be there about another murder."

"He didn't think that. He knew there would have been more action around the place if another one of the women had been murdered."

"He put on a good show, though."

Ball's glanced at me, a touch of disgust registering on his face. "He's an actor, remember?"

I felt like I wasn't such a damn hotshot investigator after all.

Balls backed into the parking space near his room where my Saab was parked. My car was looking dusty and grimy from the sand and ocean mist that seemed to carry for miles. I could see it on the windshield.

"You going to call the Pedersen girl about tonight?" Balls said.

"Yeah. See if I can come over to see her now. I want to talk to her in person about it."

"It'll be all right. We'll be watching you." He seemed subdued. "Come on in. Use the phone."

His room was on the first floor. It surprised me; he had made it his own. He wasn't living out of a suitcase, as I assumed he would be. His clothes were hung in the closet. Some of his personal belongings were arranged on the dresser and his shaving gear was neatly placed in the bathroom. I was sure the dresser drawers contained his other clothes. A wind-up travel alarm sat on the bedside table, atop the clock-radio supplied by the motel. A yellow legal pad and two pencils lay by the telephone. His soft-leather briefcase leaned against the table.

Ellen Pedersen was listed in the small Outer Banks telephone directory. Seeing her name surprised me because I was so used to the big city phone books in which women listed no more than their initials and last name, if that.

Balls went into the bathroom and closed the door.

On the first ring the phone was picked up. I heard fumbling as if the receiver was dropped, then a child's soft voice saying, "Hello?"

"Well, hello there. This is Harrison Weaver. Is your mother home?"

There was no sound on the other end of the line, then the tiny voice said, "Yes."

Silence again. I waited a moment. "Hello, are you there?"

The tiny voice: "Yes."

"Would you get your mother? Ask her to come to the phone?"

A pause. "Yes."

I could tell nothing was happening. The phone was still being held. I waited. Tentatively, I said again, "Hello?"

"Yes?"

Then I heard a grown woman's voice, tinged with

laughter. "Hello? I'm sorry. Did you wish . . ."

"Elly? This is Harrison Weaver. Was that your little boy?"

She laughed and I could see her mouth and throat, the hazel eyes sparkling. "No, that was Lauren. The little girl next door. She's over here today. She's not quite three but she loves the telephone." She laughed again. "She's got the answering part down real well. It's from then on that she sort of falls down."

"Reason I called, Elly. . . ." Balls had come out of the bathroom, glanced at me and then sat in the chair by the window. "Reason I called is because I want to talk to you about tonight."

"Oh?" There may have been the slightest trace of disappointment in her voice. I heard Balls shifting impatiently in his chair.

I figured I'd better blurt it out quickly before she got the idea I was trying to get out of our date. I sketched it in briefly, assured her I was just fine, and said I would like to talk to her in person.

"By all means," she said.

Balls walked out with me. "When you get through at your girlfriend's, swing on by the sheriff's office. I'll be there."

I ignored the remark about girlfriend and said okay.

"If you get detained, I'll understand." He stopped at his car and let his grin fade. "I want to have a little sit-down-come-to-Jesus chat with Deputy Sammy Foster. And I want him to see you. Look you in the eye."

My car's interior was hot but the heat made the leather smell good. I had been brought up to believe that attachment to material possessions was vaguely, if not outright, sinful. Still, I took pride in this one possession, my Saab 9000, and rubbed my hand across the leather and touched the solid dash, warm from the indirect sun. I lowered the windows and let the motor idle a minute. Balls waved as he gunned out of the parking lot in his yellow and white Thunderbird.

I drove west on Highway 64, retracing, for a short distance, our route toward Fort Raleigh before turning left off the highway. I glanced in the rear-view mirror to see how my head looked. Not bad, really. Also, I realized I'd been checking the rear-view more frequently than usual. But I saw nothing suspicious. I felt buoyed, optimistic, convinced Balls was right. There wouldn't be another attempt.

I turned again. The short road had only about five houses on it. Elly said hers was at the end. In certain areas of the Outer Banks, in Manteo and especially around Wanchese or on the mainland at Manns Harbor, people's yards resemble land-locked marinas. Boats in need of repair and painting sit on trailers or lie tilted on their sides, and dozens of rusted wire crab pots are stacked haphazardly among the weeds, along with anchors, busted oars, propellers, and the ubiquitous fish net the owner intends to mend, someday.

Only one of the houses on Elly's street was a storage site for discarded nautical gear. The other houses were neat and tended: a small ranch style, three almost square bungalows, and Elly's and her mother's at the end. A narrow lot separated their house from its nearest neighbors. The vacant lot had been mowed recently. Elly's place was what's called the Sears-Roebuck house, sold in the 1930s as a complete kit ready to be assembled. A story-and-a-half, two gabled windows upstairs, and a porch across the front. A tin roof slanted down toward the porch. White paint and two large pots of petunias on the front porch offset the lowered-brow appearance of the slanted roof. A white Pontiac sedan, six or seven years old, sat in the driveway, and a small tricycle waited near the front steps. I parked behind the Pontiac.

Elly was on the front porch before I got out of the car. She smiled but a look of concern quickly took over. I felt she was looking me up and down to see if she could discern any bodily damage.

"Hello, Harrison." We shook hands. She studied my face and the side of my head.

"Here." I touched my fingers to the right side of my head.

"I can see. Swollen, getting sort of yellow, the bruise. Lucky it wasn't closer to your eye. You'd be getting a black eye, too." She touched her fingers lightly to my scalp and I could smell a flowery scent of soap on her hand. She looked around. "Want to sit here? Or go inside?"

"Here's fine."

We sat on the edge of a three-cushioned wicker porch settee. She sat at one end, knees together in faded tan shorts, her hair pulled back.

"I want to know," she said. "All of it."

I went through it, in detail this time. She watched my face the entire time I talked.

She sat a moment longer before speaking, turning to look at the yard and the pine trees that enclosed the street and made it private. "Sammy," she said. "Sammy Foster. He's the one who caused this. With his talk."

"That's what Agent Twiddy and I think. He called Sammy last night and he's probably having a talk with him right now. He doesn't think anything else will happen. So Agent Twiddy thinks, and I guess I agree with him, that there's no danger, with, you know, going with me tonight to *The Lost Colony*."

She smiled.

The screen door opened and Elly's mother stepped out on the porch, holding the hand of a small boy with curly, sun-bleached, light brown hair. I stood and held out my hand to Mrs. Pedersen, then bent slightly to speak to the boy.

"This is Martin," Elly said.

He was hesitant about giving me his hand and withdrew it as soon as I let him. He came to his mother and leaned against her legs. She patted his back.

Mrs. Pedersen said, "Marty and I are going back in so you two can talk. He's helping me, aren't you, Marty?"

He shook his head. But he let his grandmother lead him back inside.

"Nice to see you, Martin."

He wouldn't look at me.

Elly watched her son as he was led back into the house. "Shy," she said, the pronunciation sounding vaguely Cockney.

She waited for me to speak. "About tonight," I said. "I want to leave it up to you."

"I'd love to go, Harrison. Hundreds of people around. He can't do a sneak attack with hundreds of people around."

When I stood to go, Elly stood, too, the slightest glaze of perspiration at her hairline near her ear. I could tell she wanted to say something further. "Harrison, it's about Sammy. He's shy and all, but he's stubborn. And he won't just, just speculate. He won't say anything until he's sure. I don't care how much the sheriff or Agent Twiddy tries to get him to say more than he wants to say."

"Balls is awfully good at getting people to talk," I said.

"Might be. But maybe you are the one Sammy would talk to. I think he would relate to you, more likely."

"I'll talk to him," I promised, and started toward the car.

She stayed on the front porch, smiling, as I backed out of the driveway.

The pine trees were a vivid green against the blue sky. I felt great. Maybe the Outer Banks would come back again and not seem spoiled once we got this thing solved.

I drove to the courthouse, figuring I'd join in on the talk with Deputy Sammy Foster.

# Chapter Twenty-Four

Maybe it was the sense of normalcy at Elly's house, with her mother, the child, and a front porch settee, that made me feel good. I turned off Highway 64 onto Budleigh Street and parked beside a WVOD Radio news truck near the courthouse.

I locked my car and involuntarily looked toward the Manteo Waterfront, remembering. The fear returned and flooded over me, as if I were drowning.

Someone on the sidewalk spoke to me, startling me back to the here and now.

It was Linda, who worked at the newspaper.

"Lost in thought. Didn't see you."

"I figured you were solving the mystery." She flashed those strong white teeth at me.

"No way," I said.

"You and Elly have fun tonight," she said, and hurried across the street. "I'm on my way to Wilson."

Since it was Saturday, the courthouse was quieter than usual. I figured Mabel was not around. Although a fixture at the courthouse, she didn't stay there twenty-four hours a day. I heard Balls laugh just before I tapped on the door to the sheriff's office.

"Come on in." Albright sat tilted back in his chair. He looked different in his casual, open necked short-sleeved shirt. His forearms were white and freckled. He appeared more comfortable about my being in his office.

Deputy Creech stood near the window, cleaning his fingernails with a pocket knife.

Balls lounged in a chair to the side of the sheriff's desk.

Albright nodded toward Balls as he spoke to me, the smile still playing across his big face. "I was just telling Balls about the time that hippie woman camped out on the front porch of the courthouse and wouldn't leave. Became a national story with the newspapers and television. She was giving interviews to everybody. It was under Sheriff Claxton. He tell you about it?"

"Oh, yeah," I said. "She about drove him crazy."

"She was the one who was crazy."

"It didn't end too happily, as I recall."

Albright's face saddened. "No, it didn't." He turned to Balls, as if Balls was not already familiar with the story. "She overdosed. Deliberately. Died sometime during the night sitting in a lawn chair right in the middle of the courthouse porch with an Indian blanket wrapped around her shoulders."

Creech looked up from his fingernails, grinning, wanting to get the mirth back in the story again. "I heard she threw her arms around Sheriff Claxton, tried to kiss the hell out of him while he was trying to get her to move off the porch, with all the TV cameras around and everything." Creech stood there, the big smile on his face beginning to fade because the fun had gone out of the story.

Albright was looking at me with his large, kind eyes. "You had sort of a rough time of it last night, didn't you, son?" He used the term "son" for any male ten years his junior, and it seemed totally appropriate, coming from him.

I nodded. "It scared me then, and it scares me now thinking about it." I touched the side of my head. "Hurt, too."

Balls said, "Sheriff and I were talking about some other angles. I haven't talked in person with Deputy Foster yet."

Creech said, "I just saw Linda Shackleford from the

paper. She said Sammy was down there earlier looking at back issues or something."

"He'll be back directly," Albright said. "I sent him over to Manns Harbor a little bit ago." Albright chewed lightly on his lower lip. "I talked with Sammy first thing this morning." He looked at me. "He was real upset you got hurt. But I don't think he has any good idea who did it. At least he didn't let on that he did. He said he had just sort of spread the word that you *might*, you know, know more than people suspected, and he really didn't think it was going to backfire. You know how Sammy is. He was standing there twisting his hands together and hanging his head."

Balls sat up straighter. "Sammy's already supposed to be getting the word out that you really don't know nothing. Hell, that ought not to be hard to convince folks of anyway."

"Thanks, Balls."

I was not convinced that what Sammy told the sheriff was the truth. He targeted where he spread the word. But it was clear I was not going to talk to Deputy Sammy Foster myself unless I hung around all day. No sense in that. I decided to go back to my place, so I left the courthouse and walked to my car. I couldn't keep from looking toward the Manteo Waterfront.

Sandra Nance stood directly across the street beside her parked Buick staring at me. She wasn't smiling, and she looked like she wanted to speak.

I raised my hand and waved. "Hello!"

She raised one hand slightly. "Hi." Her mouth moved quickly in what was supposed to be a smile.

I hesitated before getting into my car because I thought she was about to say something. Instead, she seemed flustered, half-heartedly waved the one hand again, and got into her car. She turned her head momentarily toward me again, nodded, then focused all of her attention on starting the car and driving away.

I got into my car and watched as she drove slowly around the corner at the Manteo Post Office.

What was all that about? I'm attuned to people enough to be certain she wanted to speak to me. Something held her back.

Driving back toward the beach, I thought about a comment Balls had made as I left the courthouse. I'd asked him if he planned to go home on Sunday.

He said, "No, I've got a feeling something just might break this weekend. It's got to. But if it doesn't break soon, well, I can't stay around here waiting four years for another murder."

I don't believe in jinxes, I tell myself, but I wish Balls hadn't said that. The sense of foreboding lingered.

The afternoon was sunny and the wind had shifted, making the day less humid. I thought I would drive up the Beach Road, rather than the Bypass.

I parked in the small paved parking lot at the end of Ocean Bay Boulevard. The wooden walkway to the bath house passes two outdoor showers and heads straight to the ocean. At the end of the walk, the structure widens into a deck with benches. I stood there and looked toward the ocean.

I needed to breathe in the softness of the warm air that came off the water. I needed to feel it on my face. In my short time back at the Outer Banks, I had become so attuned once again to the ocean and it had become such a part of everything about life here, that I made listening for its sound part of my day. If I stopped and stood still, no matter where I was, it seemed to me that I could hear the waves breaking on the sand, the whisper and the surge, and sometimes the angry crash of the surf, churning white or muddy and green with sand and seaweed.

The beach was moderately crowded, but I gazed beyond the sunbathers to the waves, which swelled gently, then broke into three or four rows of white breakers reaching for the shore. The water receded, chased by jerky-legged sandpipers. Out beyond the breakers I saw two dolphins heading south. Their fins surfaced every so often, and twice they came completely out of the water in graceful high leaps.

I realized I was smiling, standing there smiling at the ocean. I breathed deeply one more time before heading home.

Catching sight of my house, nestled at the end of the cul-de-sac, the break-in seemed a long time ago, and I knew that within a few days it would fade like a half-remembered dream.

Reliable Jerry had repaired my side door. It was better than before. Janey started chirping as I came in. My busted computer was stacked to one side and the place looked neater. Jerry's wife had surely come with him and helped, as she often did.

I stepped over the neck of my bass and went to my compact stereo. No Windham Hill or New Age today. The beach air and thoughts of seeing Elly tonight put me in a much more robust mood. So I chose a CD of Lester Young playing tenor with the Oscar Peterson Trio, Ray Brown on bass, Ed Thigpen using brushes on drums. Originally cut in 1957, great old gutsy standards: "These Foolish Things," "I Can't Get Started," "Confessing," the works. That's what I was in the mood for.

A few tunes later I remembered I'd promised to call Balls after checking out my house. Reluctantly, I turned down the stereo.

"Everything's fine here. Any enlightenment in your conversation with Deputy Sammy Foster?"

Balls said, "I've been trying to figure out how to describe that conversation, if you can even call it a conversation. More like me talking and him saying 'Aw, shucks' and 'Yep' and 'Nope.'"

I laughed, knowing exactly what Balls had been going through. "Come up with anything?"

"Well, nope and yep."

"Catching, huh?"

"He did say that on several occasions at several places he

'deliberately sort of mentioned,' as he put it, that you had the case pretty well solved. That you had been working on the first one all these years and with this latest murder you knew how to sew the whole thing up, and that he wouldn't be surprised if you didn't spill the beans any day or any hour."

"Jeez, that's laying it on thick."

"Here's more of the 'Yep' part: The 'various places' included—you guessed it—the Diane's Courthouse Cafe, the Green Dolphin, where she was last seen, Saber's, where cast and locals and other assorted tourist types go, plus Ferguson's Drug Store, Ace Hardware. You want any more?"

"That's the 'Yep' part. What about the 'Nope'?"

"He claims he had no one in mind when he started spreading the word. No individual or even two or three that he was keeping an eye on to see if they got edgy."

"He claims?"

"I don't think I believe him."

"You think he's got an idea?"

"Yep."

I told Balls what Elly said about Sammy clamming up so we couldn't get anything out of him unless he was sure.

"She's probably right," Balls said.

I was more convinced than ever that Sammy was targeting someone.

I cut the stereo off and picked up my bass. At first, still feeling the effects of the Lester Young-Oscar Peterson CD, I put the bow aside and played a few jazz riffs and then fast blues in B-flat, C and D. I sighed, applied rosin to the bow, and warmed up once again with the Mozart piece. Then I switched to a fun section of a Haydn work that was much easier. I avoided saying "shit," but "bitch" could be heard every so often.

Janey liked the commotion and hopped around in her cage, doing her head-bobbing dance and either chirping or muttering something. Hard to tell.

When it was time to get dressed a flash of brilliance hit me that Elly and I ought to eat before the play. You're a great date, Harrison. Tell the girl you'll pick her up at seven and don't mention anything about eating.

I dialed her number.

After the first ring, a small voice answered, "Hello?"

"Hello, is this Lauren? The little girl next door?"

A pause. "No."

"Martin? Is that you?"

Another pause. "Yes."

"Well, how are you? Is your mother in?"

"Yes."

Okay, here we go again. But then Elly came to the phone.

"I think they're putting you through the test," she said.

"My great intellect tells me we've got to eat."

We settled on getting a sandwich or burger and I'd come by a half-hour early so we could grab something quick. Not exactly New York-style dinner and theater.

But I sensed a new stage in my life opening up.

# Chapter Twenty-Five

Dressing in high fashion for the Outer Banks, I put on khakis and an oxford weave button-down shirt. I took along an unlined windbreaker, always a good idea in the evening near the water where it can sometimes get a bit chilly. You never know when the wind will shift, bringing a change in the weather that you can actually see coming at you across the sound or the sea.

I got to Elly's a few minutes early. Martin came to the front door. He didn't respond to my greeting, but he did hold open the screen door, and I stepped into a bright and cheery living room. Two large lamps highlighted a couch and easy chairs upholstered in splashes of yellow and white. A crossword puzzle magazine lay open on a table by one of the chairs. The house smelled like apples, maybe being cooked or peeled.

I smiled at Martin, who stared up at me. I thought he was about to smile but he turned and walked toward the rear of the house.

Elly came into the living room, while at the same time looking back over her shoulder to say something reassuring to Martin. She brought an overall impression of freshness with her, like the first time I saw her at the courthouse. The trim, sand-colored slacks and peach silk blouse, made me realize anew what a petite young woman she was. She wore hardly any makeup, and she looked great.

"Hello, Harrison." The top of her head was even with my eyes.

I thought we were going to shake hands again but we didn't. My impulse was to give her a big-city hug. I come from a long line of huggers. But I wasn't sure how that would go over with Martin. I gave her a modified hug anyway. Martin eyed me coldly.

She laid her lightweight white sweater across the back of one of the chairs and held up a finger. "Just a minute." She went back toward the rear of the house, to the kitchen, I presumed, and returned carrying a small wicker basket and Thermos. Mrs. Pedersen came behind her, smiling and nibbling on a piece of peeled apple.

Elly held up the basket. "Dinner," she said.

"Oh, for goodness sakes. . . ."

"If it suits you, we'll go out to *The Lost Colony*, get our tickets, and have our picnic. Like a tailgate party."

"I should have thought of something like that. Thought I was being creative suggesting McDonald's or Butch's Hot Dog stand."

"Come on and hush up," she said, snagging her sweater with her free hand.

"Want to take your crossword?"

She grinned. "A decorative needle case? *Etui.* They use that a lot. Just in case you needed that in conversation."

She gave Martin a kiss. He started to protest her leaving. His face began the slow, agonized contortions that signaled a good heart-rending cry. But Mrs. Pedersen took his hand. "Okay, now we can have some of the ice cream," she said, "and they don't get any."

"See you, Martin," I said. He ignored me.


Elly pointed in the general direction under the trees where we would have our little picnic. A number of cars were already filling the parking area, and many other picnickers had the same idea as my date.

When I returned with the tickets, Elly had spread a plastic tablecloth on the ground away from the main flow of foot traffic and was sitting cross-legged and waving to get my attention. I flopped down on the grass beside her. "This is nice," I said. "I haven't done anything like this since . . . hardly ever."

We finished the thin boiled ham sandwiches, along with peeled apple slices and cheese. She leaned back on her elbows and I said something about what a beautiful setting for a theater, but I was really stealing looks at her breasts. Perfectly formed, and just the right size for her.

Maybe she sensed I was looking at her. She sat up and said, "We'd better put this away and stroll on over to the theater."

Near the parking lot, I saw Deputy Creech, in sport shirt and slacks, leaning against a pine tree and smoking a cigarette. He raised one finger in greeting. I figured there were other security people around, as well.

His presence brought me back to reality. I had dismissed the entire crime investigation from my mind. I'd been doing the la-la-la with Elly, while Balls and other lawmen were keeping an eye out for anything suspicious—and watching over me.

Just the same, it was nice acting like normal folks on an outing.

Elly and I put the picnic basket in the trunk of my Saab, and standing side by side I could smell the late afternoon sun on her hair, a pleasant human smell, and a trace of cologne. She glanced up and saw me looking at her, smiled. We both looked away.

"It's going to be a beautiful evening," she said. She held her face up to feel the breeze. "Wind from the north, or north-west. I don't think we'll have any bugs tonight."

People were standing by their cars, liberally spraying insect repellant.

We followed a gently curving paved path to the theater through a dark growth of pines, live oaks, and shrubs. At dark, low-level lights along the path came on.

As we approached the amphitheater, I was reminded of how much it resembles a wooden stockade, a fort made of upright timbers. The seats, or benches, are wooden and the floor is sand. Rays from the setting sun glistened on the water visible beyond the stage.

We rented two padded plastic cushions for the seats. I handed Elly her cushion and saw she was looking over my shoulder. "Hello, Mr. Twiddy," she said.

I turned. Balls stood there wearing a loose-fitting sport shirt not tucked into his slacks, a big grin on his face. I knew his sidearm was under the shirt. "Like to sit with us?" I said.

"Appreciate it. But I'm going to sort of mosey around and visit. Besides," he said, "the seats are reserved." He glanced at my tickets. "I'm not far away." He looked around as if appraising the good attendance for the season's last performance. "Quite a turnout," he said.

I saw another of Sheriff Albright's deputies at the left exit.

We went about halfway down into the large bowl of the theater and took our seats. Elly cast her eyes around at the crowd, picking out one or two deputies she knew. "Body-guards?" she whispered.

"Oh, no, they just want to keep an eye open. Maybe see the show."

"Comforting."

I wasn't sure what she meant. Then I realized that was exactly what she meant. Nice having Balls and the deputies around.

She nodded toward the stage. "You know the story, don't you?"

"*The Lost Colony*? Yes, but I get a little mixed up some-times. Dates." Actually, I knew the story well, but I never tired of hearing the mystery surrounding the colony's dis-appearance. I wanted to hear her version, and have an excuse to study her as she spoke.

She summarized Sir Walter Raleigh's sending an

exploratory group here three years before the arrival in 1587 of eighty-nine men, seventeen women, and eleven children. It was a voyage intended to establish a permanent settlement.

Elly lifted her head proudly. "That was here on Roanoke Island, the first one, not Plymouth Rock, not Jamestown, but here."

She said, "The colonists were supposed to receive more supplies from England the next year, but because of trouble with Spain, the Spanish Armada, Queen Elizabeth wouldn't let any ships come back. It was three more years before Governor John White arrived with supplies from England."

She leaned toward me and spoke more softly, "When White and his party got here, they didn't find any people left. Only the remains of that little fort and the word 'Croatoan' carved on a post. Those are the Indians. And it's a mystery to this day as to what happened to this 'Lost Colony.'"

"What do *you* think happened to the people? All die?"

A slow, sly smile. "Eventually."

"You know what I mean."

"Old folks say they moved inland. The sound was said to be even shallower then. They could have practically walked across and lived and intermarried with the Indians. The Indians were friendly, at least in the beginning."

I concentrated on the delicate bow of her upper lip, and how her mouth moved when she talked.

"Some of the names—I don't know what they are, Davis is one I think—turned up early on in that section of North Carolina. And some of the Indians had gray eyes, it was said. Like my great granddaddy."

No one has ever been able to find out for sure what happened to this band of people. Four hundred years later and still a mystery.

I said, "You know your history well."

She smiled. "My major, you know. You want to hear me tell about the Punic Wars? Linda almost throws up when I start on the Punic Wars."

People arrived in a steady flow, taking their seats, filling the theater quickly.

She said, "They took Chief Manteo, the local Indian chief, back to England to show him off. Made a Christian out of him. Don't you know that was a strange, strange voyage for Chief Manteo, like a trip to Mars."

I looked up at the sky. Dusk was coming on fast. "I always think about how dark it must have been here on the island for those settlers, and how terribly lonesome and homesick they must have been."

"It still gets dark and lonesome here," she said. Then, with the slightest downward movement of her eyes, I got the impression that she wished she hadn't said those words, that they might be misinterpreted. She shrugged. "In the winter, I guess. That's what I mean. And that's part of the charm of the place, right?"

The theater crowd began to hush. I wasn't sure whether I'd missed a signal. It had grown fairly dark and maybe that is what settled the crowd.

Through the theater's sound system came a deep, sonorous voice, slightly softened by a Southern accent. "Ladies and gentlemen, before we begin tonight's performance of *The Lost Colony*, the outdoor drama by the late Pulitzer Prize-winner Paul Green, which has run continuously since 1937—with the exception of four years during World War II when this entire coast was blacked out because of enemy submarines off the coast—all of us with *The Lost Colony* wish to make it known that this last performance of the season is dedicated to the memory of Sally Jean Pearson, a member of the cast, who met her death so tragically and senselessly just a little over a week ago."

I recognized the voice as that of the general manager, Ken Cavanaugh.

He continued. "We have all been deeply saddened by this event. In the beginning, there were those of us especially close to Sally Jean who felt we couldn't go on, that the tragedy had covered us with a melancholia from which we could not recover. Our sadness and shock was so severe it was as if a tide of darkness had swept over us."

Cavanaugh's voice broke slightly. He paused, composed himself, and said, "But the cast of actors and the staff have gone forward with the performances and with their duties, just as we know Sally Jean Pearson would have wanted. This performance, then, this last performance of the season is dedicated to the memory of Sally Jean Pearson. Her memory will live on in our hearts."

The audience was reverently quiet.

After a moment of silence, the play began.

# Chapter Twenty-Six

The play opened with a prologue by the "historian," who strolled on stage right. Then our attention switched to a replica of an Indian village on Roanoke Island in 1584, where Chief Manteo, Wanchese, and other Indians were introduced. Early in the play, the Indian Uppowoc, played with hostile intensity by Eric Denny, came on stage. As principal dancer, and the instructor in stage combat, he moved with grace and strength.

The scene switched to England and preparations for the initial journey to the New World. A headstrong Queen Elizabeth was introduced, along with Sir Walter Raleigh, Governor John White and his daughter, Eleanor White-Dare, and her husband, Ananaias Dare, the soon-to-be parents of the first child of English parentage born in the New World.

The staging was good, especially considering the simple outdoor structures. Behind the facade at the rear of the stage, the mast of a ship, no doubt being towed along on a hidden track by out-of-sight stagehands, appeared to be moving along the sound.

A character called Old Tom provided comic relief in being pursued by the amorous Indian squaw Agona. As the play proceeded, it became obvious that the colony was in desperate need of supplies and food and was, in fact, doomed. At one point in the play, when no one was expecting it, one of the English soldiers fired a musket off-stage, the report so loud that everyone in the audience jumped and gasped in surprise, including Elly. So did I, and my heart beat faster. The deputy at the exit watched the crowd. I was on edge more than I realized.

At intermission we stretched and headed back to the restrooms. When I came out, Elly stood nearby, looking up at the sky. "Too much of a line. I'll wait."

It was after ten when I realized the colonists still had some tragedies and hard luck to go through, but the drama was nearing its end. Eric Denny, muscular and vigorous, performed an impressive solo dance.

When the play ended, despite the audience's applause, the actors did not reappear for a curtain call, reinforcing the sense that they had disappeared forever. I'm enough of a theater buff that I love the whole process, the excitement and the magic of pretend.

We made our way up the aisle, and I noticed Balls standing there, his eyes sweeping the crowd. When he saw us he said, "And we think we've got it rough."

Elly said, "If you two will excuse me, that line doesn't look as long as at intermission."

Balls glanced at her as she walked away. "Nice gal. Call me when you get back to your house." Balls shook his head as he surveyed the diminishing crowd. "This case is really a bitch! Nothing. I mean nada."

"I saw Creech and fellow deputies here tonight."

"Yeah, but I don't think you saw that one this afternoon when you stopped at Kill Devil Hills Beach House."

"Huh?"

"Or the Jeep parked in the cul-de-sac that backs up to the rear of your lot."

"You gotta' be kidding."

"Albright lent me some fellows in plainclothes. Been keeping an eye on you all day."

"Jeeze, I had no idea."

"You need to stay more alert, my man." His eyes crinkled with a smile. "Quit thinking about a certain pretty gal."

The house lights were up and crew members lingered about impatiently. I sensed they were ready to begin breaking down equipment as soon as all of us left.

Balls turned serious again. "We've seen nothing all day that looks suspicious. I'm calling off the deputies."

Elly came back from the restroom.

"Shall we?" I said.

With a smile and something of a flourish, she hooked her arm in mine and we strolled off.

"Have fun," Balls called.

Elly raised one hand and wiggled her fingers at him without looking back. I was becoming fond of the gesture.

As we walked to the parking lot, I was silent.

She said, "You okay?"

"Yeah, sure. Fine." I lied. I was embarrassed that I had not noticed I was being shadowed all day. Hell, like it or not, I was in the midst of this investigation, and I wasn't paying the attention I needed to. I rationalized that my work began *after* crimes were wrapped up and I was able to write about them. Usually, I was not involved to this extent. As if that was an excuse.


With the help of law enforcement officers, the traffic moved steadily out of Fort Raleigh, most of it heading east toward the beach. We were with the flow when I said, "Want any coffee? Dessert?"

"Oh, thanks so much, Harrison. But I'm just fine." The accent made her last word come out softly as "foine."

I looked at her. "You're okay, Elly . . . Ellen."

"Very few people say Ellen anymore. Even Mother."

"I like both of your names."

"Tomorrow morning Martin is in the children's program early at church, so. . . ."

"I got the picture." I swung the Saab onto the road that led toward her house. A short distance ahead I knew I had to make a left, but it looked different in the dark.

"It's just a little farther," she said. "I guess I'm not much of a night owl. Maybe not the most exciting, ah, date."

I slowed the car to look at her, to thank her for coming tonight.

We turned into her street and stopped behind her Pontiac. I cut the engine. The porch light was on but it didn't cast illumination much beyond the steps. I came around to her side of the car just as she was getting out. "Thank you," she said. I got the picnic basket from the trunk and held her elbow as we stepped up on the porch. I sensed we were both feeling awkward. Neither of us was practiced at the dating game. She glanced up at the light on the porch, and I followed as she opened the screen door and the unlocked main door. We stepped into the living room, where only one low-wattage lamp burned. She pushed the front door partly closed and we stood there for a moment. No other sounds could be heard in the house. "We don't want to wake the house with raucous laughter," I said.

She smiled. In the light I could see her upper lip move slightly.

"I think I'm supposed to ask you if I can kiss you goodnight."

She smiled and nodded her head quickly, as if we were sort of cutting up.

I kissed her, and I swear to God it started out as a fun kiss, just a way to tell her goodnight like boys and girls are supposed to do on a date. But suddenly we were melting together, and I held her so tight I was afraid I might hurt her, but I didn't let her go and my heart was racing. Our mouths were open wide against each other and I could feel her trembling as well. She came up against me, seeming small and vulnerable. Yet there was an incredible strength, determination, insistence in her body. Then, almost as suddenly, we got control of ourselves and our faces parted, but we stood looking at each other.

Her eyes had a surprised, stunned look, and surely mine

did as well. We had stumbled onto something we hadn't expected.

She swallowed and smiled wanly, but kept searching my face as if to make sure what we had just experienced wasn't all some trick. I think she could tell it wasn't.

I said, "I didn't really expect that . . ."

"Neither did I."

"Well . . ."

"Well, I certainly enjoyed the evening," she said, and swallowed again.

"I guess I'd better go." My hands were trembling. Jeeze, I had not had a kiss affect me like that since I was fifteen.

She nodded and kept looking at my face.

"Harrison, I don't know what happened. Please, nothing like that . . . I usually don't even like to kiss. I don't."

I managed to smile for the first time. "Kind of caught me by surprise, too."

She managed a more relaxed smile, shook her head, and rolled her eyes upward. She put her hand on the doorknob. I was careful not to stand too close to her once we were framed in the light of the door. Neighbors in these small towns have incredible eyesight.

"I've enjoyed it, Ellen . . . Elly."

"So have I."

I breathed in deeply and turned to go.

"Harrison?" she said.

I had one foot on the steps. "Yes?"

"That was *some* kiss," she whispered.

"I'll always remember it."

"So will I." Quickly, she blew me a kiss before closing the door. She really did.


I got in the car with my emotions churning like a Maytag on the sturdy cycle. I was happy and disturbed at the same time. I wanted to rush back to her and I wanted to run away. I wondered if I should kick myself for not trying to go further.

That's what it's all supposed to be about, isn't it? At the same time I was worried because I felt like a smitten teenager.

I drove to the highway and headed toward the darkened beach, and my feelings began to sink. Maybe it was backlash from the emotional high. I couldn't figure out why in the hell depression would begin to wash over me. There seemed nothing I could do about the growing melancholia, either. Was the feeling because I had such a strong attraction for Elly, quite unexpectedly, and that made me feel guilty, as if I were being unfaithful to Keely's memory? I had been in love with Keely, but not once did our kisses do for me what Elly's kiss had done. My reaction to that kiss knocked me for a loop, and inexplicably depressed me. Maybe, deep down, I was afraid to feel anything.

For the first time in months, I wanted something to drink. No, not just something to drink. I wanted to belt down a few beers or a couple of shots and become semi-anesthetized again.

If I drank just a little, calmed myself down, I wouldn't have to get blotto. But I'd been under a strain this week. Maybe a beer or two, enough to take the edge off things. Nobody ever said I couldn't handle booze.

I pulled into Saber's parking lot. There was a space near the front. I sat in the car a few minutes, thinking. Tomorrow's Sunday and I can sleep late. A couple of beers and that'll be it.

I locked the car, stretched like I had all the time in the world. I studied the sky a moment or two, then shook my shoulders loose. All this to convince myself that taking a drink was no big deal.

# Chapter Twenty-Seven

The place was Saturday-night noisy, smelling like beer, sweat, seafood, and wet wood. There were a couple of empty stools midway down the bar. Trying to look casual, I strolled to the bar and perched a hip on one of the empty barstools. I kept one foot on the floor. I turned to look around the room. I was sure some of the cast members from *The Lost Colony* were celebrating the end of the season. Everyone seemed young and in complete control of everything. Young and cocky. That's the way the world is, I thought.

"What'll it be?" asked the blond-headed young guy behind the bar.

Before I could answer he shouted to someone in the rear. He turned back to me with a smile, and raised his eyebrows as a way of repeating the question.

"Oh, beer. Heineken'll be fine."

I wasn't sure what Heineken sold for here so I put a five dollar bill on the counter.

"Glass?"

"Please."

He set the glass and change on the bar. I let the change lie there. I put my fingers on the cold, moist bottle and turned it around to look at the label. I was reaching for the glass when I sensed the presence of someone entering and walking straight toward me.

"Well, well. Look who is bellied up to the bar." Eric Denny looked as if he had rushed from the theater with just a minimum of attention to removing all the makeup. His face was slightly cold-cream greasy. Two male members of the cast were with him, as was the red-headed young woman who'd been with him at his apartment that morning.

He got right in my face. I could smell whiskey and maybe marijuana on his breath. "It's our hack writer. The typist. Where's your big buddy? I didn't know you could go anywhere without him."

I still had one foot on the floor, and poised the other toe to drop to the floor to give me leverage. I took my hand away from the beer.

Denny got even closer in my face. With one finger he started to poke me in the chest. "Maybe you make some sort of a living writing your crap about other people's misery but let me tell you one—"

He shouldn't have poked me.

I took a step forward at the same time I swung, and I knew I was hitting him solid with the weight of my body behind the blow. My right fist caught him just above his lip and below his left cheekbone. The blow couldn't have been any cleaner. Solid and hard. His eyes blinked, and he staggered backwards, knees buckling, and went down. He ended up in a pile on the floor, stretched out on his back, shaking his head to clear.

A couple of guys jumped at me, as if to stop me if I planned something further, which I didn't.

To this day I can't say whether the finger in the chest or what he said triggered my hitting him. Maybe that kiss with Elly—not knowing what to do about it—had built up in me. Maybe I was striking out against the beer that sat on the bar.

Whatever it was, I knocked the living daylights out of tough guy Eric Denny.

He kept shaking his head, as he started getting to his feet. I stood with muscles tensed, not knowing what might happen next. The blond kid behind the bar barked, "Okay, you two cowboys just cool it."

Eric Denny got to his feet, rubbing his face. The red-headed young woman moved Denny's hand away from his face and looked at where I had hit him. "It's starting to swell some." To the barkeep she said, "Get me some ice."

Denny kept looking at me but spoke to the redhead. "That's okay. Show's over for the season and I don't need to look pretty until six days from now when I get to New York."

Then to my amazement—because I stood braced for what I figured was going to be a real fight—a slow smile spread across his face, even though he winced once, and then it became a full grin.

"Well, *The Typist* becomes *The Tiger*."

"Two one-act plays," I said. "Only it's *The Typists*, plural."

He cocked his chin up as if to indicate he was impressed. "Well done! By Murray Schisgal. Popular in the sixties. Revived every so often."

"Dinner theaters," I said.

One of Denny's buddies said to him, "You wanna' take him outside?"

Denny waved a hand. "Certainly not." Still looking at me, the grin was there, but favoring his lip. "I deserved it. I pushed too hard." To me, "Want a beer?"

I picked up the Heineken and offered it to him. "On me," I said.

"That's yours."

"I decided I want a Coke." The barkeep had one opened and handed it to me in flash. I turned the Coke bottle up and drank as if I was dying of thirst. I drank it down like they do in the commercials. It tasted better than any I'd ever had.


The phone was ringing as I opened the door at my house. I scurried to pick it up.

"What do you do, go around picking fistfights with

suspects soon as I turn my back?" It was Balls.

"How the hell did you hear about that so quick? It just happened."

"Balls sees all and knows all."

"Bullshit. How'd you find out?"

Janey chirped away happily at the activity. I heard her say, "Shit," as plain as day.

"Understand you clobbered the bejesus out of Tom Cruise." He chuckled. "Congratulations. Something I wanted to do myself."

For the first time I'd heard it, Janey chirped out what sounded like, "Sumbitch . . . bitch."

"It was a good punch," I said. "You have somebody planted there?"

"Not exactly planted. But one of the female plainclothes from Nags Head, Jamie Davis—is that your parakeet making all that noise?—was sitting at a table near the barber's chair, the one with the mannequin, nursing a Coke. She recognized you and called the sheriff's office and they called me."

"Jeeze!"

"You okay?"

"Yeah. Sure. I probably shouldn't have hit him but he kept on pushing. And then, I don't know. He was right in my face and poked me with his finger, and that did it."

"I sort of figured he'd pushed you about as much as he was going to be able to."

"Well, I keep pretty cool most of the time." I laughed. "We're buddies now. By the way, did you have some of your people tailing me as I took Elly home?"

He chuckled. "No, but we were timing you."

"I'm sure you were. Okay, I'm home now being a good boy. Everything looks fine. I'm going to bed. I'll call you tomorrow."

"Weav?"

"Yeah?"

"Elly's a nice gal, isn't she?"

"She sure is."

After I hung up I looked at Janey. "You've got to watch your language, girl."

She bobbed her head. "Shit."

I lay in bed and thought about Elly and thought about kissing her. The intensity of the kiss remained very real and disturbing even now. Hitting Eric Denny was another surprise of the evening. I was glad I hadn't had a beer; deep down I knew I was afraid of drink taking over again. Was the good Lord intervening? First time I've known God to promote a fistfight, but what do I know? Mysterious ways and all that.


I jumped awake when the phone rang, fumbled with it, but got it before the second ring. The illuminated dial on the clock showed five-twenty A.M.

"Yeah?"

"Weav, this is Balls."

He didn't need to say that because he knew I would recognize his voice. That, the time, and the tone of his voice told me to brace myself.

"It's Sammy. Deputy Sammy Foster. He's been blown away with a shotgun." He said it quietly as if he were bone-weary.

I sat up on the edge of the bed. I'm sure I said something, asked something.

"Early morning fishermen found him about four at the parking area at Coquina Beach. His personal vehicle, his pickup, was nosed-in at one of the spaces and he was in front of it. You wouldn't see him just riding by. Prelim-inaries indicate he was shot as he stood near the driver's side of the vehicle. Blood and stuff right there, and then dragged around to the front so he wouldn't be seen as easily. Medics say looks like it happened about one A.M. Maybe one-thirty."

"Oh, shit." The universal exclamation of distress.

To the next question, I was afraid I knew the answer before I asked, "Suspect?"

"You got it," he said wearily. "Zilch. We're trying to retrace Sammy's activities, who he talked with. His mother's too distraught to tell us much. She doesn't know where he was going or doing. He was just as much of a 'yep' and 'nope' guy at home as he was on the job. Like trying to trace the movement of, I don't know, a leaf that's blowing along in the wind. Sammy meandered, or seemed to, anyway. But he wasn't meandering as much as some folks might think. He was going straight toward something." I heard him exhale heavily. "And whatever it was, got him instead."

"It's all connected, isn't it, Balls?"

"Has to be."

"So Sammy knew, or at least suspected, who's behind the murders."

"Yeah, last person he saw."

Who the hell was that last person?

Balls said, "I think Sammy's death means you're out of the line of fire, Weav. Just the same, it's best we know where you are."

I said I'd come to the sheriff's office right away.

I'd just gotten out of the shower when the phone rang again. Automatically checked the time. Five of six.

"Oh, Harrison . . ." There was a sob in her voice. I could tell she was fighting to control her voice. "This is Elly." Her voice sounded small. The close network of courthouse people operated at high speed. Add to that the way word can travel in a small town and you've got communications at warp speed.

"I know, Elly," I said softly. "Agent Twiddy called me about Sammy."

"Oh, it's so horrible, so horrible. I practically grew up with Sammy. Mabel called me. She sounded like she might have a heart attack."

I kept saying, "I'm so sorry, Elly." I wanted to say more

but didn't know what.

"When did it happen?"

"They think one or one-thirty."

"Oh, that's so horrible. I almost wish I didn't know when it was. I couldn't sleep last night. I was lying in bed thinking. Well, I was thinking about last night and, you know, when we said goodnight."

"I thought a lot about that, too."

"So, I'm lying in bed thinking about, about telling you goodnight and how nothing like that had ever, and I mean this, had never ever come over me before, not like that, and then, all the time I'm thinking this beautiful thing, something horrible is going on at the same time." Her voice had trembled; now, her words surged with anger and strength. "Oh, why is it, Harrison? Why is it? Every time God gives you something nice, a little something to make life sweet and wonderful, He turns around and takes something away."

"I'm not sure it's God who does the taking," I said.

I told her I was getting dressed to go the sheriff's office to meet Balls and would call her if I learned anything. Even if I learned nothing, I promised to call her by the time church was over. Yes, she wasn't going to disappoint Martin. The Methodist Church would have the children's program, and Martin and the other Manteo children would be part of it.

In the meantime, we would be trying to figure out who had blasted a hole the size of a dinner plate in Sammy Foster's chest.

# Chapter Twenty-Eight

Traffic was light at that hour on the Bypass, but I kept a wary lookout around me in all directions.

Two reporters were already at the front door of the courthouse when I arrived. A third one came up about the same time I did. They looked somber and saddened, not at all pushy and insensitive as Hollywood portrays them. I recognized the one from *The Virginian-Pilot* Outer Banks Bureau. I'm sure they knew Sammy, at least casually. Before long there would be a television crew or two. A radio newsman had his recorder in hand. Because a couple of them knew I was a writer, they apparently believed that was my reason for being there. They were busy trying to catch a glimpse of the sheriff, get a statement from him. I heard one of the reporters mention that the sheriff had promised a briefing by eight o'clock.

Deputy Creech opened the front door of the courthouse. The reporters approached him but he said he was just going to his car for something. His eyes were red. There was no swagger in his walk. He looked older. I stood off to the side of the porch. He saw me and inclined his head toward the side door at the far end of the building. "Balls," he whispered. I strolled toward the side door. It opened slightly and Odell Wright, the black deputy who met Balls and me at *The Lost Colony*, crooked his finger at me. I slipped inside and went upstairs.

Balls was in slacks and sport shirt, his 9mm riding high in plain view on his belt. He was all business, standing in the center of the room, giving orders. Another plainclothes SBI agent I didn't know nodded at what Balls was saying.

Sheriff Albright sat at his desk. He looked stunned. But then he rose from his desk and stood beside Balls to be part of that discussion. He kept chewing at his lower lip.

I kept as far out of the way against one wall as I could. I heard Balls say to one of the uniformed deputies, "See if you can find anybody else who was out there early this morning going fishing. Keep hanging out there." To the other SBI agent, "The crime scene boys are going over the car and looking for shotgun shell packing. Wind was blowing so any footprints are gone, but they're trying."

The activity continued, with people coming and going. From bits of conversation, I learned that Sammy was not on duty at the time, nor was he in uniform. His mother said he'd gotten a call last night shortly before she'd gone to bed, close to eleven. Said he talked for only a few minutes on the phone and didn't seem upset. Would he, anyway? When she went to bed she thought he'd be coming to bed right after watching the eleven o'clock news. She thought maybe he'd made a phone call just before she fell asleep. She slept soundly, she said, and didn't hear him go out.

The other SBI agent said, "The call he received? Caller ID?"

"We've checked," Balls said. "Pay phone. One of the fast-food marts on Highway 64. Got somebody out there asking questions see if the guy on duty remembers who used the outside phone. Fat chance."

Prosecutor Rick Schweikert strode into the sheriff's office. He looked dressed for church. He spotted me, glared, and greeted Albright.

Balls continued. "Sammy sure didn't leave home just to drive over to Coquina Beach to look at the ocean. He drove over there to meet someone—and he met them all right."

Balls sat down heavily in what was becoming his usual

chair beside the sheriff's desk. He smacked one of his big hands on the edge of the desk. "Damn! This is what happens when an officer goes off on his own, playing the Lone Ranger. If Sammy was on to something, he should have let one of us know, damn it! He probably told this guy that Weaver here didn't know anything but that *he did*. That's just asking for it. This cowboy crap of doing it alone is what gets you killed. And it leaves the rest of us standing around with our thumbs up our asses." He saw the pained expression on Sheriff Albright's face. "Sorry, Sheriff. I know that kind of sounding off doesn't do us any good." Then, "You've got a statement to make to the press out there in just a couple of minutes."

"I know."

"As prosecuting attorney, I'll accompany you," Schweikert said.

Yeah sure, there'll be TV cameras there.

Balls said, "I suggest don't let any of them draw a connection between his killing and that of the Pearson girl. And maybe they won't. No obvious connection. Could have been a random killing for all we know—officially. Maybe the deputy came up on something that looked suspicious, got out of his vehicle and was—was assaulted."

When the sheriff, Schweikert, and Balls, along with Deputy Creech, went down to the front porch, I went out the rear door and came around to the front so I could listen to the press conference from the sidelines.

Two television crews already had their equipment set up. Two radio reporters as well as four print journalists were waiting.

A reporter holding a tape recorder asked, "Sheriff Albright, is there a possible connection between this killing and that of the Pearson woman from *The Lost Colony?*"

"We have no reason to believe there is any connection," he told her. "But we are just in the initial stages of an investigation. We will explore all possibilities."

The young reporter from *The Virginian-Pilot* asked,

"Was Deputy Foster on duty? Was he in uniform? What was he doing out at Coquina Beach?"

"No, he was off duty, and as far as we know was just enjoying the beach on a warm summer night."

After a couple of more questions, Schweikert indicated to the sheriff that he wanted to speak. "The citizens of this county, as well as all of our visitors to this area, can rest assured that we will not stop our vigilant manhunt until the perpetrator of this heinous crime is arrested, tried, and convicted."

The first reporter spoke up again. "What about funeral arrangements?"

Albright's face momentarily registered a tug of surprise, as if no one had thought there might be a burial, the same as under normal conditions. "I don't think the arrangements have been . . ."

"Wednesday, I think," Creech said softly.

When it was over, I strolled to the side door and waited for Deputy Wright to open it.

Schweikert had left. Balls looked very tired. "This is a hell of a business."

We went into the small empty office next to the sheriff's. I said, "I know you've been checking what Sammy did the last few hours. You know he stopped by the newspaper office Saturday afternoon."

"Yeah, I know. That Shackleford girl said something to Creech. Creech checked it out. Sammy stopped by and paid a bill for a classified ad he had taken out a couple of weeks ago trying to sell an old outboard motor."

I said, "Shotgun blast isn't exactly quiet. No one has come forward saying they heard anything?"

"Not yet. Happened down at the far end of the parking area. Pretty deserted that time of night."

I nodded. "Have they moved his vehicle? His pickup?"

"Yeah. Little while ago. They roped off the area first thing and went over everything they could there at the scene, and they are going to go over it some more. But they're not going to find anything. Nothing much to trace. And that area's going to be swarming with people before long. Sunday, late summer. Would have to be a shotgun. No real way to trace it. Can narrow it somewhat by size and type of packing in the shell but that's about it. Practically every household on the Outer Banks got a shotgun."

"But not many tourists bring them down here, I'll bet."

"True."

"And I'll wager Eric Denny and *The Lost Colony* actors don't have shotguns."

"A townsperson," Balls said quietly. "Someone Sammy knew. Someone who lives here." He shook his head slowly, wearily. "But who?"

I stayed on with Balls at the sheriff's office, trying to keep in the background. About twelve-twenty I called Elly as I had promised but got no answer. I waited fifteen minutes and called again.

She answered the phone after the first ring.

"This is Harrison."

"Are you all right?"

"Oh, yes, fine. I'm still at the sheriff's office with Agent Twiddy."

"You got in a fight last night after you left me?"

I was startled. "Well, it wasn't really a fight. How in the world did you find out about it?"

"Jamie Davis with the Nags Head Police Department goes to my church. She was at Saber's last night. Jamie said you knocked him down. Someone from *The Lost Colony.* That dancer."

"It was over before it really started," I said.

In a softer voice, Elly said, "Sammy was a member of our church, too. The minister this morning had a long prayer for Sammy and he talked about him before the prayer. It was nice but very emotional. I couldn't help but cry." She sounded as if she were about to cry now.

"Children's program?"

"They had it. Not as happy as I'd thought it would be, but I'm glad they had it. The children would have been so disappointed."

We talked a bit longer and she told me the funeral was going to be at ten o'clock on Wednesday at the church. He would be buried at East Lake, on the mainland, where he was born and where most of his folks were buried. "There's just his mother, a married older sister, and a kid brother. In college at Greenville." Sammy was barely thirty-one years old, never married.

I asked her if there was something I could do for her. "Yes," she said. "Take care of yourself."

Before we hung up I asked if we could have lunch together tomorrow.

There was the slightest hesitation before she said yes. She suggested we meet at Sugar Creek Restaurant, where she and Mabel and I had eaten, because there was no sense in my driving to the courthouse and having to double back. The conversation ended and I wasn't too happy with it. I knew depression from Sammy's death weighed on her, but there was something else. A deliberate distancing.

I wondered why.

# Chapter Twenty-Nine

"Jesus God," Rose said. "Sounds like you're right in the middle of a friggin' war zone."

It was Monday morning and I was on the phone talking with Rose Mandowski, one of my New York editors, about the ongoing murder investigation.

I heard her throaty chuckle. "That's supposed to be the South with all that magnolia and moonlight, where you were going to soak it all up and take it easy."

Born in the Bronx, Rose had moved to Brooklyn as a young girl. She started work at one of the detective magazines on 34th Street in Manhattan while she was going to night school. She lived and breathed the crime magazines, and kept moving up. She was a good editor. I couldn't imagine her outside the confines of the magazine's office.

She said, "I read about the deputy in one of the dispatches, and that maybe this killing was tied in with the death of the girl they fished out of the water." Her accent was strong, a mixture of Bronx, Brooklyn, and who knows what.

"Good opportunity, Weaver, for a double-lengther. When do you think we can have something?"

"Well, you know, Rose, we got to have an arrest. You want a trial, too, before we actually publish, don't you, as usual?"

She was excited. "This is such a great first-person piece

that maybe we can do something different."

"Rose, hold on now. We don't know there's any connection between the young woman's killing and that of the deputy sheriff. And it's not just *material*. These are murders, and I know these people, and knew the deputy."

"I know, I know." She tried, not quite successfully, to sound more sympathetic. "It's just that it's such great materia . . . information. And this deputy was investigating the young woman's slaying, wasn't he? Dispatches said he was."

"So was about everybody on the force. I'm going to keep you posted on developments."

I could imagine her pursing her lips, then a smile must have spread across her face. "Hey, Weaver?"

"Yo?"

She chuckled. "Don't get yourself all shot up down there in this place you figured was going to be peace and quiet. Remember, you're about my best writer. I don't want to lose you."

"I thought I was *the* best."

"Get back to work," she said, and I could hear the smile in her voice as she hung up.

I arrived early at Sugar Creek's and got a table on the porch overlooking the water. The wind was soft and mostly from the north, making the air clear and pleasant for late summer. I was staring at the water when, from the corner of my eye, I spotted the hostess leading Elly to the table. Elly glowed, slim and lovely in a medium blue dress, straight up and down with a narrow belt at her waist. She appeared prim and proper, and I loved knowing that she'd been breathing heavily and panting with passion Saturday night. No one would look at her and suspect that at all.

I stood until she sat down. She smiled, and I think she started to reach over and touch my hand. Instead, she picked up the menu as if she were studying it. She looked up at my face again and saw how serious I was.

I knew it was something besides Sammy's killing. I didn't know how to start asking her.

We ordered after the waitress brought us both sweet iced tea. "What is it, Elly?"

She stared at her tea, then at me and smiled brightly. "I guess I'm just sort of scared."

I wasn't sure what she meant. "Danger?"

"Not, you know, *danger* danger."

Then it began to dawn on me. "You mean, us?"

"It may sound silly to you, but yes. It's like things are moving too fast. Everything has speeded up since I met you. I've been a widow now for four years, and I haven't really been out with anyone." She smiled, and arched one eyebrow. "Not that there are that many people to go out with."

I waited, trying vainly to think of what I could say to reassure her.

"And, Saturday night. Well, it may not be much to you, but it really, really . . . affected me. What I'm saying is it *scared* me."

I wanted to tell her how greatly what was supposed to be our simple goodnight kiss affected me, too, but I could tell she had practiced a speech and wanted to move forward.

She looked at me with a trace of pleading in her eyes, those hazel eyes with flecks of gold. "You're here now, but you've come into town, a writer, doing all this exciting stuff, all these things happening. Poor Sammy gets killed. God knows what else will happen. And then I'll look around and you'll be gone somewhere else, where there's more excitement in another place."

I touched her hand lightly, a quick caress.

She said, "I don't want to let myself get too close. I could hurt real easy." She turned her mouth up in a self-deprecating smile. "I'm better off to stick with my history books and crossword puzzles."

The waitress brought our food and said she would check with us later. "You guys enjoy," she said.

I did my best to convince Elly that things weren't really moving too fast and that I planned, indeed, to stay at the Outer Banks, and we could spend a long time getting to know each other, and all that sort of thing. I said let's just give things a chance. She nodded and acted like she was agreeing but I wasn't sure.

She said, "Maybe I'm just depressed right now."

"There's plenty to be depressed about."


I didn't want to go back to the house. I decided to look Balls up at the sheriff's office. So I drove to Manteo after all.

Since the attack on me at the Manteo Waterfront, my access to the sheriff's office had been more accepted, thanks to words from Balls, I'm sure. The sheriff's door was open and he motioned me in with a sideways jerk of his head. I didn't see Balls.

Albright slapped a newspaper down on his desk, as if he were swatting flies. "Editorial," he muttered. "Says we need more experienced lawmen here in the county if we expect to be able to solve crimes. Let those blasted pinhead editorial writers come solve a few crimes. We'll see."

Balls came in. He had been closeted down the hall on the telephone. He flopped into his usual chair with a sigh.

Albright said, "That fancy profiler tell you what kind of killer we're looking for?" First time I witnessed the ire and bitterness beginning to rise in Albright.

"Yeah. Actually, got a lot of respect for this guy in Chapel Hill. Psychiatric profiler." Balls puffed out air between his lips. "But didn't tell me much more'n we already suspect—that the murderer kills the women as a substitute for some other aggression that he has 'failed to actuate.' That was his phrase."

I couldn't keep quiet. "What about Deputy Foster?"

"The killer feels like everything is closing in on him. He feels trapped. And he's more dangerous."

Albright raised his eyebrows. "Closing in on him? I wish

we were."

"He feels like we are, though," Balls said. "This could cause him to come completely unglued, start taking chances, go berserk. That's not exactly how the doc described it, but that's what he was saying."

I spoke up again. "He say anything about the murder of the women being four years apart?"

"It was the profiler's opinion that whatever it was that triggered the guy, to push him over the edge, hadn't 'actuated' his ass for four years—that we know of."

Albright and I watched Balls, silently. I knew Balls had checked into unsolved slayings of young women. He said, "There's that one in Raleigh a year ago that is somewhat similar. Strangled, thrown into a lake. Bunch of unsolved up in Norfolk, but not the same trademark."

I said, "If what the profiler said is true, that the killer thinks we're closing in on him and that has caused him to panic—to come unglued, as you said—I believe he's going to do something else. I just hope it's something that gives him away—before he hurts somebody else."

Late in the afternoon I told Balls I was going back to the house, review my notes, eat in.

Balls said, "Keep your eyes open. I think you're safe, but don't take any chances." Under his breath he said, "Sort of wish you hadn't given away that old .32."


Tuesday morning I got an early start for the two-hour trip to Norfolk to shop for a new computer, printer, and an answering machine. As I got on a stretch of Route 168, I noticed a pickup truck coming up fast behind me. I couldn't see the driver because of the way the sun hit the truck's windshield. Though I was traveling in the right lane, instead of passing, he stayed close behind me. I increased my speed, and he did too; I slowed, he slowed. My heart beat faster.

I saw a small farm road off to the right. I felt panicky, but believed I could outmaneuver the pickup. I waited to the last second, hit my brakes, and swung quickly into the farm road. A few yards into the road, I took advantage of the Saab's sharp turning radius and whipped around in a U-turn, hitting grass and weeds on the one side.

But the pickup truck had turned into the farm road behind me, partially blocking my exit.

The truck window rolled down.

The driver was an elderly man in work shirt and cap that advertised a brand of fertilizer. "You crazy, young feller? This is the road to my farm . . . everybody knows that."

I mumbled something and tried not to look at him as I eased out onto the highway and vowed not to be so paranoid.

That afternoon I was glad to be back at my own house, the Saab loaded with all kinds of office equipment, reams of copy paper, and more software that I would ever use.

In between unloading the car, I called Balls at the sheriff's office. Not there. I caught up with him at his motel later and learned that he was going to the funeral home visitation that night.

"I'm not going," I said. "Services tomorrow, yes."

"I'll be there to see who else shows up." He added, "Lock up good and stay out of trouble."

I knew his friends from Kill Devil Hills police would be cruising by during the night.

I spent the evening getting my new computer and stuff set up. Taking a break, I played the bass, mostly pizzicato, some blues, and practiced fast riffs. I thought about Elly a lot, and every time I thought about her I got vaguely depressed about our conversation at lunch Monday. I knew I would see her at the funeral tomorrow.

The next morning I checked again with Balls.

"Nothing unusual at the visitation," he said. "The expected townspeople, courthouse crowd. Your girlfriend and her mother were there, briefly." He sighed heavily. "Nothing but dead-ends on this case."

"I'll see you at the funeral."

"Yeah. Then right after that I gotta go to Edenton for the rest of the day. Back late in the afternoon." I could hear the weariness, the frustration in his voice.

After a while I showered and dressed for the funeral.

I wished it was Sammy's murderer we were laying to rest.

# Chapter Thirty

The downtown Methodist Church parking lot was packed. The whole county seemed to be filing into the church, along with more spit-n-polish police uniforms than I had ever seen. Sheriff Albright wore a dress uniform that I didn't know he even owned. As I expected, the television news crews were on hand outside the church. I knew they would want to get a shot of the coffin being carried out by the uniformed pallbearers, with the grief-stricken mother and other family members following behind. I buried myself in a cluster of townspeople going in. I saw Balls near the back. He nodded.

The closed casket rested near the altar. Despite myself, I thought about Sammy's chest blown open by the shotgun blast.

I saw Linda Shackleford seated half-way down the aisle in front of me. She was turned around looking at the crowd. When she saw me, she silently mouthed the words, "I want to see you later," and pointed at herself, then at me. I gestured with my head to the side of the church where the parking lot was.

I kept looking for Elly.

Mabel came in with another woman approximately her age. Poor Mabel looked extremely distraught, and I could tell she was having trouble with her legs. I'm sure she felt as if she had practically raised Sammy. She limped down front,

right behind where the family would be seated. I saw
Charlie Ferguson and his wife, both all dressed up, and Jules
Hinson, looking uncomfortable in tie and coat. Mr. King, the
motel-owner, was there, and his big, lumbering son with
skin the color of biscuit dough. This may have been the first
time the son had been in the daylight in years. He kept
glancing around, as if not used to being out in public.

Elly and her mother arrived together with another
woman. Although Elly gave a solemn nod in my direction, I
wasn't sure if she saw me. She wore a dark blue silk dress
and hose and heels. She carried a small pocketbook, and
walked tall and erect.

The minister, a balding athletic man in his forties with a
short reddish beard, sat waiting gravely and patiently in his
large chair. The organist played something softly.

Thankfully, the service wasn't overly long. The minister
had kind words about Sammy's honor and humbleness and
how humility was a virtue. He made reference to the tragic
way Sammy died while bravely performing his duty as a law
enforcement officer. He didn't mention how stupid it was to
be performing it as a solo act, if that's what it was.

At the end of the service, I made my way through the
crowd to the side parking lot and waited.

Balls came by on his way to his car. He said he couldn't
go to the graveside. Glanced at his watch and said he had to
high-tail it to Edenton. "How many suspects have you
spotted?" he asked.

"About fifty," I said, "not counting the minister."

"Yeah, I know." That heavy sigh again.

Elly and her mother and the other woman came by on
their way to Elly's car. They stopped only briefly. Elly and
Mrs. Pedersen spoke to me softly, as if they were still in
church. The woman with them was more talkative. She
reminded Mrs. Pedersen that they had to stop by the house
to pick up the food to take to Mrs. Foster's after the
graveside service. Lots of food connected with funerals.
Save the grieving family from the burden of having to

"entertain" all the people who came to give their condolences—and try to fill the void of death by stuffing it full of honey-baked ham with pineapple, coconut cake, and Rice Krispy treats.

The crowd was thinning. Linda came hurrying up to me carrying a large brown envelope that she'd retrieved from her car. Perspiration stood out on her forehead. She flashed those big teeth at me. "I've been waiting for you or somebody to ask me about Sammy stopping by the paper on Saturday."

I said, "Balls said that Creech checked, and Sammy went by to pay a classified ad bill. Selling an outboard motor."

"Yeah, maybe that was one of the reasons he stopped by. And probably the woman up front that day didn't remember that he talked to me. He also wanted to look at some back issues of the paper. He looked at these two." She tapped a finger on the envelope. "We keep a supply of back issues for a year before we start to archive them. These aren't our only copies."

I slid the papers partly out of the large envelope and noted the dates—the second week in February. Linda stood there expectantly. "Any significance that you know of?" I asked.

"If there is, I don't see it. And you know how Sammy was. He didn't spend that much time with the papers and didn't say anything. I wasn't really watching him all the time but I think he leafed all the way through them. Then he was out of there in sort of a hurry, like he remembered somewhere he needed to go. He left these right there on the counter." She nodded toward the envelope. "You take them. Maybe you can see something I don't . . ." Then she flashed that big, toothy grin, "But you gotta promise me you'll give me the scoop."

I promised, thanked her, and tucked the envelope under my arm. I would go over the papers as soon as I got home, thoroughly, then turn them over to Balls when I saw him tomorrow. I felt a touch of excitement. Maybe, just maybe. . . .

Most of the cars were lined up and leaving. I decided to skip the graveside service.

At home, I put the envelope containing the newspapers on the coffee table, where I could spread them out and go through them page by page. Too, I needed to activate my answering machine. I laid my suit jacket across one of the chairs and re-read the instructions about how to record and to change your outgoing message—all that stuff.

That done, I fixed a pimento cheese sandwich, iced tea. I stood leaning against the counter in the kitchen to eat. I thought about Elly and about living at the Outer Banks, and how I wanted things to be simple and happy. That's all I ever really wanted, yet somehow it always eluded me. Once in a while, happiness gave me a brief hug and kiss and a promise.

For a long time I stood at the kitchen counter, staring off into God-knows where. After a while I picked up my suit coat from the back of the chair, took it to the bedroom, and hung it up properly. Took my tie off, and went into the bathroom, splashed water on my face, and brushed my teeth. Made me feel better. Still, a vague depression tugged at the edges.

I sat on the sofa, the coffee table in front of me. I took the newspapers out of the envelope. One was dated Thursday, February 13, the other Sunday, February 16. The Thursday paper carried a lead story about future plans to build a new Dare County Government Center to replace the old courthouse and various offices scattered throughout the town. The second section of the paper was devoted to schools and athletic activities. I did a quick perusal of the other paper.

I folded the one neatly, then began a story-by-story check of the Thursday paper. Sammy had to have been looking for something, checking something. I believed it was a key to understanding what he was up to, who he might have confronted. I went through the other paper, as well. Then I started again with the first one, going over headlines, and pictures, and scanning through the stories. I paid close attention to the court docket stories. Nothing jumped out at me.

I had been at it with no luck for close to two hours when I stood up to stretch and ward off drowsiness. I rubbed the back of my neck, glanced out the sliding glass door.

A white Pontiac turned into the cul-de-sac. I walked quickly to the glass door and slid it open. Elly. I was surprised. As she pulled into my driveway I stepped onto the deck and leaned forward on the railing, smiling at her.

She got out of her car, looked up at me, and shrugged. "After we visited at Mrs. Foster's, I took Mother home and just had to get out. I started driving, just driving." She shrugged again. "And here I am."

# Chapter Thirty-One

She still wore the clothes she had on at the church, the navy blue silk dress, hose, and heels. She had small earrings on and a simple necklace of some sort.

She stood in the living room and cast her gaze about the room, probably taking in more about my décor, or lack thereof, than the average man would in forty years. "This is very nice, Harrison. You've made a little home here, haven't you? Your big bass fiddle, and that cute parakeet." Like a small boy, I showed her my new computer, printer, all my office stuff.

"Something to drink? I've only got iced tea, maybe fruit juice, Diet Coke."

"I'd love some water. My mouth feels sort of dry." She sat on the edge of the sofa.

Holding the glass with both hands in front of her she stared into my eyes and said, "Harrison, I'm not much on coyness and that sort of thing. I'm a straight-forward Outer Banks girl and I really don't know how to play games." She took a sip of the water. "I wasn't just driving around and happened to come here. I knew exactly where your house was, and I knew I was coming here as soon as I let Mother out." She tilted her chin upward, a hint of defiance. "I figured that if life is moving too fast, well, you just got to start running to keep ahead of it. I don't want life to go passing me by."

I came around the coffee table and sat on the sofa with her. I folded the newspapers out of the way. "Elly, I've been thinking about you a whole lot more than I've got any right to. And I don't want to stop thinking about you."

She stared down at her hands. "I know," she said miserably. "Me, too. And today, today was so bad. Seemed like death was all around us." I thought her voice would break. "I don't want any more death around. It comes so quickly, when it shouldn't."

I put my hand on her wrist and rubbed it lightly. I looked at the side of her face. She remained perched on the edge of the sofa. Delicate strands of her dark hair drifted upwards on her white neck. I touched her neck with my fingers. I could see the pulse in her throat, and her upper lip moved a bit as she took a breath. She put the glass down on the coffee table.

Then she turned and searched my face.

Our lips came together very gently, just barely touching, and I could feel her lips moving as if she were telling me something as we kissed, lightly at first, then opening wide. We kissed and leaned back against the sofa and kept kissing, and the intensity was every bit as strong as the first time.

We sat up. She tried to smile and held one of her hands out to show me how much she was trembling.

I hugged her toward me and we leaned to one side, half lying on the sofa.

Then the goddamn telephone rang.

She jumped.

My years of training as a reporter and my natural instincts make it impossible for me to ignore a telephone. Even at a time like this. I got up to answer it by the second ring, before the answering machine kicked in.

The line went dead.

I put the handset back in its cradle. "Shit," I said softly.

Elly sat up straight on the sofa, looking prim. The spell broken. She gave that smile of hers. "Do I say something corny like 'Saved by the bell'?"

"I'm sorry." I sat down dejectedly on the sofa.

She drained her glass. "Mind if I get some more?"

She waved my hand away when I tried to get the water for her. When she came back, she sat in the easy chair near Janey's cage. "Hello, little bird."

Janey eyed her suspiciously.

I pointed to the newspapers and told her about Linda's approaching me with them, how I was going through them.

Elly said, "I ought to let you get back to work."

"Oh, no," I protested. "I can do that tonight."

Janey chirped and made more of those soft, almost human sounds.

Elly turned toward the cage, cocked her head, a half-smile on her face. "What did the bird just say?"

"Huh? Well, female parakeets don't really talk."

"*She* did. She said, 'Bitch.' I know that's what she said." Elly was laughing. "You jealous little devil."

She stood and took her glass to the kitchen sink.

She shook her head slightly when I came up behind her and put my hands on her shoulders. "Let's don't get me started again. I really feel better now, Harrison." Then, "I hope you're not upset."

I leaned back from her, holding both of her hands. "Another time?"

"I'm sure," she said.

I didn't want her to leave, but I figured we've got time, time to take it slow, do it right.

I walked to the car with her and watched her back out of the driveway. She wiggled a goodbye with her fingers, but she looked very serious. Then she turned left out of the cul-de-sac and headed toward the Bypass.

I climbed the outside stairs and stood on the deck a long while before going inside. Janey was chirping and doing her head-bobbing dance. "What's this you said? You're not supposed to be able to talk. Elly's my friend. You might as well get used to it."

Janey turned her head to one side. "Shit," she said. I

didn't imagine it. Then she began happily bobbing her head.

I was feeling pretty good about things.

Then the phone rang again.

At first, I thought the caller wouldn't say anything, that the line would go dead on me again. I was ready hang up when a soft, well-modulated woman's voice, with just a trace of Southern accent, said, "Harrison Weaver?"

"Yes?"

"This is Sandra Nance. Mrs. Dixon Nance. I need to talk to you. It's urgent . . . I think."

# Chapter Thirty-Two

As I held the phone, I pictured Sandra Nance's handsome, unsmiling face, her hair parted in the middle and brushed down at the sides, her eyebrows straight, giving her a somewhat severe countenance.

I caught my breath. That's why she looked familiar, why I wasn't sure that I had met her. Christ! She's an older version of the two murdered young women. Same coloring, same shaped face and eyebrows, hair close to the same color and worn the same way.

"Mr. Weaver? Harrison, are you there?"

"Yes."

"I need to talk to you in person."

I struggled to find my voice.

She said, "There's something I need to show you."

I knew I was going to meet her. "What?"

She was silent momentarily. When she spoke again it was to whisper, "I'll call you back." Click.

I sat there puzzled, looking at my new combo-phone and answering machine. I pushed two buttons, not sure I was doing it right, but wanting the conversation taped if she called back. In less than a minute the phone rang, startling me even though I was expecting the call.

"It's Sandra Nance again. I can't get away just now. But can I meet you at seven-thirty? At *The Lost Colony*? Up inside the theater entrance. It's closed now. It'll be private."

"Sandra . . . tell me now."

She hesitated. "You know what it's about. I'm just not sure it means anything. It may not, so I don't want to talk to anyone but you. Then if you think it's something, we'll talk to the authorities. SBI and the sheriff. If it's nothing, then please, please let's drop it and not let it go further."

The tiny red light on the answering machine blinked in the recording mode.

She said, "I don't know anybody else I might talk to, someone who knows all about this kind of stuff—what has happened—but isn't the police. Someone I can trust. I think I can trust you. Please tell me I can."

I checked my watch. "Can't we do it sooner?"

"I thought I could. Now I can't. Please. Seven-thirty. At *The Lost Colony*, just inside. I'll be there. Come by yourself, please."

"Okay, Sandra. But if it has anything to do with . . . with what's been going on, the events here with Sammy Foster and the Pearson girl and the other one, this is something that the authorities need to . . . not just you and me."

"I know that," she hissed. "Don't you think I know that?" Then, "I'm sorry. I need to talk and ask you about it first. Maybe it's nothing."

I took a breath and let it out slowly. "I'll be there."

I pushed *rewind* on the answering machine and then *play*. Though I was more puzzled than before, at least the machine worked. I rewound the tape.

Aloud I said, "Balls where are you when I need you?"


What was left of the afternoon went fast. I kept going back to the newspapers, hoping a fresh approach would pay off. I was beginning to think they held no clue after all.

I kept busy. I was determined not to speculate excessively over what Sandra Nance wanted to talk about. Obviously she thought she knew something.

I ended up having to rush to take a shower and get

dressed again. I didn't want to go to a practically deserted amphitheater without leaving word with someone. At the same time, I didn't want to get anyone excited unnecessarily. Not being sure whether I would tell her, I called Elly. The phone rang several times. I was about to hang up when Mrs. Pedersen answered. She said that she and Martin had been next door and that Elly hadn't come home yet.

"She hasn't?" My voice was loud.

"She went out driving this afternoon, and probably got up with her friend Linda. I'm sure she'll be along directly. It's getting late." I could hear a touch of concern in her voice. "She usually calls, and she probably did but we were next door and all. . . ."

When I hung up, I was torn between keeping the date with Sandra Dixon or going to look for Elly. For Christ's sake, Weaver, if her own mother isn't all that worried, cool it. She's a grown woman. No reason to assume she'd go straight home. I tried to put her out of my mind.

On the off chance that Balls might be back from Edenton, I called the sheriff's office. The second-shift dis-patcher was a young man I didn't know, and who apparently didn't know me. I asked him if he would give Agent Twiddy a message. He seemed less than eager to do so but said, "Hold on a minute."

When he came back on the line he was more cooperative. "One of the other offices said Agent Twiddy contacted here a short time back and said he was going from Edenton up toward Sunbury, and then would be coming back this way via Highway 158. What's your message?"

I realized Balls would be coming to the Outer Banks from the north, practically passing my house on his way back to his motel. Knowing Balls, I felt sure he would radio the sheriff's office for messages at least once more before he returned.

"Sir, what's your message?"

"Sorry. Please tell Agent Twiddy that Harrison Weaver said there's a message for him on my answering machine.

Tell him to come in and play it."

I could tell the dispatcher was laboriously writing it down. "On your answering machine? He knows where this is at?"

"Yes."

Another pause. "I've got it," he said.

I thanked him and made sure the machine was working. I hoped that by the time Balls got the message from the sheriff's office and stopped by here, I would be back to personally greet him. Then we could go get a late bite to eat while I filled him in on my outstanding investigative efforts.

If, by chance, I was not here . . . well, it wouldn't hurt that he knew where I had gone.

I left the side door unlocked. What the hell, nobody was going to bust in again.

My watch showed a couple of minutes till seven. I needed to hurry. I started out the door, came back, picked up the newspapers from the coffee table to take with me. I laid them out on the passenger seat so I could glance at them from time to time as I drove. I've found over the years that if I keep bouncing a puzzle around in my mind, amazing how often the solution clicks. I was hoping.

At French Fry Alley on the Bypass it seemed every car slowed to a crawl to make a turn. Past Jockey's Ridge I was able to speed up, nudging the speedometer up to fifty-three, fifty-four. I knew I'd get ticketed if I pushed it too much along the Bypass. Rounding the curve at Whalebone Junction I saw traffic backed up all the way to the bridge.

We inched along. The dashboard clock read seven twenty-one. I saw a wreck had occurred on the bridge between a recreational van—one of the larger sleepers—and an older model gray sedan. Police were letting one of the four lanes go at a time.

During the stop-and-go, I glanced at the newspapers. I had gone over the front sections so often, I started on the second sections—schools and sports. With one eye keeping watch on the car ahead of me, I flipped pages. I focused on a story I had only scanned earlier. In February the high school basketball team had participated in an invitational exhibition tournament at Littleton, near Lake Gaston. Dixon Nance, coach.

A chill came over me.

February. The same month, and the same damn place, where Sammy said Bobby Ford, the suspect in the first murder, had drowned. He had fallen off a pier into Lake Gaston, a bump on his head.

Christ. Hit in the head, just like I was, and pushed into Lake Gaston.

The car behind me tooted lightly. I lurched forward a few yards. Traffic was beginning to clear and we moved steadily. Seven thirty-two.

I remembered something Sammy had said at the sheriff's office when we were talking about Bobby Ford. He mentioned that Ford had come back to town every July 5th to see the show on the anniversary of Joyce Brendle's death— something Balls and I both knew—and Sammy said that this past year Ford had come to town shortly after Christmas vacation and was seen around, including standing across the street near the Pioneer Theater. Sammy said he'd also been seen later that night at the high school basketball game.

This guy comes to town to see a high school basketball game? No way. There was something else, and I knew the events were related. I just didn't know exactly how. But I realized Bobby Ford had gone to the game because Dixon Nance was coaching. A few weeks after that, late at night, Bobby Ford falls in the lake and drowns when Coach Nance is in the area with his basketball team.

I believed Bobby Ford had started to suspect that Joyce Brendle's death—in which he had been a prime suspect— was connected with Dixon Nance. And Bobby Ford ended up dead.

I believed Sammy Foster had begun to suspect the connection, also. Then Sammy Foster ended up dead.

What did Sandra Nance have to do with it all? Was she suspicious of her husband's role? Or was she in this with her husband and luring me into a trap at *The Lost Colony* theater? I felt a trickle of nervous perspiration run down the side of my chest. No, I couldn't believe that she was setting me up. Just the same . . .

I sped through town faster than I should have. At Fort Raleigh, only four cars, all with out-of-state tags, were parked in the lot near the Elizabethan Gardens. A man and woman and three children were just getting into a van. By the time I parked and started walking the path to the theater, it was a quarter to eight. I didn't know where Sandra Nance might have parked. I remembered seeing her drive a Buick, but I didn't see it in the main lot, though there were other places she could have parked.

The days approaching Labor Day were definitely getting shorter. The tree-lined path to the theater had darkened. I could smell the woodsy odor of pine and live oak. All was quiet. It was also spooky. I knew I had no damn business being here. But no way was I not going to be here.

Twilight was coming on fast. I reached the entrance to the theater. There's hardly anything more lonesome than a theater that's closed. Any time a theater has nothing scheduled its ad says the theater is "dark." They ain't kidding. Yet an amphitheater like this one is never closed.

A bird fluttered away from a branch as I walked up the slight incline, past the control booth tower. At the top of the bowl, I looked around in the growing dusk at—nothing.

The rows of seats were empty. The stage was empty. In the distance beyond the stage, weak flickers of light still reflected off the water in the sound, but it, too, was losing its luster and becoming a dark gray. I looked to the sides of the amphitheater and up at the light tower. No one. I glanced again at my watch. Six of eight. I didn't like it here.

Then I heard soft footsteps. I wheeled around, and there was Sandra Nance.

# Chapter Thirty-Three

She had become haggard: her eyes, the drag on her mouth, her whole manner. Sandra had aged twenty years since I had seen her Saturday with her father at Diane's Courthouse Cafe. She was in slacks and a cotton blouse that needed pressing. She carried a tan plastic bag, which she clutched tightly. "I had to be careful," she said. "I haven't known where he is." She tried to moisten her lips with the tip of her tongue.

She walked close to me, then stared toward the stage, as if getting up her nerve to talk We stood at the last row of seats, close to the center and the control booth.

"Here," she said, and offered me the plastic bag. It appeared old and felt limp and dusty. "I found this in the garage, high up behind the rafters."

I opened the plastic bag. "Oh, Jesus." I swallowed. The bag contained a coil of leather thong, probably several feet long—the type of thong used to lace hiking boots, or that was used years ago to lace footballs or basketballs. Or to strangle young women. At the bottom of the bag lay four tubes of lipstick, the big, garish, dime-store variety. Flaming red.

"I knew Dixon had something hidden in the garage but I couldn't find it. Until today, during the funeral."

"Does Dixon have a shotgun?"

"Yes, but I looked for that after . . . after Sammy. I can't find it."

"Do you think Sammy suspected Dixon?"

She nodded. "I do now."

"What about Bobby Ford? The guy they questioned in the first murder, the one who drowned last February—when Dixon was up near Lake Gaston with the team. Do you think Dixon did that?"

She nodded. "And I believe Sammy began to think that, too."

"I was almost drowned the other night. Someone hit me and knocked me in the water at the Manteo Waterfront."

She compressed her lips. "I heard. They said it was an attempted mugging. But I wondered. That's why I was standing out there on the street the other day. I was trying to get up enough nerve to face this and say something to someone."

"The first young woman? Four years ago?" We remained standing, close. I held on the plastic bag.

"She was killed the same night that Dixon and I had a really bad, yelling argument. I threatened to leave him, or force him to leave."

She took a deep breath and straightened her shoulders as if steeling herself to proceed. "We used to drink together. But I quit." She breathed in deeply again and stared at her hands before she continued. "I didn't think I'd ever tell anyone this . . ." I waited. She gave a shake to her head and shivered, as if a chill had come over her. "When we were drinking he would get me to dress up, you know, real floozy like . . . like a whore, I guess, with garter belt and black stockings and . . . and a lot of red lipstick. Not just on my lips but . . . on my breasts. Other places, you know."

Her voice dropped to a near whisper, and her eyes couldn't meet mine. "It was sort of a lark at first and then I saw it was really getting sick. And I wanted to stop it. Then when the Brendle girl was found, they said there was lipstick on her face. I almost threw up when I heard it, but Dixon convinced me it was just a coincidence. He laughed and said it just goes to show that a lot of people like to get a little kinky. That doesn't mean they're all sick-o killers."

She appeared so weakened by what she was going through and with what she was telling me, I thought she might fall. I motioned for her to sit down. She leaned against the back row of seats but remained standing.

"I quit drinking about then and stopped playing the games with Dixon. We got into arguments but not like when I was drinking. Then about three years ago he started pestering me again to get dressed up and do that sort of thing and I wanted him to leave. He grabbed my shoulders and shook me so violently I thought my head would snap off. He's real strong. I yelled at him that he was sick and getting sicker. He stormed out of the house and was gone for a couple of days. He came back all apologetic and said he wouldn't ask me to do that anymore. He said he was afraid to leave me. Real weird dependence. And everybody thinks he's so independent. Self-made man. He is, except when it comes to this. And I can tell when it's coming over him. Like something he can't control."

"Do you think he killed someone when he left you those couple of days?"

"I don't know. I know that about the same time a woman was killed, strangled. In Raleigh. But it didn't sound like quite the same thing. So I don't know." She stared at my face, a pleading in her eyes. "I haven't been able to face all of this until now—I guess when Sammy Foster was killed I couldn't keep shutting my mind."

Darkness came in steadily as she talked. The woods that surrounded us on three sides were black. The stage, with the water behind it, held on to a glimmer of fading light. The air was more hot and humid, too, with a breeze moving clouds in from the southeast.

I felt perspiration on my back and I noticed that traces of moisture stood on Sandra's forehead and upper lip.

"Two weeks ago," she said, her voice sounding normal again, "Dixon started acting really nervous, agitated." She stopped, looked back at her hands and rubbed the knuckles of one hand with the fingers of the other. "I came upstairs and caught him going through my . . . my lingerie drawer. He actually snarled at me, like some sort of animal, and threw lingerie at me and said, 'You're a bitch. Why don't you wear that good stuff anymore?'"

She took a couple of deep breaths. Her eyes met mine. "You must know how difficult it is for me to be telling all of this. But I have to. I know that."

"Yes," I said, "and all of this needs to be told to the authorities, not just to me."

She nodded and touched the back of the row of seats with her fingers as if steadying herself. "Let me finish. The night the Pearson girl disappeared, Dixon was drinking heavily. I begged him to stay home. He went into the garage, and I heard him fumbling around. Then he started his van and drove out. It was late when he came back. I pretended to be asleep. Then they found her . . . strangled and with the lipstick. I know I'm not supposed to know what she was strangled with. But I do. One of the deputies let it slip to Daddy. But that was before I found that stuff." She nodded toward the plastic bag I held.

She stared at me, her eyes showing all the hurt she carried, to pose the final question. In that faded light the pain etched lines in her face. "Am I being crazy? Putting all this together? Making something out of what may be nothing?"

Slowly, I shook my head and spoke softly. "I'm afraid not. I think you're right on target." I wanted to get the hell out of there. With the darkness enveloping the woods leading to the parking lot, the images she conjured up were too unnerving. "I think your instincts are right. Authorities can take what's here in this bag . . ." We both glanced at the plastic bag, as if it were something alive. "They can find out something real quick. They can see if this cord matches anything. It may be common. But I expect if it's cut, they can match the cut with the piece here and the piece found on the victims. And the lipstick, too. It sure looks bad." I realized my speech had speeded up because I wanted to end this and get to the sheriff's office with this bag.

As I talked and watched her face, she turned toward the stage and leaned heavily against the back of the last row of seats.

Suddenly she seemed to crumple. Her body sagged and she gave a muffled, barely audible, high-pitched groan.

"You okay?"

Her head wobbled as if it had come loose from her neck and she was trying to keep it up. Her mouth was moving but no sound was coming out. Then, "Oh, my God."

I followed her gaze.

My whole body froze. On the stage, looking up at us, stood Dixon Nance.

He was not alone.

He had Elly. She was tethered on a leash wrapped around her neck.

He held the leash, along with a bottle of whiskey, in one hand. In the other he held a battery-operated lamp, like campers use, and he cradled a shotgun under his arm.

Even from that distance I felt I could see the terror in Elly's eyes, beseeching, begging. Her hands were bound behind her, and duct tape covered her mouth. Shoeless, she wore what remained of her dark blue silk dress. Its left shoulder had been ripped down, exposing one breast.

And something was attached to her bare nipple.

# Chapter Thirty-Four

Sandra let out an eerie wail. "Dixon, for God's sake what have you done?"

As if mocking Sandra's question, he lifted the bottle quickly and took a slug from it. The movement tugged the leash, snapping Elly's head. My muscles tensed as if I expected to cover the distance between us with a single movement.

He placed the lamp on the stage at his feet, keeping his eyes on us the whole time. The shotgun pointed in our direction.

I knew I had to get down there. I didn't know what the hell I was going to do, but I had to try.

He took another swallow from the bottle, saw it was empty, and tossed it underhanded behind him to the stage floor, snapping Elly's head.

Sandra spoke, "Dixon, listen to me."

"Shut up, bitch. Look at this." He tilted his head toward Elly, and gave a sharp pull on the leash. I saw the pain on Elly's face. She looked small and her breast very white in the glow from the lamp. "This is the way you're supposed to be. You're supposed to dress more like this." He reached out and grabbed the right sleeve of Elly's dress and ripped it several inches. The movement pulled Elly off balance.

I struggled to control my voice. "Dixon, I'm coming down to talk to you."

To Sandra, I whispered, "When I start down there, you run back to the car. Get help."

I took a step toward the aisle.

Dixon bellowed, "Stay right there, Sandy, baby." He swung the shotgun up to Elly's head, poking her ear with the barrel. "You try to run and I'll blow her head off." He snickered. It wasn't a real laugh. The sound came through his nose. "Come on down here on the stage, Sandy, baby, and put on a show for me like you used to." He nodded toward me. "You tell lover boy there about how you used to like to get all dressed up? Like the whore you are?"

"We're coming down there, Dixon," I said, taking slow and deliberate steps to the aisle and starting a measured walk down to the stage, not taking my eyes off him.

Just under her breath, Sandra said, "I'm coming, too. He'll shoot her if I try to run." She walked on my left, a step or two behind me.

We were half-way to the stage, with Dixon and Elly directly in front of us. I could make out what was attached to Elly's left breast—a two-inch metal C-clamp. It was screwed tightly to her nipple. The C-clamp weighed her breast down. Elly trembled as if she couldn't stop.

That son of a bitch. I was determined to kill him. I didn't know how, but I was going to do it. That I knew. I didn't care what happened as I did it, but I was going to kill this bastard.

He kept the shotgun cradled in his right arm, finger on the trigger. He swung the gun slowly from Sandra to me as we walked toward him.

We were about twenty feet from the apron of the stage.

"Stop there. I want to show lover boy something." He yanked hard on the duct tape that covered Elly's mouth. I heard the painful sound of the tape as it stripped from her face. She twisted her head away from him and spit something from her mouth. It was a wad of cloth or cotton. She slowly turned her face toward us. At first I thought her mouth was bleeding. Then I saw it wasn't blood. It was painted grotesquely with lipstick. Some of the lipstick had stuck to the tape, which lay adhesive-side up at her bare feet. The knees of her pantyhose were torn out and there was a long run in the stockings down one leg.

The leash was a coil of nylon rope tight around her neck, imbedding itself into her flesh. She looked at me, her eyes filled with pain and terror. She opened her mouth to try to speak.

Dixon jerked on the leash. "Don't say a fucking word," he hissed. "I can jerk just a little harder on this cord and you're not going to have any vocal chords you can ever use again." His lips parted loosely in a grotesque grin. "You start making noise and I'll blow him to hell and back." He poked at her side with the shotgun. "Or I'll blow both your tits off."

I tensed, but took a couple of tentative steps toward the stage.

Sandra came up beside me. She stood straighter, squaring her shoulders before deliberately starting toward the stage. "We're coming up there," she said flatly.

Dixon eyed her as if he didn't know exactly what he should do next. I took advantage of the moment to move quickly toward the stage, too. At that section, it was an easy step up to the stage. The two of us stood not five yards from Dixon and from Elly. Elly kept staring at me with tear-filled eyes.

Dixon advanced toward us in a shuffling, stiff-legged walk. He jerked on Elly's leash, and she took a step or two also. The battery-operated lamp cast its glow upward, distorting Dixon's face. If I didn't know it was Dixon Nance, I would not have recognized him.

I could see that Elly's nipple looked angry and purple. It hurt me to look at it, and I couldn't begin to imagine how much it hurt and humiliated her.

Sandra held herself erect, shoulders squared. With firmness in her voice, a firmness I had no idea she was able to summon, she ordered, "Dixon, put that gun down!"

He stared at her, didn't move. Slowly he turned toward me, his head low and jaw thrust forward. To me he said, "I should have made sure you were dead there at the Waterfront."

"So that was you, and my house, and the van. . . . Now, listen, Dixon—"

"Shut up!" He swung the double-barreled shotgun at my chest and took a couple of more shuffling steps toward us, keeping Elly's leash tight.

I felt perspiration roll down my neck. I breathed shallow, quick gulps of air. My heart pounded in my chest. I still held the plastic bag in my hand. I must have glanced down at it because his eyes followed mine.

"I know what that is," he said. His eyes on my face again, he spoke to Sandra. "You didn't want to play our games any more, did you? Don't you know there are others I could get to play?" A grin touched his face for an instant, making him look even more grotesque. "Even if they didn't *want* to play."

Sandra took a step forward.

He swung the gun toward her. "Stay right there, Sandy, baby . . ."

She stopped and he slowly moved the gun back to me, aimed at my belt. He shuffled a half-step closer. The humid breeze came from the southeast behind him and I smelled the sour sweat and whiskey odor that enveloped him.

I knew this was the time when you're supposed to try to talk the gunman out of doing what it looks like he's intent on doing. The best I could come up with was, "Look, Dixon, we can get you help . . ." That sounded absurdly lame, even to me.

He snarled at me, his lip curling upward. "What the fuck do you know about help? What sort of bullshit do you think I'm going to buy from you, huh?" He started to lean forward as he spit the words at me. His odor gagged me.

Jesus, I had really set him off.

His chest heaved with his breathing. The gun barrel came

slowly toward my chest, then my neck, my face.

I figured this was it, and no matter how unlikely it would be to succeed, I had to try something, or stand there helpless while he blew us all away.

I stared at Dixon's face, but out of the corner of my eye I saw Elly tense her body, nod her head ever so slightly.

She was going to be part of it, too. Not just stand there. With my eyes, I tried to signal her that I understood. Time it right, Elly, I prayed silently.

I held up the plastic bag for him to see. "Here, Dixon. Keep this as a souvenir," and I tossed it lightly toward him. It was enough to distract him, cause him to swing the gun barrel away from my chest.

With a blur of energy, Elly lowered her right shoulder, crouched and threw the weight of her body and every ounce of her strength into one hell of a body block to Dixon's side.

Dixon gave a startled grunt as Elly's blow knocked him off balance. He dropped the leash but his finger pulled the trigger and the shotgun blasted once into the air.

I lunged with all my might at Dixon before he regained his balance. I think my feet even left the stage. It was that kind of lunge.

The full power of my shoulder hit Dixon in his upper chest and we tumbled onto the floor of the stage, both us grappling for the shotgun. It lay across his chest. My hands were on the gun, pressing the length of it down against his chest. He rolled back and forth, trying to get out from under me. His hot, stale breath felt tangible against my face.

Sandra came up fast on the other side. Dixon still had his hand near the trigger guard and before I could yell to Sandra he managed to squeeze the trigger again.

The blast pounded my ears as if my head were inside a bell. I heard Sandra scream and saw her slowly sink to her knees, both hands near her left shoulder. The double-barreled gun was now empty.

The body block Elly threw knocked her off her feet, and with her hands tied behind her she struggled to get up. She got to one knee, lost her balance and fell again.

I kept pressing the shotgun against Dixon's chest, putting as much weight on it as I could, slowly gaining on him. I wanted to get it to his throat, strangle the life out of the son of a bitch. I wanted to make him die.

Dixon got a knee and then a foot under my body. He flipped me over him like tumblers in a Chinese acrobat show. I landed on my back with a thud.

But I had managed to hold onto the shotgun. I scrambled, trying to get on my feet; he got up a split-second ahead of me. On my knees, holding the shotgun by the barrel, I swung it with what strength I could from that position.

The blow caught him across the shins. He crumbled into a half-crouch. That gave enough time for me to spring to my feet. Like a baseball player standing at the plate, I hauled back and swung the shotgun straight at his head.

He glared up at me with hatred, that snarl on his face, just as the stock of the gun smashed broadside into the side of his head. I heard bone crunch. His head snapped. He went over backwards, a side of beef, dead weight.

He didn't move.

I stood over him and raised the shotgun to hit him again, to pound his head into pulp.

A loud electrical swoosh sounded and the entire theater exploded into light. I squinted, the gun still raised over Dixon's form.

"Hold it," Balls' voice shouted. "It's all over."

I fought the impulse to smash the gun into Dixon's face. His eyes, dull and sightless, stared up at me.

"Weav, put it down." Balls and others were now up on the stage. Balls held his 9mm Glock. He knelt beside Dixon Nance and with his free hand he felt for a pulse. "It's done now," he said softly.

I dropped the shotgun and raced over to Elly. Deputy Wright had helped her to her feet. Standing behind her, Wright used a pen knife to carefully cut the duct tape that bound her wrists. She turned toward me, her back to the others, and I gently unscrewed the clamp. Gingerly she covered her breast with the piece of her dress. Wright handed me his windbreaker, and I draped it over Elly's shoulders.

Deputy Creech used his portable radio to call for two ambulances. Sheriff Albright and two deputies tended to Sandra. Blood covered her left shoulder and side. She was dazed but conscious. The main force of the blast had missed her.

Balls had gotten slowly to his feet. "You swing a mean bat there, son," he said.

I stood with my arm around Elly, holding her close. I could feel her tremble. "And Elly throws a mean body block."

I heard the wail of the ambulances. I held Elly very tight. She put her head against my shoulder. I wasn't going to let her go. Ever.

# Epilogue

As I hoped he would, Balls had checked with the sheriff's office for messages on his way back to the Outer Banks, and gunned the hell out of his Thunderbird to get to my house and listen to the message on the machine. He must have gotten there not too long after I left for the theater. He called the sheriff and they rounded up Creech and the others. It was Creech's idea to grab Pernell Hunnicutt and take him along to flood the theater with lights. Pernell walked up toward the stage when it was over, and I saw Balls nod at him and smile; Pernell nodded in return and showed a trace of a smile himself.

Sandra Nance recovered. The shotgun blast caught her in the upper shoulder and chest. She lost a lot of muscle in her shoulder and will have to go through extensive physical therapy. It's sad and it's ironic, too, I think, but she lost part of her left breast from the blast. But I understand reconstructive surgery can do miracles.

The town is getting back to normal after the kind of tragedies that in time get absorbed into the fabric of a place. On Labor Day weekend a cold, rainy northeaster blew in and stayed through Monday night. Beach-goers were disappointed but the merchants did all right, because people didn't have much else to do but shop. The days after the front moved out, the weather was beautiful and the fishing on the piers and in the surf picked up. I went surf fishing one afternoon and did okay. School started and the yellow buses are going up and down the Bypass. Tourist traffic has lightened considerably.

Balls managed to stay home a couple or three days after this thing was over. Now he's in the middle of another case. I think it's a biggie. I know that he's spending some time talking with officials from the Norfolk area and maybe federal types. He won't tell me about it. Says it's none of my business, and I should stay out of trouble. That's Balls for you.

Prosecutor Schweikert grumbled considerably about the fact that Dixon Nance would not stand trial because I had killed him. Once again, Schweikert blamed me for making his life less than glorious. The publicity he would have received from the trial would have kept him pumped for years. He glares at me every time he sees me. I wink and grin.

I'm getting my writing going again. My new computer is set up in the dinette. I like looking out the windows toward the road and watching the sun as it makes its journey all the way across the entire front of my house. I've got the birdseeds out on the deck railing. The little flying pigs make a mess with the seed hulls, I realize, but I get to look at a lot of sassy birds. I've got a pair of cardinals and black-capped Carolina chickadees as regulars. At times I move Janey's cage so she can watch the birds. She tries vainly to get their attention by bobbing her head, occasionally muttering what sounds like the two cuss words she picked up from me. I can't be sure.

My bass playing is coming along. I've finally got that Mozart section so that it sounds good, and I continue to use it as an exercise. I'm practicing regularly on a Brahms etude. I figure it won't be long before I meet a few other musicians and maybe we form a chamber group.

As for Elly, thank God she wasn't really hurt. It took a while for the soreness to leave her breast, but she had her doctor look at it and she said no real damage was done. Elly still has nightmares about coming up on Dixon Nance standing in the middle of the quiet road to her house, waving her down, and her stopping, not suspecting anything. She wakes up terrified. The dreams are less frequent now, and she says she is determined to put it all behind her. I think she'll be able to do just that. After all, she's a tough Outer Banks gal. I give her full credit for saving us, for she was the one whose body block set in motion our salvation.

I'm going over to Elly's this afternoon to have Sunday dinner with her and Martin and Mrs. Pedersen. Martin is getting so he will speak to me, some of the time.

I'm already showered and dressed and ready to go. When I get there, I know Elly will be standing on the porch as I get out of my car.

She'll smile, and raising one hand, she'll wiggle her fingers at me and speak my name with that wonderful soft and enchanting Outer Banks accent.

PHOTO: CHRISTOPHER TERRELL

## About the Author

Joseph L.S. Terrell makes his home on the Outer Banks of North Carolina, his native state, where he continues the craft of fiction-writing—with a little fishing, golfing and boating thrown in.

He may be reached through Bella Rosa Books or via email at JLSTERRELL@aol.com.

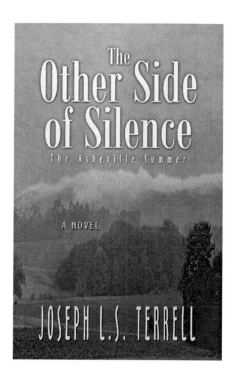

# The Other Side Of Silence
## The Asheville Summer

ISBN 978-1-933523-10-1

That summer in the mountains near Asheville, North Carolina, between the end of the Great Depression and the onset of World War II promised to be an enchanted one for ten-year-old Jonathan Clayton and his family. But almost from the beginning, Jonathan sensed that something sinister lived across the meadow at the base of Clown Mountain in the Dennihan's pigpen of a house. Before the summer ended, violence erupted in that house and Jonathan, his brother, sister, and cousins have to race ahead of a crazed, hatchet-wielding mountain man in a frantic flight to save their lives and stop their pursuer—by any means they can.

LaVergne, TN USA
30 October 2010
202871LV00002B/17/P

9 781933 523668